THE BUSINESS OF LOVE

It was almost midnight when Trajan and Maya entered the lobby of the Empire Hotel. After the hansom cab ride, they walked the few blocks to the hotel, all the while Trajan talking about his adopted home, the people he knew and the things he'd done. Maya hadn't grown a bit tired of it, and she had to admit she was sorry to see the night end. Still she knew it had to.

"Tre," she said, turning to him as they approached the elevator. "I had a good time. The tour was very impressive."

Trajan stepped only inches from her, compelled by something other than his common sense. "What about the company?"

Maya felt her pulse quicken, and she searched desperately for words. They were alone at the moment, but if there had been people in the dark elevator hall, she wouldn't have noticed.

"Tre." His name barely came out. "I'm . . . not sure . . ."

It was too late for uncertainty as Trajan reached out for her. He was already feeling the heat as he pulled her to him, but it turned to fire as soon as his mouth touched hers.

Maya felt her head swirl, her stomach twirl and her knees go weak as his lips pressed against hers. A flame ran through her body as he kissed her deeply. His lips were rough, but pleasing against her own. She felt a moan rise in her throat from the pit of her belly as he slid his hands down her arms slowly. She felt a tingle rush through her body down to her toes.

BOOK YOUR PLACE ON OUR WEBSITE AND MAKE THE ARABESQUE ROMANCE CONNECTION!

We've created a customized website just for our very special Arabesque readers, where you can get the inside scoop on everything that's going on with Arabesque romance novels.

When you come online, you'll have the exciting opportunity to:

- View covers of upcoming books

- Learn about our future publishing schedule (listed by publication month and author)

- Find out when your favorite authors will be visiting a city near you

- Search for and order backlist books

- Check out author bios and background information

- Send e-mail to your favorite authors

- Join us in weekly chats with authors, readers and other guests

- Get writing guidelines

- AND MUCH MORE!

Visit our website at
http://www.arabesquebooks.com

THE BUSINESS OF LOVE

Angela Winters

ARABESQUE
☆BET.
BOOKS

BET Publications, LLC
www.bet.com
www.arabesquebooks.com

ARABESQUE BOOKS are published by

BET Publications, LLC
c/o BET BOOKS
One BET Plaza
1900 W Place NE
Washington, D.C. 20018-1211

First Printing: August, 2000
10 9 8 7 6 5 4 3 2 1

Printed in the United States of America

This book is dedicated to "Harriett" for lighting the spark that made an eleven-year-old pick up a pen and pad for the first time, and see so clearly what she was meant to do for the rest of her life.

One

Maya Woodson slid her Toyota into her reserved parking space in Pharaoh Hotel's parking garage. She was swirling with a mixture of excitement and nausea. She'd felt it since waking up that morning in her Georgetown condo. The usually horrifying D.C. metro traffic only made it worse.

Today was it, she thought, as she grabbed her briefcase off of the backseat. Pharaoh Hotel Corporation was starting its road show, the most important part of going from privately owned status to a publicly traded company. Maya was scared to death, but so proud. She'd been itching to be a part of it from the beginning, but a public relations director wasn't of need-to-know importance until now. So she'd kept her distance, feeding off news that slipped out of the finance department or the senior management group. But now that public perception and buy-in was necessary, Maya was going to be in the mix, and she was rearing to go. She could only think of how proud her father would be of her if he were still here. Pharaoh was his baby.

Maya checked her watch. Nine fifteen. She had to hurry. There was so much to do before the big meeting at eleven.

When she saw him slam the door to his black Lexus, the first thing Maya noticed was how classically gorgeous he was. Well over six feet tall with a rich caramel-colored complexion, he had sharp features and a strong build. He had a hard jaw line and distinguished nose, and his perfectly tailored navy blue suit hinted at a very fit figure.

Before having the chance to take this attraction in, Maya realized he was so busy tidying his tie and very expensive suit and checking his watch at the same time, he had no idea he was walking right into her.

"Hey!" she yelled to him, but it was too late.

He bumped into her only a second after he looked up. It was only a slight bump, but he was large, and Maya's 5'5", 125-lb. frame was pushed back. Her briefcase fell out of her hands to the floor. The impact jarred it open, a few files falling out.

His light eyes blinked as he reached for her. He hadn't even seen her. "Where did you come from?"

"Where did *I* come from?" Surprised at his response, Maya pulled away from his grip. It was too strong anyway. "Do you mean how dare I be in your way?"

He ignored her snide remark. There was too much on his mind. Too much to let this pretty young sister get to him right now.

He knelt down to help with her papers. "I didn't mean . . ."

"No." Maya shooed his hands away, picking up the last file. "I've got it. I've got it."

He didn't have the time to argue with her. He ran his hands over naturally curly black hair. "Look, I'm just . . . I mean I'm running late for a meeting."

Maya closed her briefcase and stood up to face him. His full lips were pressed together. He appeared annoyed at the necessity of acknowledging that he caused this. "Plan better."

He caught that, his head lifting back a little. Spicy little thing, and he could swear she looked familiar.

"Excuse me?" he asked, taking in a gander. She was a little thin for his taste, but shapely with a smooth and beautiful milk chocolate complexion. Her shoulder length, jet black hair was shiny and healthy, her large, dark eyes catching, and her nose like a rosebud with elegant, promising lips.

"Plan better," Maya repeated, not at all happy with his roving eyes, no matter how appealing they were. "The license plate on your car says New York. Our traffic is worse than yours, believe it or not. If you're going to do business here, plan to leave earlier. Nothing appears worse than being late for a meeting."

"Thanks for the advice," he answered. "I'd love to hear more of your business tips, but my meeting starts in fifteen minutes, so I'll be going."

Maya eyed him cynically as he walked away. "New Yorkers. Always in a rush."

She brushed him off. She had no time to concern herself with rude men, no matter how fine. She had a lot to do before her meeting, and she wasn't about to be late for that.

"Hey, Maya."

Alexandra Hampton, all of twenty-five, not looking a day over sixteen, sauntered lazily into Maya's office in the business corridors of the hotel. She sat comfortably in the royal blue chair, her eyes gazing around the sleekly designed office.

Maya Woodson had been director of public relations for Pharaoh Hotel Corporation for three years now. The small hotel chain, specializing in extended stays, was started by her father, Nick Woodson, and Jerome Newman, his former apprentice. Already successful in real estate, Nick foresaw the technology migration to the northern Virginia and D.C. metro area. With his protégé turned partner, Jerome, he started a hotel for businessmen and women who would be in the area for more than a week. Long-term contractors, consultants, business commuters and new hires needing a home until they found a permanent one made up their clientele.

That was twenty years ago, and the idea of a home away from home with the quality service of a hotel was just catching on. The only black-owned hotel of its kind, Pharaoh Hotel Corporation grew faster than anyone expected, expanding to other metropolitan areas. Then Nick was killed in a tragic car accident ten years ago, and Jerome Newman took over the reins himself. Maya had worshiped her father, and thought she and her mother would have fallen to pieces if Jerome hadn't been there for them. Almost ten years younger than Nick, he gave up any idea of a normal personal life and made Pharaoh famous while becoming a surrogate father for Maya.

Jerome had taken Maya under his wing. He'd wanted to groom her for senior management, preferably through the world of finance. But Maya wasn't interested in that. She was a creative soul, more interested in writing and special events than accounting and finance or sales. Although she knew more about the company than anyone short of Jerome, she moved into public relations and Jerome had let her spread her wings and take over. She played a major part in the success of the chain, leading public investors to want a piece of the private pie.

Maya was going over a first draft release, waiting for Alexandra to say something. It wasn't going to happen. The girl could sit there forever and just stare.

"What's up, Alex?" Maya leaned over the desk, her hands entwined in front of her.

Alexandra shrugged. "Just saying hey. You look nice today. More . . ."

"Corporate?"

She had on her best black suit, tapered to fit her perfectly and end just above her knee. Corporate offices were on the first floor of the D.C. hotel. To fit in with the guests, the dress code was business casual, so an outfit such as this, with pumps no less, brought on attention.

"Yes, corporate." Alexandra nodded, her braids, which seemed to be in the thousands, each thinner than strings, moving with her head. "What's up? Job interview?"

"Like I would ever work anywhere but here." Maya laughed at the thought. She would devote the rest of her life to seeing the continued success of her daddy's dream. "You know my life is Pharaoh."

"That's your problem." Alexandra slid a pen over her right ear. "You're always here. You were supposed to hire a public relations manager to help out, but that was months ago."

"I have public relations contacts at every Pharaoh hotel. I'm doing fine."

"Still, you spend all your time here. You're twenty-eight and very single. Very, very single."

"Don't go there." Maya leaned back. The pictures on her desk told it all. Daddy, Mama, her best friend Alissa's daughters, Amani and Winnie. No man. "I'm still looking for a man like Daddy, Alex. Haven't found him yet. I've come close once or twice. You gotta give me points for trying. I'm not giving up. I'm just in a little drought."

"You can say that again."

"Alex, did you come in here to remind me of my manless state?"

She slowly crossed her legs. Alexandra did everything slowly. "No. That was for me. You know, misery loves company and all. What's up with your short temper?"

"I'm not upset," Maya said. She'd grown used to Alexandra's interference in her personal life, her nagging habits, her too short skirts and too much makeup. She was Jerome's niece and an okay secretary if one didn't need anything in too much of a hurry.

"Your hands are clenched in a fist, Maya. Chill out. I wasn't criticizing. I know you could have ten men if you wanted one."

Maya shook her head, leaning back in her chair. "I'm sorry. This isn't about you or men. It's about today. I'm nervous and excited. Anxious, all that."

"You and Uncle Jerome." Alexandra rolled her eyes. "IPO, IPO, IPO. I don't even know what IPO is an abbreviation for anymore."

Maya sighed. They'd gone over this several times. Alexandra had a selective memory. "Initial public offering. When a company goes public and . . ."

"Wants to sell shares of stock, they do an IPO." Alexandra nodded. "I know what it means. More money for investments, acquisitions and stuff."

"Stuff?" Maya asked. "This is more than stuff. It's big time. Stockbrokers, analysts, big spenders, power people, NASDAQ."

"Whatever NASDAQ is." Alexandra looked bored. "All I know is Uncle Jerome says it's going to make a few people, including you and him, rich because you own both your parents' stake in the company."

"That's a plus." Maya wouldn't deny that. "But getting rich has never been the issue for me. Furthering what Daddy started is what this is all about."

"Back to you," Alexandra said. "If this is all about the investors, big spenders and all that, what are you doing in it? You're public relations, not NASDAQ."

"The road show is when the company goes to the investment community to shore up interest, ensuring a successful opening day and a great stock price." Maya felt her stomach swirling just thinking about it. "It involves Investor Relations, which is just financial public relations. My expertise is needed."

Alexandra frowned, seeming a little confused. "But Uncle Jerome hired that guy. That Tre . . . Tragan . . ."

"Trajan," Maya corrected. "Trajan Matthews, and I know."

"What in the world kind of name is that?"

Maya shrugged. "Something about Roman emperors. At least that's what Jerome told me. I wasn't interested in an explanation of his name, just his credentials."

"I thought he was black." Alexandra shifted in her seat. "I thought that was the point. A black-owned Investor Relations firm for a black-owned company."

"TM Investor Relations is black-owned, and Mr. Matthews is black, but your uncle wasn't looking for a black-owned firm only. He was looking for the best firm. He seems to be satisfied with Mr. Matthews."

"Hide your true feelings, Ms. Bitter," Alexandra said. "I take it my uncle didn't ask your opinion of the emperor."

Maya smiled. "You know I wanted to be a part of that, but the NAACP banquet was coming up. The San Francisco promotion was hitting stride. We had that issue in Philadelphia."

"What do you think of him?"

"Matthews?" Maya frowned, fidgeting with her pen. "Never met him. I got a report from Jerome. He showed me some articles. Trajan Matthews has the inside on Wall Street, a history in investment banking, and a strong reputation. I'll be meeting him today. I'm sure I'll like him since Jerome seems to love him so much."

"Have you seen him?"

"Not yet. The photos weren't supported by my web browser when I visited TM's Web site. The articles

Jerome gave me were faxed copies of copies. The pictures were unviewable."

"Uncle Jerome's secretary says he's steaming serious sexy hot. He's a little lighter than she generally likes her men, but . . ."

"That's not important," Maya said. "He just better get the job done. We all better get the job done. Which reminds me. I have to contact the catering manager for the NAACP banquet. We'll have to finish this dynamic, stimulating conversation later."

With Alexandra gone, Maya went back to work. She found it weird that, with her hectic schedule and all that was on her mind, an image of the New Yorker with the Lexus flashed in her mind. She laughed at herself, creating a character from stereotypes. Obnoxious New Yorker with a foul mouth and bad manners. However, a paying guest was a paying guest, so as far as she was concerned, he was a king.

"Hello, young one."

Maya's smile was cheek to cheek as Elaine Cramer entered her office. The woman always brought her joy.

"Hey, Elaine." Maya quickly stood up and went to hug the seventy-year-old permanent resident of the hotel. She loved the nosy woman.

They sat on the sofa near the window. Maya knew she was running short on time, but she never refused Elaine. Elaine was a wealthy old widow whose three ungrateful children never called, except to ask for money. She had no close friends, only acquaintances, and all her other family was dead. When Maya's mother, Rose, died of breast cancer two years ago, Elaine became a surrogate mother of sorts. Maya knew she was all Elaine had.

"Now Elaine." Maya accepted the small plate covered with a paper towel. She lifted the towel. Brownies. "What did I tell you about baking for me?"

"I'm an old lady," she said, gently tapping Maya's arm. A caring gesture. "We have to bake for someone. It's an old lady rule. Who would I bake for if not you? My god-awful children?"

"What have they done now?" Maya felt for Elaine. Her children were a constant source of disappointment and regret.

Elaine sighed, shaking her head. She gently placed her peach-colored hands on the lap of her paisley dress. "They've got the kids into it now. My own grandchildren. Do you know Linda said I wasn't welcomed to Debra's junior high graduation ceremony? I mean the girl is almost as horrid as her mama, but she's one of only two grandkids I have."

"Why would she do that?"

"Guess." Elaine rolled her eyes.

"Of course," Maya said, nodding. "Money. What else?"

Elaine Cramer's husband of thirty-two years won a multimillion-dollar lawsuit from the company he worked for for thirty years. The company exposed him to radiation as a laborer in their Maryland plants. James Cramer died a month after receiving a check for three million dollars. The kids, who were already worthless, became worse. They wanted more than Elaine gave them, which was already more than their father indicated they should have in his hastily drawn up will. Never a call for just a hello. No invitations to visit over the holidays. Just requests for more money.

"Because I didn't send Linda five thousand dollars to pay for her trip to Hawaii, I can't see my grandchild graduate. Who needs five thousand for Hawaii? It's in the U.S., not Africa."

"I'm so sorry, Elaine." Maya placed the plate on the table next to them both and wrapped Elaine's hands in hers. "That was painful, but are you sure you can't go?

Can you contact the school directly? Maybe one of
Debra's friends graduating with her has an extra ticket
she can give you."

"That's just it." Elaine looked away, her pink face
drained. "I was thinking of that when Debra called yesterday. I thought . . . I guess I'm still too hopeful."

"You're an optimist, honey." Maya respected that
quality, but knew it only made her more vulnerable.
"What did Debra say?"

Elaine's eyes welled up with tears. "She told me she'd
never speak to me again if I didn't give her mama the
money."

"Oh Elaine." Maya felt her pain. Her own family had
been so close, although their time together was too
short. She couldn't imagine such betrayal.

"She went the whole route. Sobbing, sniffling, all of
it. Said since Jim left them two years ago, they were
broke. Don't know how that could be 'cause he never
worked a steady job for more than a month when he
was with them."

"You know her mother put her up to this, Elaine.
She's only thirteen."

Elaine nodded unconvincingly. "I don't care anymore. I'm through with all of them. That's what I came
to talk to you about."

Alexandra slipped in the room. "Hey, Ms. Anticipation. It's eleven. Do you know where your senior management team is?"

Maya jumped up from the sofa in a panic.

"Oh dear," Elaine said. "I've left you late for a meeting again."

Maya ran to her desk, grabbing her papers and files.
"I have to go, Elaine. We'll talk later."

She smiled at the woman, feeling guilty as she saw
her somber expression. Her heart was broken and that

should mean more than a meeting. But this wasn't an ordinary meeting.

"I wish you didn't have to go," Elaine said. "I have such good news for you."

"I'm so sorry, Elaine. It'll have to be later. I am eager to hear the news."

Elaine nodded, standing slowly with Maya's help. "I understand. You'll come by later?"

Maya led Elaine out of her office. "I'll stop by before my dinner with Jerome."

"Now where is he?" Elaine frowned, confused. "I've been looking for him all morning. I've left messages for him telling him that the front desk is messing up with the mail again. I want to lodge a complaint."

"Later, Elaine." Maya kissed the older woman's cheek before darting down the corridors to the meeting room on the fifth floor.

It was only five after when she reached the door, but Maya still cursed herself. As she walked into the conference room, all eyes turned to her.

Jerome Newman stood up and headed for her immediately. There was an urgency in his step. At forty-five, Jerome Newman looked relatively well for his age. Fit with the exception of a belly, his dark brown skin and gray temples were distinguished.

"Where were you?" he whispered in her ear as he led her to the seat next to him. "Is everything okay?"

"Sorry." Maya felt comfort at his touch. She knew him so well, she could tell he was concerned, not angry. "I'm sorry I was late."

He smiled at her, all care and forgiveness in his eyes. "Don't worry. We're the client, remember?"

Jerome faced the group at the long table, head held high. "To get back to work here, I think of couple of you have yet to meet our business partner in the investor relations effort of this venture, Trajan Matthews. He's at the end of the table."

Trajan had gotten over the initial shock, recalling his earlier sense of familiarity. He stood and smiled kindly, focusing on Maya's tightened lips. He saw her swallow hard, and he smiled wider.

The New Yorker! Maya took a split second to compose herself. She nodded a curt hello with a forced smile. As he stood up and walked toward her, Maya felt her anxiety grow. She did her best to hide it as she slowly stood up to greet him.

"Ms. Woodson." Trajan took her hand, shaking it vigorously. Her hand was silky soft, her eyes were tempting without effort. "I've been looking forward to meeting you especially, after hearing so many great things of your father. It's nice to finally do so . . . formally I mean."

Maya felt his grip was way too strong for her taste and quickly pulled her hand away. "Mr. Matthews, we're all happy to do business with you."

He stepped closer, planning to be gentle. However, he wasn't going to let her get away scot-free.

"You would be proud of me," he whispered in his strong voice "I took your advice. I was early for this meeting. Nothing worse was what you said, right?"

Maya felt her veins heat up with embarrassment and resentment, but she kept the smile on her face. "Good for you, Mr. Matthews."

Maya returned to her seat as he returned to his. She looked at Jerome, who winked at her with a proud smile. She'd never questioned Jerome's judgment before. She'd give him the benefit of the doubt for now.

"Now that we have the introduction out of the way," Jerome said, "let's get back to business"

Maya felt Trajan's eyes bearing into her, but she refused to look at him. She was certain he thought she was a hypocrite or incompetent, but she shouldn't care. As Jerome said, she was the client. With the exception of Trajan and Cynthia Hodges, the representative from the financial firm underwriting the public offering, everyone at the table knew she was excellent at what she did, and very capable.

Trajan was conflicted. A part of him was excited about working with this woman, but he wondered if she was committed. After all, attraction aside, this had to work. He only wanted players, not soft PR cheerleaders.

"First order of business," Jerome said as he slapped his hands together, rubbing them in excitement. "The road show agenda. I think Maya wants to set the tone."

Trajan blinked, surprised Jerome let her go instead of him.

Maya nodded a thank-you to Jerome and stood up. She didn't need notes; she was prepared for this.

"I don't need to tell you all that this road show means everything," she said. "It's a combination of public buy-in through media strategy and investor support. We know—"

"Can I just say something?" Trajan held up an impatient finger.

Maya was caught off guard by the interruption. She sensed impatience in his tone. "Mr. Matthews, I . . . yes, go right ahead."

"Thank you." He nodded appreciatively, turning his attention to the group. "The road show will make or break Pharaoh's public offering. It's a test of you, senior management's, mental and physical endurance and competence. As important as public buy-in is, it's secondary."

Maya was certain that was a jab at her. She'd been warned that these investor relations folks looked down on traditional public relations people. Saw them as puff

pastry. She thought to be the big one and give him
room.

"When I say that," Trajan continued, noticing Maya's
lips were getting smaller and smaller as she pursed them
tighter together, "I mean that it's unlikely that the general public will be buying shares in the first days, weeks
or months of your going public. They will watch the
professional investment community and look for their
reviews and reactions. When I talk about endurance,
I'm not just talking about travel. You're going to be
questioned intensely by brokers, traders, analysts and
portfolio managers of the most powerful firms in the
country who work for some very demanding and
wealthy folks. You'll probably be asked a lot of questions
by people that are none of their business. Media reps
from the leading financial and business magazines and
newspapers are going to investigate you all, ask grilling
questions. You'll have to be on your toes and sharper
than sharp."

Maya glanced at Jerome. She knew him so well and
could spot his emotions. He turned to her with a wink.
He was ready. He was excited, but she saw he was nervous as well. She kept her mouth shut for his sake. For
now.

"This is not intended to insult anyone here," Trajan
continued, "but the less of you involved, the better. Of
course, Jerome and David Hanley, your chief financial
officer, must be at every city. The rest of you can alter-
nate appearances."

Maya knew he was talking about her. She wondered
why she was taking his insinuations so personally, grip-
ping her pen tightly. "Thank you, Mr. Matthews."

Trajan didn't like her very kind way of telling him to
shut up, but he showed no signs of it. She was his client,
but he wasn't about to let a PR puff give the real ex-

THE BUSINESS OF LOVE

ecutives in the room the impression that this was a warm, fuzzy-feeling mission.

Maya cleared her throat. "Mr. Matthews's administrative staff has handled all the reservations and general logistics of the trip, and I've put together a schedule for everyone which should've been passed to you by Alexandra Hampton this morning. We'll be hitting the major cities. New York, San Francisco, Boston, Chicago, Los Angeles, Philadelphia, Dallas, Denver, Atlanta, Miami, Seattle and of course D.C.

"As of now, we have at least thirty people confirmed for all our luncheons. Most of the small breakfast meetings and dinners have been filled as well. Your assistants all have the presentation on Power Point and your booklets show your contribution to these meetings. I've set up several media interviews and sessions and your booklets show who will be contacting you for comments. Mr. Matthews will discuss further what is and isn't appropriate to say as it particularly pertains to a public offering. In general, no promises."

As the others leafed through their booklets while Jerome gave encouraging, motivating direction, Maya's eyes turned to Trajan. Puff pastry? She didn't think so. She saw a brief smile of respect form at the edges of his mouth. His very attractive mouth. Maya had met many men like him. He was smug and self-absorbed, a power-hungry man used to putting people in their places, keeping the limelight for himself. Maya realized if they were going to work together, she would have to put her foot down now.

Questions came, most answered by Trajan. He was prepared for them all, especially the one posed by Holly Priesler, director of sales and marketing. He knew about this topic all too well.

"Yes," he answered. "Wall Street still has pockets of that good ol' boy network. A lot of it actually. I know

you've all read in the news about the absence of blacks
in power positions in the investment banking community. I was deep into it, and it can get pretty bad. There
are a lot of people on Wall Street who think African-
Americans can make a lot of money, but we can't manage it. We can't be intelligent about it. Things have been
changing, but you'll get questions that a white or Japa-
nese-owned company probably wouldn't get. You'll be
held to a higher standard. Your mistakes won't be made
because mistakes are made, but because you're black-
owned. You'll have to deal with it."

"We can take it," Jerome said as he stood up again.

Maya smiled at his confidence. She had complete
faith in him. He understood exactly what her father
had in mind when he envisioned Pharaoh Hotel Corporation's future.

"Nick and I faced some ugly discrimination twenty
years ago when we started this company. We were told
white folks won't patronize a black-owned hotel and
black folks didn't have the money to keep us going.
Two black men, despite our college educations,
couldn't manage a business of hotel proportions. Look
at us now. We can deal with anything."

Maya was beaming with pride, a sight that hadn't escaped Trajan. How he'd thought Maya was familiar earlier in the garage was due to a picture of her Jerome
had shown him. He'd had it in his wallet and introduced her as his public relations director, whom he
would be working closely with. She'd looked different
in the picture, much younger, hair more out of place,
still attractive. Trajan was surprised her picture was in
the wallet. Jerome explained that they were "close." It
was left at that. What he remembered most was the look
on Jerome's face as he spoke of her. His care for and
confidence in the woman was very personal. Now, as he
watched her staring, Trajan sensed something much

more than business and he didn't like it. It wasn't at all professional.

The meeting wound down, and others left. Trajan was in the corner on his cellular phone. Maya headed for Jerome, who was standing at the floor-to-ceiling window that was the artistic center of the sharply designed room.

"Jerome." She placed a comforting hand on his shoulder and looked into his hazel eyes. He had a broad nose and thin lips that contrasted each other. Jerome always hated his small lips. Blamed it on an Irish grandmother. He'd gained fifteen extra pounds his entire adult life, but he carried them well.

"You did good today, kid." He smiled at her, his eyes warm.

"Thanks." Maya leaned against the window. "What's wrong? I'm sensing more than nervous excitement here."

Jerome shook his head. "We had another burglary last night."

"Oh no." This would be the third in two months. The first was jewelry taken from a room, the second was a credit card receipt stolen from the bar counter and the number used to purchase more than a thousand dollars worth of goods before the criminal was caught and the card canceled. "What happened this time?"

"This wasn't a room, thank God. Someone left their purse on the bathroom counter when they went to use the stall. It was taken."

"Are there any leads?"

Jerome shrugged. "I've been in these meetings all day. To add to that, I'm going to have to fire Randy Bagwell."

"Why?" Maya couldn't imagine that. "Randy's a

harmless mail sorter, not a thief. He couldn't steal a thing."

"He's messing up the mail again." Jerome's expression was exasperation. "I got two messages on my phone this morning from guests. He's had too many warnings. Now, of all times."

"Calm down." Maya rubbed his back, remembering Elaine's complaint earlier today. "Do me a favor and hold off on that."

As Trajan approached them, the sight of Maya almost caressing Jerome's back confirmed his suspicions. He'd have to talk to Jerome about this. He didn't expect Maya to be receptive to reason. If the press got ahold of this . . . no, not on his watch, not on his reputation.

"Excuse me." He waited for the two to turn to him. "Sorry to interrupt, but Jerome and I have a meeting to get to. We'll all see each other for dinner downstairs at seven?"

"Let me check messages with my admin," Jerome said. "I'll be ready in a second."

As Jerome went to the wall phone, Maya felt a sudden uneasiness alone with Trajan. She was still very angry with him, and his constant staring at her didn't help the situation. It was as if he was waiting, expecting something from her. Maybe an apology? Not in this lifetime, she thought.

"If you'll excuse me, Mr. Matthews, I have . . ."

Trajan stepped to his right, halting Maya's attempt to leave. He could smell her perfume, fresh and wild at the same time. He didn't appreciate the distraction. Never one to let things simmer, he had to get some things straight with her. "Look Ms. Woodson. First of all, if we're going to be working closely together over the next month or so, we should at least be on a first-name basis."

"That's fine with me, Trajan." He was too close and

Maya had to admit she was a little intimidated. It was weird. She was usually one to warm to others immediately. She wasn't warming to Trajan Matthews. That was generally a sign to her that she never would.

"No, Maya." He sensed her discomfort, and saw it as possibly impeding their work. "Call me Tre. All my friends and business associates call me Tre."

"Fine." Maya nodded. She would be spending almost every day with this man for over a month. Worth a try. "Fine, Tre."

"Second." Trajan wasn't satisfied with her response, and he knew he wasn't making it any easier. But he hadn't gotten where he was by concerning himself with feelings. "I don't want you to take this the wrong way, because I know you're the client and you know public relations. But this isn't public relations. This is hard-nosed money, financial statements, acquisitions and some high-stakes gambling."

"What's your point?" Maya asked, knowing where this was going. She tried to get a hold of her temper beforehand.

Trajan couldn't ignore that she'd interrupted him again. "My point is that public relations is about making people like you, making them feel connected to you, believe that you care. Here, it doesn't matter who likes you, and nobody cares if you care. Connecting? You can be from two different planets. You can be the devil in human form. All that matters is if you can make them money."

"Are you suggesting I don't understand that?" Maya was starting to hate the condescending look on his face, although she couldn't ignore its appeal.

"No, I'm not saying you don't understand this," he answered, not taking at all to her stubbornness. "I'm saying that I understand it better than anyone, so you need to let me lead this."

"I'll let you lead this . . . Tre," Maya said, staring hard into his eyes, making sure her tone was impatient. "I'll let you lead this because that's what we're paying you to do. But get this straight. I'm not about touchy-feely, handing out T-shirts with smiley faces, or whatever your interpretation of public relations is. I'm a business-woman. No, I'm a good businesswoman, and this business is my life. It's my family. So don't underestimate me or my ability to deal with you and all your Wall Street sharks."

"Are you sure of that?" He couldn't help but feel a little spark from her attitude. It was unavoidable. "Using family and Wall Street sharks in the same statement makes me worry about that."

Maya's hands formed in fists. He was insulting her to her face. He needed to be put in his place. "I appreciate your concern, Tre, but you don't have to worry about me or anything I say. You just do your job and make us money."

Trajan's eyes held hers for a moment. She was forcing a power play and was going to be trouble. He wasn't sure if it was good or bad trouble, but his instinct said it would be bad. If she saw this as a family thing, she'd be a liability. He'd have to make it clear to her it's not a family thing, but a money thing.

"Tre." Jerome gripped the shoulder of the man younger by ten years. "I need to speak to Maya, then I'm ready to roll."

Trajan nodded at Maya before turning to Jerome. "I'll meet you out front of the hotel. Maya, see you at dinner."

Maya nodded her good-bye, struck by the utter charm in his smile. He was a dangerous one—thought he was smooth.

"What now?" Jerome asked.

Maya's eyes widened as she turned to him.

"You got that keep-it-up-and-I'll-smack-you look on your face," Jerome said after Trajan left. "I've seen it too many times for it to get past me. Now, I know Trajan is very aggressive, but you will play nice, won't you?"

Maya's hands were on her hips. "You know I always play nice, but are you certain he's the guy?"

"Look, he's a money-hungry Wall Street go-getter. He's left all his morals behind for the sake of money. That's what we want. We want a fighter. Besides, he's spent ten years on Wall Street after his Wharton MBA. He's an insider, and his company is young, fresh and exciting. He knows his stuff. So yeah, he's the guy. Now, play nice."

"You need to tell him that." Maya headed out the room and down the hallway with Jerome at her side. "I think he has a problem working with women."

"I hear he's a hit with the ladies in New York."

"I don't doubt his social dominance, with that player smile he's got on him. I'm just worried about the boardroom."

"To put it plainly," Jerome said. "He's not your type either inside or outside the office."

"Not in the least."

"Then again, who is? It appears nobody qualifies."

Maya laughed out loud. "Alex and I were having a similar conversation this morning. My drought."

"Let me refer to George. This guy—"

"George is history," Maya said of her last lover. "I know it breaks everyone's hearts, but it was a mutual thing."

"Maya, I liked the guy."

"So did I," she said regretfully. "But I didn't love him, and I only frustrated him."

"Fine. George is not up for discussion."

"Thanks." Maya didn't enjoy discussing him. She regretted that it hadn't worked out. She was a traditional girl at heart, and wanted the husband, the family, all of it. It just wasn't working out too well.

Jerome stopped her at the elevators, holding her at her shoulders as she faced him. "Well, whenever that knight finally comes, you know I have to approve first."

Maya beamed. "I love you too, and I'll be sure to send him your way as soon as I find one. I know you'll be nice, not like Daddy was with my dates in high school."

"Your daddy had unreachable standards for any man who wanted his princess. No one would've ever been good." Jerome sighed. "He loved you so much."

Maya entwined his hand in hers. Jerome still occasionally got choked up when he talked about Nick. Even ten years later.

"He would be proud of you, Jerome. Of us. Daddy wanted what was best for this company. He wanted a black-owned company to be a force in the market, in this industry. This is going to make that happen for Pharaoh."

Jerome laughed. " 'All in good time' was what he always said. Used to drive me crazy. I was so eager. But not Nick. No, he was the voice of reason. He knew when we were getting too far ahead of ourselves. He was a genius."

"He was." Maya noticed a distant look in Jerome's face. She saw it so often when he talked about what Nick wanted for Pharaoh. "A genius and a good man. And I know there's a Nick Woodson out there for me. I'm going to find him. And when you approve of him, I'll know that means Daddy would've approved."

Outside the hotel, Trajan anticipated the familiar sights he expected to come across, and they all touched a nerve in him. A hotel employee approached him, an African-American man not a day over eighteen.

"Can I get you a cab, sir?" he asked.

Trajan shook his head. "I have my car in the garage across the street. I'm waiting on someone."

"Are you new to D.C., or a visitor?"

"Neither," Trajan said, glancing at his watch. He hoped Jerome wouldn't make them late. "I grew up in D.C."

"Really? What parts?"

Trajan smiled. "The hood."

The boy nodded. "You, a crazy kid from the hood? I would've thought you were from one of the secluded suburbs in Virginia or Maryland."

"No way. I grew up in one of the worst neighborhoods down here. The kind that—"

"You don't have to tell me, sir. I'm from there too."

Trajan looked at the young man for the first time. He reminded him of himself a little bit. He wondered if this kid grew up without a father, like he had. Like too many young black children. His own mother, Maria, had done it all by herself. She did it without the help of most of the neighborhood, because she wasn't like them. Still, there were those who took her in even though she was an outsider.

"It ain't all bad," the kid said, his eyes watching as the cars drove by. "There were some good times. The neighborhood is the neighborhood. Running with my boys, the corner drama."

"Well, I could focus on the good things," Trajan said, surprised he was opening up to a stranger. Or maybe that was why he was opening up. "But they inevitably bring along the bad things. Being so poor. Always so poor. Running with my boys was fun, but toward the end they were all dropping like flies. Dead or in jail."

"You don't keep in touch with any of them? Or are you the only one to make it out?"

Trajan knew he'd purposely lost contact with the others. "Yeah. It's only me."

"How did you get out, man? Please tell me, 'cause you look like you're getting paid."

"My mama passed when I was seventeen, and I went to live with cousins in New York."

"You ain't never looked back, man?"

"Never," Trajan said with insistence. "Never have, never will."

The young man left Trajan to attend to a guest calling out to him. Trajan took a deep breath. Yeah, he had gotten out and was proud of it. New York was the best place in the world for him. So much the opposite of what he'd come from. It promised opportunity and wealth. Even though Trajan's cousins were working class, it was a huge step up from where he'd been. It offered him exposure to a life that the D.C. ghetto did not.

Trajan had found his niche in finance, and his ambition couldn't be rivaled. Now running his own IR firm on Wall Street, the past three years had been a nonstop ladder to success. He'd handled smaller hospitality accounts, but Pharaoh was big enough to add another specialty to his list of areas of expertise.

He'd reassigned all other accounts to the five professionals he had working for him, and was determined to focus his attention on Pharaoh and turn it into much more than could have ever been expected. This had to be a 100 percent success. There was no room for mistakes or distractions. This was all business.

He checked his watch again. What was keeping Jerome? Couldn't he talk to Maya another time? Trajan had a good sense of whether or not someone was with the program, and he had reservations about Maya. Yes,

she was beautiful, feisty and all that, but he had no use
for those qualities toward this purpose. He had to figure
out what he was going to do about her. She wasn't going
to be put in her place, but he'd have to get her in line,
and didn't expect that to be an easy task at all.

Maya checked herself in the hallway mirror on the
third floor of the hotel. She was a little on the thin side
and had endured teasing for it as a child. Fortunately,
a few curves had managed to form in her late teens.
All in all, she'd turned out pretty good.

Tonight, she toned it down for a business dinner. She
picked a dress over a suit, but it was conservative. Navy
blue, a high, straight neckline held with thick straps.
The dress cinched loosely at her waist, rounding her
hips and ending just above her knees.

She checked her watch for the fourth time in ten
minutes. She was doing well. Dinner downstairs was at
seven. It was six fifteen now. She wasn't about to let
Trajan catch her running late again. She'd give Elaine
a half hour and be downstairs at ten to seven.

Maya knocked on the door to Elaine's room. The
woman was a rambler and generally Maya indulged her,
but she was sticking to her guns.

Maya waited. Elaine moved slower some days than
others. After a while, she knocked again. Leaning her
head to the door, she listened. Nothing. She reached
for her key in her purse. Elaine had given her a spare
just for safety and insurance. She was becoming more
forgetful, and occasionally left home without her keys.

"Helloooo."

Maya stuck her head in, then slowly the rest of her.
The entranceway was basically empty. Most Pharaoh
rooms were set up to have a long foyer to hide the
lived-in look from anyone passing by an open door.

Walking by, they couldn't see the small kitchen, bed-room, dining room or bathroom that made up the home.

"Elaine?" Maya walked further inside. As she reached the end of the foyer, she noticed it right away.

Everything was a mess. Well, not exactly. Elaine was a neat freak, and although she had a ton of junk, it was always neatly displayed, stacked or hidden away. Now, the apartment wouldn't be considered ransacked, but "gone through."

The living room, dining room and kitchen were all confined to a 350-square-foot space. Books were un-opened, shifted about. Drawers were opened halfway, all the way, or just a little. Papers were spread out across the dining room table.

Panic hit Maya. Another burglary! She ran to the bed-room and swung the door open, screaming Elaine's name.

In the doorway, Maya fell to her knees as they buck-led under her. Elaine was sprawled across her bed, her eyes closed as if asleep. But she wasn't asleep at all. Life had left her. Her face, her arms, her hands were a mix-ture of pale white and blue. Her paisley dress was barely covered with blood, but enough to see. Her left leg hung off the side of the bed. She was wearing knee-highs and the left pair was losing its elasticity, rolling down her leg.

Maya opened her mouth, but nothing came out. Her stomach was turning and she felt dizzy. Grabbing the sides of the door, she pulled herself up. She couldn't turn her eyes away. There was no need to check for a pulse. She was definitely dead.

She forced herself to turn away, toward the bath-room. She stumbled to the door, using the wall to keep her upright. Leaning over the basin, she thought she would throw up, but only tears came.

Maya reached for the phone, installed in the bath-room for convenience after Elaine moved in. She dialed seven for security. She could barely speak through her shock. All she could think of was a poor, sweet woman who had never hurt a soul and had brought her so much comfort in her harder days. How could this have happened?

Two

Lance Snyder, director of hotel security, had Maya by the arms, assisting her to Elaine's sofa. He'd shown up with two police officers minutes after Maya called. It took him some time to calm her. Meanwhile, detective George Hobbs had arrived with questions.

"Are you able to talk now, Ms. Woodson?" Detective Hobbs took out a pen and small notebook from his back pocket.

Maya nodded at the officer. He was a massive man. Not fat, but a big brick wall. He was as dark as black coffee, with a face as friendly as a child's. He pulled up a chair, flipping the bottom of his coat jacket before sitting down.

"When was the last time you saw Mrs. Cramer?" he asked, his voice kind, patient.

Maya wiped her cheeks. "Around eleven this morning. She came . . . she came to my office to visit me. To talk to me."

"What about?"

"I don't think anything in particular." Maya couldn't think too straight right now. "She always came by to talk. I'm her . . . I was her best friend."

"Did you notice any change in her behavior?" Detective Hobbs was writing as he spoke. "Today as opposed to before."

Maya shook her head. "No. It was the usual. Although, she said she had . . . good news for me "

Lance Snyder kept a hand firmly on Maya's shoulder. "What would Mrs. Cramer's mood matter if this was a burglary?"

"It might not be," George said. "It's possible someone wanted to murder her."

Maya was astonished, her voice caught in her throat. "No. No one would want to hurt Elaine."

"The three burglaries Mr. Snyder told me you had here were very nonviolent." George paused as an officer approached and whispered in his ear. He looked at the man. "Not until the medical examiner gets here. Don't touch her."

"This is crazy," Maya said. "We found out who committed the first burglary. It was a maid. She was fired and we're in litigation now."

George paused in reflection. "There's still two other crimes, and risky purse snatching is hardly violent. Murder would seem a million miles away from that, but tiny points can bring them together. Possibly, Mrs. Cramer might've witnessed this person committing another crime."

"Petty theft to murder?" Maya shook her head. "It doesn't make sense."

"Maya!" Alexandra was struggling to free herself from an officer doing his best to keep her from entering. "Let me go. Maya."

George put up his hand to stop them. "This is a crime scene."

"She's my assistant." Maya stood up and ran to her, hugging her tightly. "It's Elaine. She's dead."

"I saw the police outside." Alexandra was shaking her hands as if they had touched something hot. "I followed one. I couldn't believe it. What are you doing here?"

"I . . . I found her." Maya looked around. There were officers everywhere, radios going.

"She has to leave," George said, approaching them both. "I'm sorry, but she has to. We haven't even fingerprinted everywhere. Only essential people can come—"

"Oh my God!" Maya gasped. "Jerome. The dinner. It's seven."

"You can't think that's important now?" Alexandra asked.

"No, but Jerome has to know." Maya tried to think, tried to get beyond her emotions. "Alexandra, Jerome is in the restaurant with potential investors. Tell him about this, but don't let anyone else at the table know. Pull him aside and keep smiling. Go, now."

Alexandra almost jumped as she turned and ran out.

"Who is Jerome?" George asked.

"He runs Pharaoh." Maya needed Jerome now. "He has to know. This is going to kill him."

"Is he the hotel manager?"

"No. Allen is on vacation for the week."

Trajan gritted his teeth and gripped the edges of his chair. It was seven fifteen. He would strangle Maya Woodson. So what if she was the client. So what if she was Nick Woodson's daughter. He didn't care if she had the cutest rosebud of a nose he'd ever seen. This was unacceptable.

Jerome shifted nervously in his seat, smiling at the three hotshots and Trajan. "Well I'm sure Ms. Woodson will be here any moment. Our hotel manager is out this week, and she's been running the place in his absence."

"We'll start without her," Trajan said. "She's not integral to the overall conversation."

Steve Jeffries, senior analyst at one of the top five

securities firms in the world, cleared his throat. "Now, hadn't you said Ms. Woodson would tell us about your plans for expansion? That's really what I want to know. I mean, what you're doing already is great, but I want to know what else you're getting into."

Jerome smiled nervously. "I can help you there. We already have plans set in action to expand into growth cities like Charlotte and Richmond. Our acquisition table definitely depends on how much money we raise, but there are at least five small hotels and one chain we've been researching extensively and have intentions on."

As Jerome spoke, Trajan tried to calm down. Jerome was good. He knew his stuff. This had to work, not just go smoothly, but knock the socks off the guys from International Leveraged Markets. He made the decision that Maya Woodson would have to be left out. This was ridiculous.

"There is no question," Trajan interjected at a pause, "that Pharaoh has the momentum. With the market inundated with technology public offerings, anyone looking to diversify is going to flock here. Let's look at the numbers."

"Excuse me."

Everyone turned to the young woman dressed in a hot pink minidress.

Jerome sighed. "Alex, where is Maya? She's supposed—"

"I need to talk to you." Nervously, she smiled at the others, only showing hesitation as she faced Trajan's dangerously disapproving stare. "It's urgent. I'm sorry."

Trajan pressed his lips together. He wasn't even going to guess why this . . . this hot pink woman was here. Nothing could be important enough to interrupt this dinner. As Jerome excused himself from the table, Trajan took a hard, quick sip of his wine. He could handle this, he told himself. He was the best at this. No problem.

"Again," he said, barely garnering the attention of his guests, "the numbers show a growth that is not only consistent and strong, but not too strong, so we know we aren't dealing with a phase here. We've seen them, the hot, hot companies that by the time we get through the due diligence and go public, the passion is gone."

As Jerome returned, Trajan noticed a definite change in his persona. He was frazzled. Trajan's first thought was how bad this looked to potential investors. His second thought was that something happened to Maya.

"What's wrong with Maya?" Trajan was surprised he asked the question, but it sprung from his lips without thought.

Jerome tapped the edge of the table, his eyes sharing time with each man. "She's fine. There's just some . . . there's something I have to handle. I have to—"

"Hold on." Trajan quickly stepped up. He looked at their guests, who were both perplexed. "Excuse us one moment. Jerome, can you follow me?"

Trajan fought to control his temper. "Jerome. I don't know what is going on, but you cannot leave."

"I have to," Jerome said. "It's Maya. Maya needs me."

"You said she was fine." Trajan glanced at the young woman who came to retrieve Jerome. She was upset. "Tell me the truth."

"She is." Jerome took a deep breath. "I have to go. There's been . . . a burglary. You can handle these guys. Promise them a one-on-one with our entire senior management team sometime later this week."

"But they're here now." Trajan was already thinking, planning how he would fix this. "A burglary is for security, not—"

"Do it, Tre," Jerome said before turning and walking away with Alexandra in tow.

Trajan composed himself, cursing Maya Woodson under his breath. It was bad enough she had to miss the dinner, but she pulled Jerome away as well. Why couldn't she have kept this from him until later?

He turned back to the men with a smile that was the definition of charm.

Maya was feeling a little better now that she'd been in Jerome's arms for some time. He held her as they sat on the sofa in the foyer of his penthouse suite in the hotel. Jerome had lived there for five years now.

"Don't worry, baby," he said. "They'll find out who did this."

Detective Hobbs entered the suite. The door was left open. He'd been coming and going for at least twenty minutes now.

Maya shook her head. "I just can't believe . . . She was my . . ."

"I know. We all loved her. We'd grown so used to her meddling in our business. Nagging us to pieces."

"This is what I'm thinking," George said. "Her room wasn't broken into, so it was someone she knew or trusted well enough to let in. Or—"

"Everyone who knew Elaine was fond of her," Jerome said.

George nodded. "I know you want to believe that, but if you search hard enough, everyone has an enemy or two. Can you think of anyone, Maya?"

Maya looked at him in surprise. Who could possibly?

"This could be my fault," Jerome said. "I fired an employee earlier today. He'd been mixing up the mail too much. I got a complaint from Elaine and another resident. I think I might've used Elaine's name when I yelled at him because he's done it to her quite a few times."

"You were going to wait on that, Jerome." Maya shook her head. "Randy wouldn't have done something like this anyway."

George was busy writing. "I need his name and access to his employee records. We're questioning current employees now, as well as the guests on Mrs. Cramer's floor."

Jerome stood up. "It's going to be a long night. Come on, Maya. I'm getting you a cab. You're not driving home."

Maya slowly stood up. "She has family. She has friends at the senior citizen center on M Street and—"

"Maya," Jerome said. "You're going home and getting some sleep. Don't worry about this anymore. If you think of anything, you can tell the detective tomorrow."

With George following behind, they silently made their way down the hotel corridor into the front lobby. As a security officer pulled George away, Jerome turned to Maya.

"Sweetheart." His stare was concrete support, concern and affection. "We'll get through this. We've gotten through worse together."

Maya was so grateful to have someone who understood the most painful moments of her life, and felt them too. She'd rather have no one here right now other than Jerome.

"Yes, we have," she whispered back.

"You stay here." He glanced outside. "It's raining. I'll get you a cab."

Maya tried to pull herself together. She came to know quite a few of the guests, as they generally stayed a month or more. She didn't want any of them to see her like this. She wiped her eyes, fluffed her hair and forced a smile. She glanced around the lobby, still full of guests. Daddy would have wanted her to put on a good front.

* * *

Trajan stepped out of the hotel bar, brooding. The analysts from International Leveraged Markets weren't too impressed. The dinner was quick, with no dessert or coffee afterward. It was a blow to his ego, which Trajan never took lightly. He'd gone to drink by himself for a while trying to plot a strategy to make up for such a bad start. He'd come up with nothing more than starting fresh tomorrow. All he wanted now was sleep as he headed for his room, before he noticed her standing in the lobby.

She was impossible to miss. She looked gorgeous in an unassumingly sexy way. The most dangerous kind. Trajan couldn't dismiss his attraction; it was slapping him in the face. But it wasn't stronger than his anger, which, mixed with the two glasses of gin he'd had, flared.

There she was, smiling. She'd just ruined the whole evening, hurt his own reputation and damaged the hotel's as well. But still, she was happy about something.

Well, that was about to end.

Maya was jolted the second she saw him walking toward her. He looked dashing in his power suit, and as angry as anyone she'd ever seen. In a split second, she remembered she'd ruined the dinner, and that was probably the last straw for her with Trajan. She braced herself.

"Now, listen to me," she started as soon as he reached her.

"No." He stood only a foot from her, his eyes glazed with anger. He couldn't see past how he felt. What he felt she had done to him. "You're not a player, young woman, and this business is only for those who come to play. You're flaky, honey, and you're not messing this up."

Maya was too tired to be enraged, but she wouldn't stand for this. "You never gave me a chance to—"

"To what?" he asked. "Explain? Explain why you were late for this morning's meeting? Who cares. Those were your own people. But tonight. Are you aware two of the most influential analysts in your hometown, where you need as much support as on Wall Street, had their valuable time wasted because of an insignificant incident?"

Maya's hand made contact with Trajan's cheek before she could even think about what she was doing.

Trajan was stung. All nearby eyes turned to them. Gasps escaped a few mouths. The slap had done him good because it removed him from his rage, and he saw Maya's eyes for the first time. She was hurt, in pain. He hadn't noticed it before, but it was so clear now. She'd been crying, and she was about to start crying again. He was taken by a sting of emotion he felt for her.

"You careless bastard." Maya's strength could only muster a bit more than a whisper. "An insignificant incident? A woman, a woman I care for very much, was murdered. Exactly what would have had to happen to qualify as significant in your book? Let me guess, it has to involve you losing money."

Trajan blinked, shaking his head. "Murdered? Here in the hotel?"

"Get away from me, Mr. Matthews " Disgusted, Maya turned her back to him.

Trajan's mind was racing. A murder. Had Maya been in danger? How would this affect everything if it got out? Was he in danger as a guest? Who was murdered? How would it affect the public offering? He struggled with the guilt of knowing what he was most concerned about.

"Maya," he said to the back of her shining black curls. "I'm . . . I'm sorry. I didn't know."

She swung around to face him. She wanted to hate him, but the look in his eyes made her believe him. "Why would you think I'd miss that dinner, take Jerome away from that dinner?"

"Jerome said it was a burglary." He watched as two officers entered the building. Guests were looking around at each other. People would start asking questions. That would hurt him. It would be on the news.

"I guess he didn't want to alarm your dinner guests," Maya said. "He didn't want them to know."

"Good thing." Trajan waited for Jerome, who was walking their way. "What's important here is that the public doesn't know about this. We can't let the press—"

"The press?" Maya's hand clenched in a fist, anger welling up inside of her. "What's important is that we find out who did this."

"Yeah." Trajan nodded. "Of course. I mean—"

"I know what you mean." Maya stared him sternly in the eyes. "For the sake of the IPO, you want us to pretend like this didn't happen."

"We can't do that exactly," Jerome said, "but we can keep this as low-profile as possible. Not just because of the public offering, but the other guests."

Trajan didn't like how uncomfortable Maya made him feel about his own priorities. Someone had to think about the public offering. "That's what I meant."

Maya nodded in agreement, understanding the logic although not liking it. "We will not sweep this under the rug."

Jerome smiled, placing a hand on her shoulder. "We'll work it out. We've beefed up security. We'll have it on every floor and all the cameras in the hotel and the garage are being monitored and reviewed. Maya, I have a cab out front for you. You need to get some rest."

Maya shared her disappointed look with both men. "Why do I feel like the little woman that's being dismissed so the men can handle the real stuff."

Trajan raised a brow, looking down at her. He shrugged and looked away. Maya knew he wanted to say something but thought better of it.

"First thing tomorrow morning, I'll have to write a press release," Maya said, her attention only on Jerome. "Hopefully by then, we'll at least have a suspect."

Trajan wasn't comfortable with the idea of a press release, but decided not to push it right now. Maya had had enough frustration today. He'd handle that on his own in the morning.

"Maya." He called to her just as she turned to head out. When she turned back to face him, he found her sadness, her loss touching, but told himself it was the liquor and feeling tired.

"Yes?" Maya found his expression unreadable. She was generally a good read at that. For a living, she gauged others' emotions, through their expressions and demeanor. With him she couldn't tell what he was feeling or if it was genuine.

"Who . . . I mean the woman who was murdered. Who was she?"

Maya held her chin up. "Her name was Elaine Cramer. She was a close friend of mine. She was a good person. Thank you for asking."

As Jerome led her away, Trajan watched the two of them. He saw an interesting relationship, although a confusing one. He knew the history of Pharaoh Hotel. The two had known each other for more than twenty years. It seemed peculiar that a romance would come of that, but Trajan knew stranger things had happened.

"Tre! Tre Matthews!"

Turned around by a strong grip to the shoulder, Trajan came face to face with a behemoth of a man who had cop written all over him. It took a few seconds, two more than it should have, before he recognized him.

"George?" He saw the same face from more than fifteen years ago, but much broader, more experienced. "Is that George Hobbs?"

"You got it, brother." Detective Hobbs's smile was ear to ear. "Man, I thought you were dead."

Trajan held out his hand to shake, but George ignored it, hugging him in a strong, tight embrace. "Forget those handshakes, man. We used to roll together. Whatever happened to my boy?"

"He's living in New York now." Trajan was feeling more than just joy at seeing his childhood friend. Everything from that broken-down neighborhood made him feel weird. "How about you?"

"I work for the man now." George flashed his badge. "Actually I'm on duty with a very serious case, so I can't shoot the breeze with you now, but what are you doing in D.C. and how long are you gonna be here doing it?"

"Off and on over the next month or so." Trajan reached into his back pocket. "Here's my card. My cell number reaches me anywhere."

George accepted the card, reaching for his own pocket. "Here's mine. Yeah, cops have business cards too. We're very businesslike now."

Jerome approached both men, wiping beads of water off his coat jacket. "How are we doing, officer?"

"You need to come with me," George answered. "We've got some antsy guests and some logistics to go over."

"Of all the times for my hotel manager to be out of town." Jerome sighed, seeming exhausted. "Okay, let's go. Tre, we'll meet up tomorrow."

The three men said their good-byes, with George

promising to keep in touch. As he headed for his hotel room, Trajan was anxious about so many things. First and foremost, he was concerned about the IPO. Could this first-day disaster be saved? He'd been so hopeful. Now he was frustrated and, thanks to Maya, confused. He found himself thinking of her the same way he thought of George and the memories his reentry into his life spurred. There was a sense of discomfort, guilt, confusion and longing.

Something told him Maya Woodson was going to be a thorn in his side for some while.

Maya opened the door to her Georgetown condo and Alissa Morney hugged her tightly as soon as she stepped in.

"Jerome called me," she said. "He told me about your friend and said you'd need me."

Maya joined her on the sofa of her living room. It was a warm, very feminine living room with soft blush, lilac, grass green and cream colors on the walls and furniture. Photos of the beloved parents she'd lost were everywhere.

Alissa Morney was Maya's best friend. A thirty-year-old, suburban, married housewife and mother of two, the women wouldn't seem to have much in common. But they'd been friends, the closest of friends, for five years. Their mothers were both in the Georgetown hospital cancer ward at the same time. Alissa lived only twenty minutes from Maya in Alexandria, Virginia, so they continued their relationship, and now considered each other family.

"Jerome is such a sweetheart," Maya said. "He's always thinking of me. Really, I'll be okay. I just need to deal with the shock."

"I never met the woman," Alissa said. Her caramel

colored skin was clean and clear. She never wore makeup. Hadn't found any that was baby-proof yet. "But you talked about her so much, I feel like I know her."

"I should be used to death," Maya said, hugging a pillow to her chest. "Mama, Daddy. Now Elaine."

"Stop that right now." Alissa frowned, her tiny nose turned up. She had small features, but a full face. She was a full-figured woman and comfortable and very confident about that. "I'll keep you company until you fall asleep. Then, you take tomorrow off. Wednesday, you'll be ready to go back to work."

Maya was already in her pajamas, and very tired. "I know. Wow. I was so caught up in this IPO, thinking it was the most important . . ."

"Understandable," Alissa said. "You and Jerome have been waiting a long time for this. Maybe with too much anticipation."

Maya frowned. "Too much? This is a big deal, you know."

"I know." Alissa said, nodding. "But I think the two of you have turned this into some kind of sacrificial offering to your father."

Maya noted the biblical reference. "We do not worship my dead father like you seem to think. But this is about making him proud. You know how much we both loved him."

"But you're both acting like he's still here. Like he's all you need. It's affecting everything. Like your love life."

Maya knew where this was going. "I've already had this conversation with Alex today. I compare every man to Daddy, and none of them stack up. That's why—"

"No." Alissa raised a cautionary finger. "You compare every man to this vision of perfection you've made up of your father. The reason no one stacks up is because you've created a father that was a perfect man."

Maya shook her head. "I know Daddy had faults. Toward the end, he drank a bit much. That's what killed him. Driving drunk. Still, he was a good man and a great daddy."

"But you shouldn't be looking for a daddy, girl. You're looking for a husband, a partner. Someone with give and take, not just give."

Maya couldn't argue. "I'm on a hiatus anyway. With work, Jerome is the only man in my life."

"You two aren't good company for each other when you immerse yourselves in work. You with your father worship, and Jerome with his guilt."

"Guilt?" Maya was surprised. Alissa was critical of Jerome at times, but this was new.

"Can't you see it?" she asked. "Jerome worships your dad just like you do, but he suffers from survivor's guilt."

"Like that syndrome people get when they've survived a plane accident where others were killed?" Maya was confused. "Jerome wasn't in that accident with Daddy?"

"No, but they were riding together on that road to success, and just as it hit, Nick died and Jerome was alive to see it all come to fruition. He feels guilty for that."

Maya saw some point to that. Jerome had said so many times how he'd wished her father had been there to share in some success or accomplishment. Or, he'd been faced with a challenge and wished for Nick's wisdom and advice. He'd always had a look of guilt on his face.

"All I know," she said stubbornly, "is my father was a great dad, husband and friend. And after Mama and me, no one was more loyal to him than Jerome. After

Mama died, I felt like he was the only one left who really understood me."

"He's not." Alissa placed a comforting hand over Maya's along the top of the sofa back. "He's not, girl. You think he is because he drowns himself in thoughts of your father like you do. Now Jerome is a good man, and he loves you like a daughter, but this isn't any good for either of you."

Maya didn't want to hear this. "That's not the point anyway. Elaine's death . . . her murder changed all of that. I just hope I can focus on this public offering and deal with that horrible man to make this work."

"What horrible man?"

"Tre Matthews." Maya sighed, rolling her eyes. "Girl, don't get me started on him. I've had enough to deal with tonight. I'll tell you about him another day."

Alissa eyed her suspiciously. "I won't let you forget that. I have a feeling I should be looking forward to it."

Maya was at the hotel at eight the next morning, Tuesday. She hadn't been able to sleep at all. If she wasn't thinking of Elaine, it was Trajan and the public offering. She headed straight for her office, mustering determination. She was going to get a fight from Trajan Matthews regarding the press release on Elaine, but she was ready for him.

She stopped by Jerome's office before continuing on to her own, hoping to gather the support of her most devoted backer, and undo some of the influence Trajan no doubt pushed last night, but he was nowhere to be found. Back at her own office, Alexandra was waiting for her, sitting at the window looking out at downtown D.C.

"Morning, Alex." Maya smiled at her, receiving a somber nod. "You're early."

Alexandra spoke slowly, sadly. "If you drive, how long does it take you?"

"It should take ten minutes, but generally a half hour." Maya knew Alexandra spoke of insignificant things such as traffic and weather when she was sad. "I take the bus when I know I don't have to go anywhere. Where's your uncle?"

"Haven't seen him." Alexandra sat across the desk from her. "I just got here five minutes before you. How are you doing?"

"All right," Maya said. "I guess the shock has worn down a little. It's still so hard to believe. Do they have a suspect?"

"Don't you know? The press release says they have several."

Maya's eyes widened. "The release? What release?"

"It went out this morning." Alexandra appeared confused. "I thought you did it last night. There was one on every desk. There's already a couple messages for you from—"

"Jerome would never . . ." Maya was fuming. "Trajan! He did it."

Alexandra's eyes were wide. "Calm down. You're screaming."

"Where is it?" Maya asked, searching her unusually messy desk. "Did I get a copy?"

She spotted it at the same time Alexandra pointed it out. Maya paced the room reading the release quickly. It was line after line of vague diversion. She was conjuring up various ways to make Trajan pay painfully for this.

"To read this," she vented, "you would think someone stole from the tip jar in the restaurant bar, it was caught on tape and the jury has already come out with a verdict of guilty."

"I think they're just trying to keep people calm. Be happy. It says the police have several suspects. I'm certain one of them is the guy."

Through her anger at being left out, all Maya could see was lies and a total disrespect for Elaine, with the only concern being for the public offering.

"Where is he?" Maya crumpled the sheet of paper in her hand. "What room is he in? He's staying here, right?"

Alexandra nodded. "He's in a suite on the eighth floor is all I know."

Maya was dialing the front desk already. She felt as if her breathing had picked up it's pace. To think that last night when he asked Elaine's name, she'd thought for a second she had misjudged Trajan Matthews. Maya vowed not to fall for that again.

Jesse Martin was exiting Trajan's room just as Maya approached the room door. Jesse managed the entire hotel cleaning crew, but still cleaned the rooms of special guests on occasion as well as Jerome's suite. She was certain no one cleaned as well as she did, and she was right.

"Good morning Ms. Woodson," she said. She was a petite woman, with a warm bronzed face. She was forty, but cleaning her whole life made her look closer to fifty. "So sorry to hear about Ms. Cramer. She was so nice to all of us."

Maya paused from her anger. "Yes. She meant so much to all of us. We'll miss her. Is this Mr. Matthews's room?"

Jesse smiled. "Yes, ma'am. He's such a charming man. Mr. Newman asked that I handle his room myself."

Maya peeked in the suite, seeing no one. "Is he gone?"

"He's in the shower now. You seem very interested. He is an attractive man. Is this a personal visit?"

"Not in the least."

Maya stepped past her into the room. "This is a strictly professional arrangement. As a matter of fact, we have a meeting now. I'm a little early."

"In his room?" Jesse didn't appear comfortable with Maya entering the room. "He's in the shower now. Shouldn't you come back later?"

Maya had already stepped into the hallway of the suite. "No, this can't wait. Thank you, Jesse."

After a slight hesitation, Jesse left, closing the door behind her. Maya let her eyes roll over one of the best suites in the hotel. It was almost 750 square feet, fully furnished with additional appliances, and a view of the city. She wondered why Trajan was getting it. After all, he should be impressing them, not the other way around. But here he was, basking in the hotel's services.

Maya listened as the water from the shower ran. She wanted to hold onto her anger despite the delay, but felt herself reluctantly calming. She went to the lounge chair next to the work table with a fax machine, phone and computer portal. She smelled the beautiful bouquet on the table next to her. Maya loved flowers.

As she gently brought the lilies to her nose, the note creased into the bouquet fell to the floor. Maya reached for it, glancing by instinct at the writing. She wouldn't have been surprised if it was from Jerome the way he'd cozied up to his new buddy.

Hope All Went Well. Miss You. Love You. ♥ *Elizabeth*

Maya smirked as she returned the note. So, Elizabeth was the lucky woman. She had to be some kind of woman to deal with this character, she thought.

Maya stood up as she heard the water cease. She was ready for him and he was going to be put in his place.

She had no intention of going easy on him and waiting for an explanation. As soon as he came out, she would—

Maya's mind, along with all her intentions, went blank as Trajan stepped out of the bathroom. Her body involuntarily reacted to the sight of his bare chest. Its rich caramel complexion glistened with water over his tight muscles. The towel wrapped around his waist parted over his left thigh. It was trim, but muscular as well. Maya had to check herself to keep her eyes from wandering like her mind just had.

When he saw her, Trajan took only a second to readjust. He was surprised, confused and pleased at the same time.

"How did you get in here?" He tightened his towel, staying at the bathroom entrance.

Maya forced herself to regain composure. "I . . . It doesn't matter. What matters is you went behind my back with that release."

Trajan nodded with a smile. "I expected this."

His careless expression reignited Maya's anger. "You find this amusing? How dare you? I'm the public relations director. That press release was my responsibility."

"Correction, Maya. I'm responsible for all releases pertaining to the public offering." Trajan stepped casually into the dining area, reaching for the pot of coffee he'd made before the shower.

"This has nothing to do with that." Maya's anger only rose as he seemed so nonchalant about the situation, about her presence. "This is a hotel issue, not—"

"I disagree," he said, taking a pause for a sip. "You can deal with the community crap, but this, this murder directly affects the public offering. I will handle it. This is not about spinning so the public adores you."

Maya's eyes turned to slits. She gripped the bottom

of her suit jacket. "And don't you dare condescend to me or call what I do crap."

Trajan placed his cup on the table. She wanted a fight, but he had no time for her thin-skinned feelings. "I didn't mean to insult you."

"Yes you did." She took a few steps closer, her eyes tight with anger. "How could you have possibly meant anything else? In addition, I don't spin. I tell the truth. You're familiar with the meaning of the word truth, aren't you? It's the exact opposite of the release you put out."

"With Jerome's approval," he added. "And that release was one hundred percent truth, making sure not to reveal anything that would make the company look weak or vulnerable. We can't afford that, Maya."

"Afford what?" she asked. "A murder? I hate the way you speak of this, of Elaine."

"I'm sorry I don't cry and feel sorry for myself like you, Maya. As sad as it all is, my priority is this public offering and that's why I put out the release. You aren't prepared for this. We're talking about powerful people who, with a whisper, can ruin everything."

"I am prepared!" Maya hated him for making her defend her right to be a part of this. "I've been prepared for this forever. Since I was a child, my daddy—"

Trajan raised his hand to stop her. "Cut the sob story. Daddy or no Daddy, this isn't the sentimental next chapter to a family saga. This is strictly business, hard knocks. So cut the melodies and sentimental flashbacks and suck it up."

"You're a heartless, arrogant ass." Maya stepped to him, wanting to slap him in the face. "You can't even feel pity for an old dead woman. What kind of a monster are you?"

Trajan was surprised at how he let her words affect him. He didn't even know or care about this woman, yet to look at her, she put him at a pause with her insults to his character. He shifted his eyes away from her to the sofa, scattered with papers.

Maya felt some sense of victory at his inability to answer her, but it was short-lived as her eyes followed his. She hadn't seen them before, but it was clear as she hurried to the sofa.

"This is my stationery," she said, exasperated. "From my office."

"I had to use it for the release."

She turned to him as he approached. "So you're a thief now too?"

"Jerome let me into your office." He grabbed the leftover stack of stationery and held it out to her.

Maya was disbelieving. "Jerome wouldn't do that. Not to me, not without my permission."

"Jerome knows what needs to be done," Trajan said. "You're the only one here who doesn't. Now take these extra sheets if you want them. I've got to work."

Surprising herself with the move, Maya slapped the papers out of Trajan's hand. They went flying over the room. She watched Trajan's angry face take over a second before he reached out, grabbing her arm.

"Don't you ever . . ." Trajan was livid as he pulled her to him. She was as light as a feather. It was that lightness that caused him to pause. He was grabbing a woman in anger and that was wrong. Only, as he pulled her to him, all anger was wiped away and replaced with desire.

Maya felt a wave of fear and excitement wash over her as he pulled her to him. She'd known she'd gone too far by slapping his hand. She felt a strange sense of desire well up in the pit of her stomach, and she was confused by its presence.

"Let me go," she said. She could smell his clean body and the scent of his fresh cologne as it traveled up her nose. Her eyes saw the beads of water leave a trail down his cheek.

Maya attempted to pull away, but somehow it only bought her closer to him. Closer to his bare chest, his face only inches from hers. Her lips parted just barely and her throat felt as dry as a desert. His eyes were still angry, and magnetic.

She was beautiful, Trajan thought. Those lips, that kissable nose, those fiery eyes. He had to fight himself to keep from kissing her. Still, he wanted to and couldn't see what could stop him.

Maya jumped when she heard the knock on the door. Trajan had a pause as well, and she took the opportunity to break free of him. Their eyes caught for a second, neither able to accept the tension that existed between them.

Trajan grabbed his robe off the edge of the sofa and put it on, heading for the door. Maya felt herself exhale. She felt so warm, she needed some air. Some cool air. She decided at that moment to forget any idea that something had been going on just a moment ago.

"Tre!"

George Hobbs hugged Trajan so tight, he could barely breathe. Maya noticed the interest in her presence as soon as he saw her.

"Ms. Woodson," he said, leaving Trajan behind and approaching her. He held out his hand to her.

"Detective Hobbs." Maya gathered herself together to speak with a nod.

"What's up, George?" Trajan couldn't remember setting up anything with George, but right now his mind was a complete blank.

George was hesitant as his eyes moved between the two of them. "I was wondering what was up for lunch with you today."

Trajan went for his schedule book, pausing a moment

as he passed Maya. She purposefully avoided eye contact with him.

"Let me check my book." Trajan sensed the coolness in his words this time, although he'd said those five words hundreds of times before. He brushed away the guilt in a second. He had gotten good at that.

Maya wanted to leave, but one thing kept her there.

"Detective." She spoke loud enough for Trajan to hear, making sure her tone was sarcastic. "What is the truth about the murder investigation?"

"I can't tell you particulars," he answered. "But I do need your help."

"Anything," she said. "I'm at your disposal for Elaine."

"Not exactly," Trajan protested. "We have an afternoon meeting. We have to discuss the media interviews for the next two weeks."

He noticed the uncomfortable looks from them both. Was he the only one who cared about business?

"I need you to look at some security videos with me," George said. "Can you meet me in the security office in a half hour?"

"Of course." Maya sent Trajan, who was staring intently at her, a cold stare. "And I'll stay however long you need me to."

Trajan blinked, otherwise appearing unfazed. "George, lunch is cool. Downstairs in the restaurant at noon?"

George nodded, his smile not as wide as before. Trajan knew why. George was catching on to how different Trajan was, so different from when he was a young man in the hood. And Trajan didn't like it that George, not to mention Maya, made him feel bad about that.

Maya was right behind George, not wanting to be left alone with Trajan anymore.

"Maya." Trajan called after her.

She took a deep breath before facing him, her hands firmly on the door.

"I . . . I understand this thing means a lot to you." He noticed the look of disgust on her face. "What? I'm trying to—"

"This thing?" Maya doubted he had any feelings at all. He was no good at pretending to have them earlier.

"Whatever." He was annoyed with how she made him so aware of his slip-ups. "I meant to say, despite this . . . our meeting . . ."

Maya turned back and headed out the door. She had no intention of answering him, let alone listen to the rest of his weak sentence.

"Looks like I'm too late," Jerome said, almost running into her in the doorway.

"For what?" Maya asked, surprised to see him.

Trajan approached them, taking care not to stand too close to Maya. He noticed, more than he should, Jerome placing his hand on Maya's shoulder.

"Alex told me you were coming here, red-hot mad," Jerome said. "I came to jump between you two."

"There is nothing to jump between," Trajan said, hearing the voice inside him that said Jerome's hand had been there too long. "Maya understands why we did what we did."

"Jerome," Maya said, after rolling her eyes at Trajan. "I wanted to write this release."

Jerome rubbed her shoulder with reassuring strokes. "Maya, I thought you'd be out today. Alissa called me after you went to sleep last night. She said you agreed to take the day off."

Maya pursed her lips together, reluctantly accepting that explanation. "It wasn't a sure promise I wouldn't come in. Well fine. I've got to get some work done and meet Detective Hobbs."

"What for?" Jerome asked, stepping aside for her.

"He's not upsetting you with details about Elaine, is he? I don't want him to bother you if you aren't ready to talk about it."

"No, he's not bothering me at all. As a matter of fact, I was hoping to talk to him today. I want to know what he thinks happened."

"All right," Jerome said. "But take it easy on this. You can't heal if you immerse yourself in this investigation."

"The only way I can heal," she said, "is when they find out who did this and get him behind bars."

Maya smiled at Jerome, ignoring Trajan before leaving.

Trajan watched as Jerome's face held concern in Maya's direction until she was out of sight. It irked him that he was developing a need to know the extent of their relationship.

Three

"I know this is boring," George said, standing over Maya's chair, "but it's important. You seem to have been closer to Ms. Cramer than anyone in the hotel. You might recognize someone who she knew or you'd seen around her."

"How is the questioning going?" Maya asked.

George frowned. "I can't give you particulars, but we might have some leads."

Maya turned, looking up at him. "One of our employees? I should know this. So should Jerome."

"I'll tell you and Mr. Newman when I can." He nodded to the screen. "Please, keep your eyes on the video."

Maya turned back. "Nothing yet. I mean I recognize some guests in the lobby, but . . ."

George nodded to Lance Snyder. "This is a tape of the camera on the third floor, where Mrs. Cramer lived."

As Lance switched the tapes, Maya shifted in her seat. She was getting a little frustrated. They'd been watching tapes for more than an hour. She wanted to help, but she was beginning to feel useless.

"How do you know Mr. Matthews?" The question slipped from her lips without thought.

George spoke with a laugh. "Tre and I grew up together. He's from the hood."

"That's hard to believe," Maya said. "He seems more like he'd be from the Upper East Side of New York."

"No," George said with a half frown. "Tre used to be cool. He's been through a lot, and I guess he let it leave him in the wrong way. I think he's a little ashamed of where he came from."

Maya kept her eyes on the video, sensing the sincerity in George's voice. "He seems so cold, so uncaring. Hard to believe he was ever different."

"I hear New York will do that to folks. He was always a little angry, but knew how to let go. I can't say he hasn't changed. We haven't kept in touch, but it seems like he has."

"Why weren't you able to keep in touch?"

"Are you paying attention, Ms. Woodson?"

"Yes I am, and my name is Maya. Please."

"Okay, Maya." George paused. "I can't tell you what happened. I tried to keep in touch, but I guess Tre got caught up in college and New York, all that."

Maya sensed George was uncomfortable, and she decided to end it there. What a cold sort Trajan appeared to be, leaving his childhood friend behind like that.

"Have you contacted Elaine's family?" she asked.

George nodded. "Her daughter is coming by today. We had the hardest time trying to reach her. There's a son in the area as well, but he's pretty transient. Can't seem to find him yet. The other boy lives in New Jersey."

Maya wondered if they had any intention of giving their mother a proper funeral. She was sure they'd rather pocket the cost instead.

"George," she asked. "How would I find out about the funeral arrangements?"

He shrugged. "You'd have to call the family about that. I'm just a detective."

Maya nodded as Lance fast forwarded through the tape of an empty hallway.

"Stop!" she yelled, leaning forward. "That woman."

Lance froze the tape to a woman thirty or so. Blond, stringy hair and a rail thin face with a body to match. She was dressed in a unisex white button-down and tight blue jeans.

"You recognize her?" George asked.

"Yes," Maya racked her brain, but was drawing a blank. "I've seen her before, but I can't remember where."

"A first name? Last name?"

Maya shook her head. "I'm trying. I just . . . I'm sorry. I do know her, though. I have seen her."

"Take your time," George said slowly. "A guest? A visitor? A vendor?"

Maya bit her lower lip. "You must think I'm useless."

George patted her on the shoulder. "It'll come to mind the second you stop trying to think of it. Let's move on. Mark it there, Lance, and go on."

"You're a liar," Alissa said as soon as Maya picked up the phone in her office.

"Hello to you too," Maya said.

"You're supposed to be at home today, resting. You promised."

"I never promised. Besides, I felt better this morning. The shock has passed and I was needed here. In more ways than one."

Alissa let out an impatient sigh. "I hate to hurt your ego, but the hotel can survive a day or two without you."

"As it stands," Maya said with a smile, "I don't trust Tre Matthews farther than I could throw him. He's trying to push me out of this IPO. I don't believe for a second that he has the hotel's best interest at heart. Only his own."

"Well, since he's working for the hotel . . . wouldn't that help you by default?"

"To serve his purposes. But will he have done us more harm after he rides off into the sunset, cash in hand?"

"This guy is getting to you. By any chance, is he cute?"

Maya spoke with irritation. "What would that have to do with anything?"

"Look, girl. I'm sitting here cleaning two loads of laundry, trying to deal with a two-year-old's tantrum, making two lunches that will be complained about no matter what I put in them, pricking my finger sewing various sized buttons to a pillowcase in order to make I don't know what for this school play, and I have starting dinner to look forward to. Humor me."

Maya laughed. "Okay Ally. Yes, Tre Matthews is attractive. He's very handsome as a matter of fact, but it's all surface. His beauty is only skin deep. There's no valuable substance there."

"Brutal."

Maya dropped the phone and practically fell out of her chair as she saw Trajan standing in her doorway. He smiled a victorious smile at having caught her off guard. She felt her face heat up on fire. Had he heard her say? . . . Just great.

"I . . . I . . ."

"You should close your door if you're going to talk nasty on the phone," he said.

It took Maya a moment to gather herself together, pick the phone up and say good-bye to Alissa. Her embarrassment was joined by anger as she noticed the sanctimonious smile on his face. This was not how she wanted to start this meeting.

"You had me excited there for a moment." Trajan strode confidently to Maya's desk and sat across from her. He wouldn't let her see how her last words had made him feel. He didn't really want to admit that to himself. "Then at the end. Well, I'm disappointed."

"Can we get to work, please?" Maya tried to calm herself down, thinking of their last encounter and how she'd felt when he pulled her to him. *Get it together, girl!*

"First things first," he said. "Who was inquiring about my appearance?"

"None of your business," she said stubbornly. Maya tried to play cool, leaning back in her chair. "And you should knock on the door when you arrive, open or closed. In addition, you're early. We weren't supposed to meet until four."

"I know being early for meetings is important to you, so I thought I'd gain some brownie points."

"Sarcasm gains you nothing." She knew he wouldn't let her arriving late for the meeting go. Trajan was a stick-it-to-them kind of guy.

"Wow," Trajan said, ignoring that he was affected by her response to him. Her eyes held a distaste that reached across at him. "You really hate me, don't you?"

"Let's put it on the table, Tre. I don't particularly like your style of business. But I can keep personal feelings out of this."

"If you could do that all around, we would be much better off." It bothered Trajan that he was so distracted by her features, by the way her peach silk top draped at her neck, revealing a smooth, glowing brown chest. He'd worked with and around beautiful women before with the ability to keep them from affecting him. Why should she be an exception? "When I say that, I'm speaking of—"

"My father," Maya interrupted. She was becoming infuriated with that charming grin of his. "You've made that clear. I don't need to repeat to you that although I'm a professional, I'm not a feelingless machine like you. I don't think that's good business. In addition, this is my daddy's business. He built this company with his blood, sweat and tears. He loved it as much as anything. So, as I have a right and obligation to, I will always carry personal feelings for every decision made regarding it."

Trajan eyed her sternly. He generally never cared that someone thought of him this way. They were wrong, but he let them be. But he didn't feel the same with Maya. "A feelingless machine? You don't really know me well enough to make such judgments about me."

Their eyes locked, both ready to go at it but thinking better of it. Maya knew it was really up to her; what she'd say next would set the tone. She thought wisely and said nothing, only stood and walked stiffly to the table near the window. She knew he was following her, watching her.

"I guess we can get started now," she said as he sat down next to her. She waited for him to push his chair away; he seemed too close. When he didn't, she made the move herself.

Trajan smirked at her gesture. "I don't bite, Maya."

Maya's eyes settled on him. A dangerous smile fought at the edges of her lips, but never came through.

"I do," she answered back, slowly.

Trajan knew she'd won that one. He was uniquely intrigued by her, this display of flirtatious aggression. Maybe she wasn't as puff pastry as he thought.

"Good. Now," Maya said, as she sensed no rebuttal. Her throat felt dry. She swallowed, shuffling her papers. "Media strategy first. The article in the *New York Times* will be in tomorrow's issue. Have you seen it? Proofed it?"

"Nothing regarding my clients goes to print without my review." He was letting it get to him that she wouldn't look at him. She was being a brat about this, so why should he let her make him feel guilty about anything? Feelingless machine. Please.

"Fine. I've set up interviews with these papers in New York tomorrow." She handed him a list. "You and Jerome need to do *Barron's* and *Bloomberg*. I've got the *New York Post*. Right now, I'm in the midsection, but I'm still working on maneuvering my way toward the front page. But I feel if we can give anywhere, the *Post* is the best for that."

"We give nowhere, Maya. Keep pushing."

Maya didn't want to let him get to her, but he was. "I wasn't suggesting that I would give. I was just saying . . . never mind. Next is Boston. I'm still working on the list for—"

"I've got the *Boston Globe*," he said. "I just need to finalize a few things. The *Herald* isn't in the cards. Now, we need to get started on these Internet trading companies. They carry their own newsletters, call them e-zines. They reach thousands, millions even. Most people check out the news and feature sections at the sites before they start their trading for the day."

He sighed, hating himself for caring so much. "Maya, you could at least look at me when I'm speaking to you."

"I'm listening to you." She couldn't tell him that she found him too distracting to concentrate. She wasn't sure what was going on. She was sure she hated the man, but let him get within a couple of feet of her, and her temperature shot up.

"I'll try to be more charming," he said, half joking. "I think you can tolerate me for an hour."

"Don't patronize me, Tre," she said. "I'm a big girl, and I can tolerate a lot worse than you."

"I'll take that as a compliment even though I'm sure it wasn't meant as one." He leaned back, his pride daring him to push it. "In any case, I'll provide the charm as a gift."

"Save your charm for Elizabeth." Maya saw his eyes widen as he sat forward, hearing her speak the name she'd seen on the card in his hotel room. She'd expected as much, and was pleased at catching him off guard.

"How do you know Liz?" Trajan was more than surprised. With the way things had been going between him and Elizabeth, he had been cautious to mention her to anyone new he'd met. He was certain he hadn't mentioned her to Jerome. So how did she know?

Maya raised her chin, victory hers now. "I know you better than you think I do. Can we get back to work now?"

"We need a level playing field, Maya. If you aren't going to tell me how you know about Liz, then I at least have a right to know the name of your paramour."

"Paramour?" Maya laughed, realizing he'd just confirmed Elizabeth was his girlfriend. "I think you're the first to use that word in two decades."

"It was on purpose," he said. "Now give."

"Wasn't it you who said 'give nothing'?" She smiled again as his frustration grew. He was used to winning any argument, and she wouldn't let him. And Maya was certain he'd thought he'd put her in her place.

Before Trajan could respond, there was a knock at the door, and they both turned their heads to see Jerome approaching, a wide smile on his face.

"Good news," he said. "They got the killer. They've got him."

Trajan made a victorious fist and Maya sighed.

"Who was it?" she asked, standing.

"His name is Lincoln Stack, a contract electrician. He came in for scheduled work today. As soon as Detective Hobbs introduced himself with his badge, the guy confessed to murder."

"You're kidding." It sounded too good to be true to Maya.

Jerome shook his head. "Vera Stanz was there. She saw the whole thing."

Trajan saw red flags. "Vera Stanz? Who is she? Press?"

"No, Tre." Maya wondered if the man thought of anything but appearances. "Vera is the human resources director for the hotel. She probably identified this murderer to Detective Hobbs. And no, she would never run to the press. I know that's all you care about."

Trajan shot her a glance and returned to his papers.

Jerome continued. "Vera said she and Detective Hobbs approached him, said hello. His eyes started shifting right away. When Hobbs pulled out his badge, the guy literally fell to his knees and yelled something like 'I killed her. I'm sorry, I killed her.' She said he started weeping like a baby. He couldn't even utter a word when he was hauled off."

"Wow." Maya leaned on the table. "Without even being asked. This is so . . . great, I suppose. Yes. Did he say why? Why he would want to kill an innocent old woman?"

"Not that Vera witnessed," Jerome said apologetically. "Vera's running a more in-depth background check on him now."

"Why wasn't this done before?" Trajan asked with caution. He didn't want Jerome to feel he was being second-guessed. "I mean, don't you do background checks on all your employees?"

"Not so in-depth for contractors," Jerome said. "They don't get room or computer access. He was only supposed to be here working in that one closet for the week."

Maya was unsatisfied. "I need to know why. Not that

any reason would make sense, but it would be something."

"Let's just be relieved it's over," Trajan said.

"I'm with you, Tre," Jerome said. He turned back with a compassionate expression to Maya. "He's caught. This should give you some peace."

Maya smiled, sitting back in her chair at her desk. "As much as anything can, I guess."

Trajan observed the exchange between the two. He had to know what was going on here. Had to.

"Can we get back to work?" he asked, pointing to the papers on the table.

Jerome winked encouragingly to Maya. "I'll leave you two to planning. I guess we'll all see each other in New York tomorrow."

"Eleven forty-five," Trajan called out. "They should start showing up for the luncheon at noon."

With a heavy sigh, Maya got up from her seat and returned to the table. Her hesitation did not pass Trajan's attention.

The next hour seemed more like five to each of them. They would start every interaction with the intention of professionalism, almost to a degree of nauseum. However, no matter what was said, every conversation would end up with sarcastic quips or judgmental comments. They wouldn't get along. That was clear to Maya. They weren't on the same page, Trajan was sure. They both realized they were control freaks, thrown together as business partners at Jerome's request. Neither was sure how to make it work, if it would work.

They finally made it through the hour, with a basic level of agreement on next steps. Trajan couldn't wait to get out of the office. He needed some fresh air, and he rolled down all his windows as he started on his long trip home. He'd considered himself rustic, doing the four-hour drive to D.C. for a change of pace. He enjoyed driving through the Atlantic states. On his way down, he'd thought of nothing but the public offering. On his way back, he thought of nothing but Maya.

Maya tried to get back to work, but if her mind wasn't focused on her obstinate new partner, it was flooded with thoughts of Elaine and the gnawing dissatisfaction of it all. She wasn't sure what made her finally decide to go to Elaine's suite, but once she was there, she couldn't go inside. It wasn't the barely visible strip of police tape over the knob that kept her out. It was the image of Elaine on her bed. Dead.

Such a waste, she thought. And no one left to—

As it hit her, Maya grabbed in her purse for her cell phone with one hand and rummaged around for Detective Hobbs's business card with the other. Her mind was racing a mile a minute as the phone rang.

"Detective Hobbs," she started. "It's Maya Woodson. It was her daughter. Elaine Cramer's daughter! Her name is Lisa, Laura . . . something like that."

"Linda Smalls," George answered slowly. "Okay, Maya. Now go a little slower and tell me what are you talking about."

"The woman in the video on Elaine's floor." Maya spoke as slowly as she could, pacing the hallway. "That was her daughter. It took me so long to remember because I'd only seen her picture a couple of times. Elaine doesn't keep them out."

"Go ahead."

"Elaine's children are horrid to her. Horrid period. All they cared about was her money. They never even visited her. For Linda to be here on the same day . . ."

George laughed a bit. "Ms. Woodson, whatever the case with Mrs. Cramer's daughter, we have the killer."

Maya was shaking her head as she spoke. "I know what you have. Jerome told me, but it doesn't fit right."

"You're a detective now?" he asked sarcastically. "The man confessed to murder."

"Maybe Linda paid him," Maya said. "What did he give as his motive?"

"I wouldn't tell you either way, but we've hit a little snag. Once we got him in the box at the station, asked him a couple of questions about Mrs. Cramer, he did a 180. Denies any involvement. Won't talk at all now."

"So this case is still open?" Maya asked.

"So you're suggesting the man makes a habit of confessing to murders he never knew about just at the sight of a badge?"

"I'm saying that Elaine's kids were after her money. I'm saying that yesterday morning Elaine had another bad story to tell involving Linda's daughter. There isn't even any video of this Lincoln something or other in Elaine's hallway."

"That camera only shows the east end of that hallway. If someone were to enter Mrs. Cramer's suite from the stairs to the west, we wouldn't see them."

"Detective Hobbs." Maya sighed.

"Call me George."

"George," she said. "You have to promise me you'll at least look into this."

There was a short pause before he spoke. "I don't have to promise you anything, but I'm developing a weakness for ya. Now, don't take that the wrong way. I'm an engaged man, but I think you're a nice sister, so I'll check it out. Linda Smalls is still scheduled to come by the station at five today."

Maya felt a mixture of apprehension, excitement and responsibility with her newfound clue. She was certain

Linda was behind Elaine's murder, and she was determined to see her pay for it.

Although it was less than a three-hour train ride from D.C., Maya had never been to New York City with the exception of a weekend at the Hamptons, but never in Manhattan.

The Tavern on the Green was the most successful restaurant in the country from a revenue standpoint. It would cost Jerome a pretty penny, but as he'd told Maya, Trajan insisted on it.

Maya was impressed. Located across the street from Central Park, it was a beautiful restaurant, the place of places for celebrities and CEOs alike. With a flourishing garden and twinkling trees outside, it had six dining rooms, each with a distinct style. Their meeting was in the Chestnut Room, a rustic baroque fantasy of brass, copper, carved mirrors and glorious art, overlooking a flourishing garden.

Trajan kept his distance from Maya. From the moment she entered the room, her sharp, intelligent businesswoman style impressed him. He would never fault her on her presentation. He felt a strong attraction to her as she walked across the room. Everyone was watching her walk across the room, and as she approached a welcoming Jerome, Trajan noticed his own jealousy. It frustrated him, because in recent years, he was usually the target of jealousy, and in this particular situation the feeling came from nowhere, with no justification.

He watched her, with Jerome at her side, greeting and networking. She was a joy to watch. Trajan had become so entranced by her, he didn't notice his own girlfriend as she approached.

"Tre." Elizabeth Davis brushed his shoulders with

her long, adorned and well-manicured hand. "Why haven't you returned my phone calls?"

She was almost six feet tall, with long legs and a voluptuous body. It was a body she dressed to her advantage to get the edge as a broker, a woman in a man's business. The money business. Her green eyes sparkled, the most alarming feature on her alarmingly beautiful café au lait face.

She flipped her just-beyond-shoulder-length auburn hair, and Trajan could smell the expensive perfume he'd bought her. It had no effect on him, and he didn't feel too good about that.

"Liz." He leaned in, whispering. "I told you I was going to be unavailable during this public offering. What are you doing here?"

She narrowed her eyes, her lips pressing together for a moment. "I'm a broker, remember? I always support your clients. You used to like that."

"I'm sorry." Trajan smiled with charm and assurance as an analyst walked by. "I'm glad you came."

"I wonder," she said. "Did you even get my flowers?"

"Yes." He found her beautiful, and knew she was everything he was so certain he wanted. Then why didn't he? "Thank you, Liz."

As Jerome approached them, an excited smile lit his face, the type of smile most men had when around Elizabeth.

Trajan had always prided himself on being perceptive. It was key to his survival in this business. Only, at this moment, he regretted that gift, because it forced him to realize that the second he saw Jerome, he got excited. He got excited because he'd thought Maya was with him. He was excited at the thought, the anticipation of her being near. Trajan cursed himself under his breath because of that anticipation, as well as the disappointment he'd felt when he realized she wasn't going to be near.

"You must be Jerome." Elizabeth held her hand out. "I'm Elizabeth Davis, broker for New York Securities. I'm also Tre's girlfriend, so I've heard a lot about you over the last couple of months."

Trajan gently squeezed at Elizabeth's elbow. They'd discussed revealing their relationship at business gatherings. She always broke the rules.

"It's time we get started," he said. "Come on to the podium. Liz, go ahead and sit down."

Maya watched as Trajan took control. He was in his element. She herself had been intimidated by the cynical stares as Jerome began his presentation. Not Trajan. He stepped in with all the confidence and charisma needed to fill the room.

He interrupted Jerome on cue, as she'd known they'd rehearsed. He wouldn't allow questions until the end. He created a smooth transition for David Hanley, the CFO of Pharaoh, as well as for Maya.

The presentation lasted a little less than a half hour. The questions lasted longer.

What is the company's market position now?

What is the stock's marketability?

Define the growth fundamentals?

What about takeover defense strategies?

It was rough, but Jerome was near perfect, Maya and David added a nice touch, and Trajan smoothed everything out.

Maya had to admit she was impressed. With all the personal reservations she'd held about him, professionally she had to hand it to him. He was in his element, and he owned that room.

After the luncheon was over and the brokers and analysts headed back to work, Maya wanted to congratulate Trajan, but decided against it. She'd worked too hard to hold her ground with him. If she showed him any deference, he'd walk all over her.

Besides, that beautiful woman was with him. The one who had been staring at him throughout the luncheon. They were close, at least friends. She'd invaded Trajan's personal space several times without objection from him. He hadn't even blinked.

"Beautiful, isn't she?" Jerome placed a hand on Maya's shoulder as he came from behind. "She's his girlfriend."

Maya ignored her negative reaction to this news. She remembered the flowers. "Elizabeth?"

"How did you know?" he asked. "And why do you seem so ticked about it?"

"I'm wondering if we should really be calling him Tre," she said. "Like we were old friends. It seems so unprofessional."

"Everyone calls him Tre. Even business associates. Why do you care about something so small, at this moment?"

Maya shrugged, ignoring the question. "I guess anything is better than Trajan. So, you happy?"

Before he could answer, David Hanley interrupted. He was a tall, lanky black man with hair that had gone white twenty years early. "Excuse me, Maya. Jerry, we need to deal with this guy over here. He's got some tough questions. Can I steal you?"

Maya knew Jerome hated being called Jerry. She stifled her laughter as he cringed.

"Maya," he said. "Ask me that question again when this is really over. So far, so good."

Trajan noticed Maya's stare as she passed him and Elizabeth on her way to the wall phone. He found himself growing angry despite the success of the luncheon. Angry because with all that was going on, he was most concerned that Maya noticed Elizabeth's hand on his lap. Noticed her, period. He didn't want her knowing more about Elizabeth than she already did. He didn't want her thinking . . . What was wrong with him? Elizabeth was his girlfriend. What did it matter that Maya knew?

"Dinner still on?" Elizabeth raised her voice. "Tre. Dinner tonight? I've got to get back to New York Securities."

Trajan shook hands with an analyst on his way out.

"Elizabeth, I can't. We've discussed this. Don't commit me to anything right now."

"This is Jennifer and Arthur Kist. You do not cancel on the Kists. You've been so eager to meet with them. More than me even."

Trajan nodded. She was right. This was what he wanted. Arthur Kist was a billionaire investor. The connections would be fruitful. Elizabeth was always doing stuff like this. Working miracles, marrying connections.

"I have dinner plans with Jerome and the guys from David Ellis Finance Company." His eyes stole quick glances at Maya on the phone. "I just can't. We'll have to do it tomorrow night."

"I sincerely doubt the Kists will rearrange their schedules for us." She snatched her purse from the table and stood up. "I'd ask you to call me, but that seems to be an impossibility for you lately. And quit blaming this public offering. It's been like pulling teeth to get your attention long before this."

She walked briskly away. Trajan's mind was already off of her, and onto something else as he stood up.

"You're kidding." Maya was shocked. This wasn't what she expected. "Lincoln Stack killed someone else?"

"You got it," George said, his voice coming over the

phone a little scratchy. "He killed his ex-girlfriend two days ago. Been racked with guilt since. That's what he confessed to when he'd seen us and my badge. We sent some boys over to his girl's place this morning. They found the body."

"So," she said. "We're back to Linda?"

"Can't tell you the details on that, but we're looking into it."

"All of Elaine's three kids were worthless. Can't stand each other, either. I know I'm no detective, but I think you'll find the answer there."

"You might be a detective after all. I'll talk to you later, Maya."

"What do you think you're doing?" Trajan started in on her the second she hung up the phone.

"Were you listening?" Maya felt herself on the defensive just by his presence. "How dare you?"

"You're preoccupied with this . . . murder still? You should be—"

"Still?" Maya asked. This man had to be the coldest jerk she'd ever met. "Still? Exactly how long would it be appropriate for me to mourn the death of someone I care about? I guess one day is all you'd give."

"I'm not talking about mourning." He stepped closer. She twisted his words, upsetting him. "I'm talking about playing private dick. Your mind needs to be here, with this public offering."

"It's so black and white to you, isn't it?" Maya could see her words weren't penetrating, but she would say her piece. "I was here today, no matter what else was on my mind. I dare you to have one criticism of my professionalism and presentation today."

Trajan stuffed his hands in his pockets. "I'm just saying that—"

"I know what you're saying." Maya felt somewhat victorious. "Besides, who are you to speak of professionalism, bringing your girlfriend to the luncheon."

Trajan gritted his teeth. "Liz is a broker. Not that it's any of your business. And how in the hell did you know that was her? I demand to know how you know about her."

"Although I'm sure most people bow to your demands, I'm not, nor will I ever be, one of them." Maya thought to mention the flowers in his hotel room, but she was reminded of the moment when he'd grabbed her, and her body slipped a message through her mind's defense that she'd liked it.

Suddenly, Trajan seemed too close for comfort, his stare too deep. Maya backed away, turning her gaze elsewhere. She was sorry she'd even brought up the topic of Elizabeth.

Trajan noticed her sudden change, her withdrawal. It confused him how he felt anger and compassion for her at the same time. He found her behavior noncommittal, but she was dealing with a lot right now with this woman's murder. He knew he wasn't making any of this better.

"I'd say this is off to a good start." Jerome wrapped an arm around Maya and slapped Trajan on the arm. "What's with the frowns? Not fighting again I hope."

"Of course not." Trajan's eyes never left Maya as he spoke. "Maya and I were discussing the success of the luncheon. But we still have a full day ahead of us before dinner tonight."

"I'll handle my end," Maya said, speaking of her media interviews. "You boys have fun."

"Wait, Maya," Jerome held her arm, turning to Trajan. He seemed perplexed at the younger man's expression. "What's wrong, Tre?"

Trajan felt his displeasure at the sight of Jerome hold-

ing on to Maya as he did. He quickly corrected himself
before it could show.

"Nothing at all," he said.

After a hesitation, Jerome said, "I need a few moments alone with Maya. Can we meet outside? In front
of the restaurant?"

Trajan nodded, although he was a little tired of this
scenario. All the privacy, the dismissals. He excused
himself and left the room, thinking only about the two
of them. What were they talking about? Was his arm
still around her? Most importantly, why did he care so
much?

Jerome and Maya sat down at a nearby table. "Sweetheart, what's wrong? You're not happy."

Maya hated that he could sense her feelings now. She
didn't want to burden him. "I'm actually very happy
about the luncheon. It's just Tre. I don't like him,
Jerome."

Jerome looked away for a moment, his expression
serious. "He seems to like you. Don't look so surprised.
I've seen him staring at you and so have you."

Maya smoothed her hair, feeling uneasy. "He's only
thinking of how he can keep me as far away from the
investors as possible."

Jerome laughed. "I don't think that's exactly what's
on his mind. What else is bugging you? Maya Woodson
never let a man ruin her day."

Maya told him what she knew of Elaine's murder investigation, and Jerome appeared disturbed by the
change of events.

"Damn," he said. "I was hoping this would be resolved. I guess this quick, easy miracle was too good to
believe."

"It was a miracle," Maya said. "But only for the loved
ones of the woman Lincoln Stack really murdered."

"You really think one of Elaine's kids did it?"

Maya nodded. "Linda never visits Elaine. None of the kids do. So she shows up on the same day she's murdered? I've never been a big believer in coincidence."

"Like your dad." He gently brushed her chin with a fist. "You're so much like him. He never believed in coincidence. Everything had a practical reason."

Maya loved hearing Jerome talk of her dad. "He would've been proud of us today."

Jerome's expression was solemn, his eyes lowering. "Yeah, he would. He should've been here."

Maya took his hand, wrapping both of hers around it. "Yeah, he should've. But Jerome . . . he'd be so proud of you. Not just today, but everything. You know, we both know this is what he would've wanted."

Jerome's eyes closed for a moment. Maya sensed his guilt, now that Alissa had made her so aware of it. Guilt for living, for reaping the benefits of what they sowed together. She wondered if he would ever get over it. She wondered if it was why he'd never started a family of his own.

Maya spent the rest of the afternoon at the *New York Post*. It was strange to her that, although the purpose of it all was for the public offering, she couldn't mention much if anything about it. Despite that, there was much to say about the popularity of the fast-growing hotel chain, and its even faster-growing niche.

She hit a couple of stores near the hotel before heading back to get dressed for her dinner with Jerome, Trajan and two vice presidents from one of the largest Internet trading companies in the country. And as she dressed, Maya felt her stomach clenching tight. There was a lot to be nervous about.

She was nervous, slipping on the jet black short dress. She was always afraid she would be perceived as bringing attention to her figure, her beauty. This simple, short-sleeved rayon dress that stopped inches above her knees seemed innocent by itself, but not so much on her.

She was nervous, putting her hair up in clips. She wanted it neat, but not tight. She applied full makeup, instead of just lipstick, which was all she usually wore. Powder, blush, mascara and a dark shade of red.

She was nervous as she turned up the air-conditioning in her room at the Empire Hotel on the Upper West Side of New York. She felt the air cool her down. She had to keep it together tonight.

She was nervous as she hailed a cab, because she knew more than anything else that even though she needed to care about tonight, she cared more about what Trajan Matthews would think of her than what any of the others would think.

Four

Trajan was all about names when it came to where to eat, have drinks and be seen. He'd picked West 63rd Street Steakhouse for that evening's dinner. He also knew the men they were meeting were beef lovers, one a native Texan.

At seven sharp, Trajan, Jerome, Dan Smith and Harry Gray were led to their table. Trajan felt confident with a half hour of drinks at the bar loosening the atmosphere. By the time they sat down, he was primed and ready to make Dan and Harry buy in to Pharaoh Hotel Corporation. Ready to make them all remember him.

But as soon as he saw her approach, Trajan wasn't thinking about himself at all. Seeing her, not just looking at how utterly beautiful she was, but just seeing her, excited him and made him less certain of everything. He wasn't ready for this, for her and the way she made him feel.

"Maya." Jerome stood up with all the men doing likewise. "Right on cue."

Maya smiled at everyone, motioning for them to sit down. She wasn't comfortable that the only seat available was next to Trajan, who pulled it out for her. She politely thanked him as he pushed her chair back in.

Maya could smell his cologne, and it was an intoxicating scent, different from the one he wore in the hotel room in D.C. This was an evening-on-the-town cologne. She wanted to regret his closeness, but too large a part of her wouldn't let her get away with that. At the sight of him in his black evening suit, she found him charming and of course attractive. Somehow, the fact that he was the most arrogant, amoral man she'd ever known didn't keep her from being pleased that she was sitting next to him.

Trajan had ordered for them all beforehand, so the courses came like clockwork. Maya interjected her usual charm and sparkle to the conversation, but Jerome was the ringleader. Trajan always seemed to tie everything together, his strong voice garnering everyone's attention. But it was the constant networker, Jerome, who really took over, answering questions before they were asked, displaying the usual mixture of flash and wisdom.

Maya felt Trajan's eyes on her more than they should have been, but she tried hard to ignore them. She wasn't getting away with it entirely, but was saved momentarily when her favorite topic, expansion, came up. Discussing it took her attention away from Trajan, although not completely.

Trajan had mixed feelings listening to Maya. He was impressed again by her sharp professionalism. He had to admit he'd underestimated her. She spoke with confidence and control, and Dan and Harry were speechless as they listened. Her beauty got their attention, and her brains kept their attention. Trajan hadn't remembered seeing them sit and listen without words like this in the five years he'd known them. He had originally thought Maya a liability, but now he knew better. If only she would be on his side.

The worst of it was that he was only becoming more attracted to her. Initially, he'd been attracted to her physically, sensing a strong sexual chemistry. It was his doubts about her professionalism that kept him from dwelling on that attraction. With those doubts gone, the attraction only got stronger.

"Good job," Trajan whispered, leaning over toward Maya. He found her scent youthful and sexy. It forced him to think before he spoke again. "You impressed them."

Maya smiled, warming to his closeness despite herself. "I know."

"Confidence," he said. "A very attractive quality."

There was a playful smile at the corners of her full lips. "Not bad for a pastry puff public relations girl?"

He lowered his head in humility for a second. "Touché. You've proven me wrong. I'm more grateful for that than anyone else."

"You'd better be."

He leaned back, appreciating her spice. She was a striking woman.

Returning to the table conversation, Trajan caught Jerome's none-too-pleasant stare. He was certain this was over Maya, and for the first time, Trajan felt a sense of competition even though he had no right to.

Daniel Smith shook his head to the waiter as he offered dessert. He ran his pale hand over his red hair. "We'll have dessert at my club. It's only a couple of blocks north of here."

Harry nodded. "I'm game. It's still early. How 'bout it, men?"

"I'm in," Jerome said, turning to Maya. "How about you?"

Maya was tired and felt she had done her part for the evening. Besides, she was enjoying her time next to Trajan too much.

"I'm going to call it a night," she said. "I think you guys can handle it from here."

Trajan knew he didn't want to see her leave, and to his surprise, he wasn't angry at himself for that.

Shouldn't he be, he thought? After all, why would he even consider being anywhere other than where the "action" was?

The bill was paid and Maya excused herself to the rest room as the others headed out front, already lighting their after dinner cigars. With no desire to inhale cigar smoke, Maya took her time. She splashed her face with water, drying, reapplying some makeup. She did a modest comb through, and stared at herself.

"What are you doing this for, girl?" she asked in the empty bathroom. "You're going to the hotel and directly to bed. Aren't you?"

Trajan was standing in the hallway as Maya exited the restaurant rest room. He said hello to two admiring women who passed him by before turning to her. He smiled wide, making Maya feel self-conscious.

"Couldn't stand to be away from me?" she asked, impressing herself with her sarcasm.

"Something like that," Trajan said. "They've gone on, so I'm responsible for you."

She stood a couple of feet from him, looking up. "I don't believe it. You left Jerome alone with them? You certain he can perform without your supervision?"

He laughed, taking her by the arm. He was halted, although only for a moment, by the softness of her skin.

"A regular comedian here." He led her out of the restaurant. It was a nice summer evening that he didn't want to end. "I'll admit I'm a bit of a control freak, but I don't take on clients I don't think can handle themselves. Jerome was a killer tonight. He'll be fine."

"You wouldn't feel the same about me." Maya tried to ignore the uneasy tension her arm, her body, felt at his touch. She made no attempt to pull away.

Trajan stopped, turning her to him. He looked at her, her beautiful eyes almost sparkling under the awning of the restaurant.

"I would now, Maya. I know I was a jerk before, but I pegged you wrong. You know what you're doing. You can handle a room of sharks just as good as the next guy."

"You'll understand if I don't say thank you." Maya was more pleased with his words than she was willing to admit. "After all, I'd be thanking you for acknowledging something you should have given me credit for in the first place."

"You're tough for a little thing," he said. He began leading her down the street, but Maya stepped back just a little.

"Hey, hey," she said. "Where are we going? The cabs are behind us."

"You ever been to New York, Maya?"

She shook her head as he pulled her to the curb. "What are you? . . ."

"We're on the Upper West Side. My side of town." He flagged down a hansom cab, the horse coming to a slow step as it approached. "I would be wrong not to show you around."

Maya didn't budge.

"Look. I heard you tell Dan you would love a chance to see New York, so you can't act as if you don't. It's literally the most beautiful place on earth on a summer night."

"Hansom cab?" the rider asked, leaning forward.

Trajan's eyes pleaded with her. She never thought of refusing him after that, even though something told her she should have.

"Yes sir." Trajan helped Maya into the cab. He wondered if it was the wine, but he felt like a kid, excited about a first date. He turned to the rider. "I'll do the tour, buddy. You can just lead the way. How about a ride around the park?"

"Where do you live, Tre?" Maya noticed his stare, a

polite expression allowing her to pick the topic of conversation.

"Right on the other side of the park." He nodded
apologetically. "I know that's where the snobs live, but
I like it. I grew up in such a . . . well, it's a change from
what I've had before, and it works well for my business."

Maya sensed that he felt guilt, and she wondered why.
She thought back on what George said. As the horse
treaded along, the breeze hitting her face kindly, she
felt comfortable probing further.

"It's home for you," she said. "Your heart is here."

Trajan nodded. "The money is here. Home is where
the money is."

Maya sent him a scornful stare. "Very heartwarming."

"I'm honest, Maya." He shrugged. "Honesty isn't always heartwarming."

"Agreed," she said, wanting to change the subject.
"So, where did you get an altogether unusual name like
Trajan?"

Trajan smiled, leaning back. "Ahh, the inevitable
question. I think you've held out longer than most. I
guess you were so busy hating me, you didn't have time
to think about my name."

"Are you avoiding the question?" At least he wasn't
thin-skinned, she thought. However, she never thought
he was. She only wanted him to know she wasn't either.

"No." He laughed at her persistence. "The name is
a long story. You don't want to hear it."

"You can't get rid of me that easily. Some kind of
Roman emperor, I remember Jerome mentioning.
Sounds interesting, and it looks like we have the time."

"Okay, Maya. I'll try to make a long story short. My
mother was Spanish, and bringing me up in a black
neighborhood, she wanted to make sure I held onto
the other half of my heritage. Marco Ulpio Trajano, or

Trajan for short, was the first Spanish emperor of Rome. Actually, he was the first non-Italian emperor of Rome. The Spanish people are very proud of him even though he didn't rule his own mother country. He's considered one of the best ever. He was a very powerful man. He also named an African as his successor."

"There was a black emperor of Rome?"

Trajan nodded. "He was only the first. Lusius Quietus was described as a man of Moorish race and considered the ablest soldier in the Roman army."

"Ohh, a history lesson and a horsey ride," Maya said, feeling giddy inside. "Must be my birthday."

He looked at her, delighting in the way she pressed her lips together flirtatiously. That bud of a nose. Any doubts he had about this ride were erased. "I disagree. I think it's my birthday."

Maya blinked, sitting up. Was he flirting with her? Was she flirting with him?

"How do you know so much about black and Spanish emperors?"

"I don't." He shrugged. "Just Trajano and Lusius. My mother thought it was important that I understand this regal merge of African and Spanish because of who I was."

"Was it hard on your mother? Being Spanish in a black neighborhood. Was it hard on you?"

Trajan shrugged. "That's not a real easy question to answer. There were some people who took out their frustrations with ugly looks and words. She was white, and that reminded them of the people who looked down on them as they served them food or shined their shoes. Overall, most people accepted her. Me too. We were all too poor to be concerned with race. Food was the big issue for us."

Maya felt for him. She'd never known what it was like to be hungry or poor. She'd been fortunate that way, in so many ways. She felt like she was beginning to get a little idea of what Trajan was about.

"What about your dad?" she asked. "How was he treated? Sometimes folks can get resentful about the interracial thing. Feel like they've been betrayed."

"I wouldn't know. My father left when I was a baby."

Maya thought she saw a glimpse of emotion on Trajan's face. She thought of how close she was to her own father, and she felt compassion for anyone who hadn't been as blessed. She sensed a pull of emotion, and was uncomfortable with that. She could see herself losing sight of her professionalism with him and felt desperate to fix it, so she changed the topic.

"Why did you leave investment banking? Jerome says you were a whiz on Wall Street."

Trajan took a deep breath. She was a quick topic jumper. At least this one was a little easier, and he enjoyed her interest immensely. "I'm still on Wall Street, but in a different arena, taking a different angle."

Maya sensed his hesitancy. "Yes, but you were an analyst with a leading investment firm, making people and companies rich and pulling in mad commissions. If you were to go on your own, why not an investment firm? Why investor relations?"

"There are a lot of reasons," he answered. "In the end, straight I-banking wasn't what I wanted. I found that my biggest successes came from creating partnerships, making introductions, for lack of a better word. And don't fool yourself, there's a lot of money in IR."

"I know. I see the checks Jerome signs for you. You've got a nice little operation going on there."

He smiled at her, connecting with her cynical sense of humor. He could fall for this woman under any other circumstances. He could fall fast.

"What about the discrimination?" Maya asked, turning away. The way he was looking at her made her a little dizzy. "I've heard and read some incredible things going on in that industry. You spoke about it before."

Trajan was certain she had no idea how bad it could get. "I've been out on my own for three years. A lot has changed since then. There is a strong group of black-owned I-banks out there now. We have our own organization, with hundreds of members. Strong networking, mentorships. They're getting up to speed on the New York Stock Exchange, with more seats than ever before. There are a few barriers in the senior management ranks at the major firms being broken. Still, the percentage is in the single digits."

He was a stubborn optimist, who would never make excuses for anything. Maya liked that, respected that. Her father was that way.

"So, you made a few million in commissions," she said, "and moved on."

"I did well. I was always going to go into business for myself. What I found in IR was a little more excitement, a lot less stress. The hours are easier, the ulcers smaller."

Maya laughed. "You're joking, right?"

He shook his head. She had a hearty laugh, and very genuine. He didn't know many genuine people.

"When people could lose millions based on your suggestions, ulcers are inevitable."

"So the appeal would be . . . ?"

"The rush," he said, his eyes lighting up, a fist forming in eagerness and passion. "The power and control. There's so much in your hands, Maya, it's intoxicating."

Maya liked the fire in his eyes, even though she wasn't so crazy about what he was fired up about. She was excited for him. "All over money?"

"Yes, money. Money is at the center of everything."

"I thought love was." Maya smiled as she realized she'd left him speechless for at least a moment.

"That's important too," he said with a nod. "However, I think money is at least as important."

Maya turned her head to the wind, closing her eyes and loving this breeze. Trajan Matthews had a lot to learn. Would he want to?

Trajan watched her for a moment, breathing in the night air. He wondered if a woman like Maya, a down-to-earth good woman, could ever understand the man he was. Would she want to?

"Tell me about your father," he asked.

Maya's eyes flew open. She should have been prepared for that, but she wasn't, and Trajan seemed to notice this by the look on his face.

"I'm sorry," he said. "Too personal?"

"No." She smiled. "Just unexpected. I thought we were talking about you."

He looked at her, in her eyes. "I find you much more interesting."

Maya was unable to tear her eyes away. Her mind scattered, her stomach pulled. "He . . . he was a great man."

"I got that much." Trajan heard himself speak in almost a whisper as he moved closer to her. "What he did for the hotel in its first ten years, with Jerome, was remarkable."

Maya remembered with love in her heart. "It was his other child. I can remember being just a baby, sitting on his lap while he told me he would start his own company one day. Then, next thing I knew I was sitting on his lap in the office of that company he promised he would have."

"Did you ever feel, you know . . . neglected?"

Maya thought about it, but not too long. "Sometimes, but I don't think more than any kid in my situation. Daddy made a point of spending time with me. He helped me with my homework, had heart-to-hearts with me on the porch, was right at church with me and Mama every Sunday, was waiting up after I got home from my dates, came to my volleyball games."

"Volleyball?" Trajan laughed, giving her a once-over. "Yeah, I can see you spiking the cover off a ball with your fist."

Maya lowered her head, blushing. "I was good too. Daddy was my number one fan, and whenever he couldn't be there, Mama cheered loud enough for the both of them."

"Sounds like a fairy tale." Trajan was touched by emotion, thoughts of his own mother. He wiped them away, knowing that the bad always followed close behind the good.

Maya ran her hand through her hair, thinking of how it was toward the end. She hated to think of it, almost refused to. "It was sometimes. Not always."

Trajan saw something deep in her eyes, a secret that was part of the key to her heart. He didn't bother asking. One would have to prove himself to Maya before earning the right to probe further into those eyes. He wanted to be one that would.

"You and your mother must've really relied on him," he said.

Maya remembered hearing her parents argue toward the end, hearing her mother threaten to leave. She wiped the thoughts from her mind as if they never happened.

"Yeah," she said. "We don't have much of an extended family, so it was the two of us. And Jerome of course."

"I'm sure he—"

"Tre," she interrupted. "Let's talk about something else. It's such a nice night. Tell me about New York."

Why didn't she want to talk more about Jerome? he wondered. Was it because their relationship had turned into something more than family? Trajan wanted to believe that was impossible. After all, how could they see each other as anything but family? But he looked at Maya, as beautiful and sexy as she was and could see how Jerome would want their relationship to change.

Trajan wiped the thought from his mind, not wanting anything to spoil the feeling he had now. He leaned back, wrapping an arm around Maya, not sure he should be enjoying himself as much as he was right now.

Maya felt a sweet excitement as Trajan's arm wrapped around her shoulders and the nape of her neck. She heard him speak of Central Park as they circled it. The zoo, the lakes, the museums, the ponds, the skating rinks, the fountains, the summer concert stage, the bikers and in-line skaters. But Maya wasn't really listening. She was just enjoying this moment. This moment in New York City at night with a charming, attractive man, trying her best to believe there would be no consequences if she let go.

It was almost midnight when Trajan and Maya entered the lobby of the Empire Hotel. After the hansom cab ride, they walked the few blocks to the hotel, all the while Trajan talking about his adopted home, the people he knew and the things he'd done. Maya hadn't grown a bit tired of it, and she had to admit she was sorry to see the night end. Still, she knew it had to.

"Tre," she said, turning to him as they approached the elevator. "I had a good time. The tour was very impressive."

Trajan stepped only inches from her, compelled by something other than his common sense. "What about the company?"

Maya felt her pulse quicken, and she searched desperately for words. They were alone at the moment, but if there had been people in the dark elevator hall, she wouldn't have noticed.

"Tre." His name barely came out. "I'm . . . I'm not sure . . ."

It was too late for uncertainty as Trajan reached out for her. He was already feeling the heat as he pulled her to him, but it turned to fire as soon as his mouth touched hers.

Maya felt her head swirl, her stomach twirl and her knees go weak as his lips pressed against hers. A flame ran through her body as he kissed her deeply. His lips were rough, but pleasing against her own. She felt a moan rise in her throat from the pit of her belly as he slid his hands down her arms slowly. She felt a tingle rush through her body down to her toes.

Trajan felt a threatening surge of desire flow through him as he felt her body against his own. Her lips were as soft as silk, full and seductive, making his mind go wild. As he deepened his kiss, separating her lips, he guided his tongue into her mouth, wanting her. Wanting her desperately.

Alarm bells went off in Maya, sensing she was at her last reserve. She pushed away, but her weak state gave her no strength. Instead, she turned her face away, parting their lips.

"Tre," she said in a tone barely audible.

Her eyes rolled back as his mouth went to her neck, kissing her slowly, deeply. Her lips parted as a tortured breath let out. She said his name again, praying for the strength.

"Maya." Her name trailed from Trajan's lips in between kisses. He felt her hands move to his chest, and he anticipated her caress. Instead, he felt pressure, he felt a push. He heard a "no" and forced himself, against his body's will, to lean away.

Trajan distanced himself from her, and through a haze of desire, saw the look of apprehension on Maya's face It was hard at this moment, but he assumed he understood.

"I know." He hit the button for the elevator, still one hand on her arm. "We're in the hallway. Let's go upst—"

"No." Maya pulled her arm from his grip. As he stepped away, she felt her mind beginning to clear. "I won't . . ."

Trajan smiled, a little confused by her jerking her arm away. "I wasn't suggesting anything too—"

"I'm sure you weren't," she said, both hands tightly on her purse, squeezing, squeezing. "I don't think we should do anything, not even this."

"This?" he asked. "This kiss?"

"I just . . ." Maya was searching hard for words. How could she explain how upset this would make Jerome, her getting involved with a business partner. "Jerome wouldn't like this."

Jealousy hit him immediately, followed right on the heels by pride. Trajan straightened himself up. He hadn't thought of Jerome, or Elizabeth for that matter, through any of this.

"I see," he said, knowing he'd been correct to think there was something between Maya and Jerome. "Just forget this ever happened."

"Well, I . . ." Maya didn't really want to forget it, wasn't sure she could if she tried.

"It was the wine at dinner," he said, stepping even farther away. "Hansom cab rides in Central Park on summer nights do that to me all the time. Besides, Liz is probably waiting for me. I promised a call when I returned home."

Maya felt like she'd been socked in the stomach. She'd forgotten about Elizabeth. Suddenly, she felt embarrassed and ashamed, and a desire to be as far away from Trajan as possible.

"Then you shouldn't keep her waiting."

"Good night, Maya." Without looking her directly in the face, Trajan nodded before turning and heading toward the lobby.

"Good night, Mr. Matthews."

Trajan turned. The sound of her voice using his formal name again really got to him. It only made him angrier, watching her cold eyes before she disappeared into the open elevator.

As he hailed a cab outside the hotel, Trajan forced himself to calm down. He was a liar. Elizabeth wasn't waiting for him to call. He didn't even want to call her, cursing himself for that. Forget Maya, he thought, forget how she made him feel. It was nothing; she wasn't his type anyway. Elizabeth was. He would make it work with her and stop thinking of Maya Woodson as anything but a business acquaintance.

Maya tossed and turned in her bed. She was trying hard not to think of Trajan, his kiss, his last words. She found herself feeling jealous of Elizabeth, a woman she didn't even know. She thought of Trajan in her bed now. Angry at herself for caring but feeling she had a right to, she couldn't get any sleep.

As hurtful as his words were, Maya hoped Trajan was right when he blamed the dinner wine and the hansom cab ride in Central Park. It was a very romantic combination. She'd hate to think it was more than that.

Back in D.C., Maya maintained an unusually high level of frustration over her encounter with Trajan. She flew right into Washington Reagan Airport and drove to the office. Thinking to bury herself in her work, she hoped to get him off her mind, but it wasn't working.

To make matters worse, she felt a sudden urge to talk to Elaine, as she had so often during the day. Elaine had been such a reliable source of comfort ripped from her so violently. Maya wasn't sure why she made the decision to visit Elaine's room again. Possibly looking around, she could feel closure, some sense of comfort.

The yellow police tape was gone from the doorknob, but all hotel employees had been told not to enter. No one knew Maya had her own key. She'd thought of handing it over to the police, but she held on to it. She wanted to hold on to something.

The key felt cold and larger than usual in her hand as she reached for the door. A chill went down her spine suddenly.

"What in the hell do you think you're doing?"

Maya jumped, turning around at the same time. She recognized the woman immediately and felt a shiver of fear reach through her as the lanky figure approached, blue eyes tiny and gleaming with contempt.

"Linda," Maya heard herself breathing as she backed up. "What are you . . . ?"

"That's my question to you." She stood with her hands on her hips, her blond hair falling in all directions.

"I was close to your mother," Maya said. "Maybe she spoke of me. Maya Woodson. I thought I would—"

"Did you point the finger at me? I bet it was you. Mom talked about you like you were the Virgin Mary."

Maya swallowed hard, thinking of Elaine. She stood up straight. "You were on the video that day. The police aren't trained to believe in coincidences."

Linda shifted hands, blinking nervously. "I told the police the truth. I was here, but I had a reason. Mom told me she was changing her will after Debra refused to let her come to her graduation."

"Whose fault is that, Linda?" Maya was eager for more information and was trying to hold her temper.

"My family's dealings are none of your business," Linda said. "I just wanted to see her will. To look out for my kid."

"Why did you leave her suite so suspiciously?" Maya asked. "You weren't on the camera leaving, only coming. So you must've left down the west end, the stairs."

Linda smiled, looking Maya up and down. "I don't have to tell you, from my vantage point, you don't appear to have a police badge."

"Since you claim to be innocent, I shouldn't need one. Should I?"

Linda paused, seeming to contemplate whether or not to answer. "I stole it while Mom was in the kitchen. The will. I knew whereabouts she kept it. I found it and ran out without her knowing. I knew she'd look out the east end for me, so I left the other way."

"How could you?" Maya was fuming, still not convinced of Linda's innocence. "And how do the police know you didn't find the will, realize she was cutting you and your daughter out and decide to prevent her from doing that?"

"Look." Linda stepped closer, pointing an angry finger. "I wasn't a perfect daughter, not even a good one. But I'm not a murderer. Can't say I wasn't waiting for the old woman to die, but I wasn't about to make it happen myself."

"So what are you doing back?" Maya asked. "If you didn't care about her."

"I got permission from security to pick up some items for her funeral. I'm waiting for them to come open the place up now."

"When is her funeral?"

Linda seemed to sense that Maya desperately needed

this information, so she took her sweet time. "Tomorrow . . . Jackson Funeral Home."

Maya added, "When?"

Linda sighed as if annoyed. "Three. But don't feel bad if you can't make it. I sure won't mind."

"Fine." Maya averted her eyes from Linda as she headed away from her. She felt her pulse calm just before the woman called out to her.

"Whatever the case," she said, not waiting for Maya to turn completely around. "You can believe what you want, but the cops aren't bothering me anymore. So they must've believed me. In that case, who gives a damn whether you do or not?"

Maya didn't really calm down until she was safely in the elevator. She left a message for George Hobbs as soon as she returned to her desk. She'd have to convince him to give her an update. She needed an explanation for why Linda was no longer a suspect.

She found it quite ironic that thoughts of Detective Hobbs brought on thoughts of Trajan Matthews, but what wasn't leading to thoughts of Trajan today? The previous night was emblazoned in her memory, and lit a spark in her body. Maya cursed Trajan under her breath, knowing his cold heart wasn't even thinking of her for a second.

Trajan looked out over Central Park from his condo. He could hear Elizabeth moving around in the dining room. The Kists were gone, and one of the longest nights of Trajan's life was closer to ending.

"Damn that Maya Woodson," he said under his breath.

He wanted more than anything to focus on impressing one of the wealthiest and most influential couples in New York and ensuring future client connections.

Instead, all he could think of was Maya, kissing her, wondering about her and Jerome. Wanting her no matter what the truth was either way.

Every second, he thought of ideas for the road show, but somehow thoughts of Maya kept slipping in. There would be no avoiding her over the next month, and he was upset that he was excited about that. It was confusing for him, because at the same time he was wishing he'd never see her again. He was contradicting his own self.

"I'm off, Tre." Elizabeth broke his concentration as she stepped on to the balcony. She looked her usual exquisite best in a satiny style silver dress.

"Leaving?" Trajan asked, feeling guilty for not caring so much if she was. Why couldn't he? He wanted to. "Why so early?"

Elizabeth's face was emotionless. "I think it's actually very late. It usually doesn't take me so long to know it's time to leave, but I guess I've gotten slower in my old age."

Trajan knew she was talking about them. "Liz, I don't want you to go."

"But that's selfish, isn't it? You want me to stay, hoping you'll eventually care about me. Because you should, right? I'm beautiful, educated, successful, intelligent, well-connected. Perfect for you."

"I do care about you," he said.

"But you don't love me." She blinked rapidly a few times, appearing to struggle with her emotions, which wanted to show themselves. "And you won't, because you can't force yourself to love anyone. Well Tre, I'm ready to love someone and I deserve it back."

"I don't want to hurt you." Trajan knew she was right. Had he grown so callous, so self-centered, that he couldn't see that?

"I know." She smiled a half smile. "It was flattering.

A man like you, one who could have any woman he wanted, fought tooth and nail for six months to make himself love me. Tells me my stock is still high at thirty-five.

"I saw you tonight, Tre. Trying. You're good. I don't think the Kists noticed you weren't actually here. But I did, and it hurt. But I gotta thank you. Something or someone was on your mind completely. I mean, taking you over. I'm assuming it's work, but I could be wrong. Now I'm going to leave and find someone who will look the way you did tonight, but because of me."

As she kissed his cheek, Trajan squeezed Elizabeth's arm. "I'm sorry."

"You should be," she said with a wink. "You missed out on a good thing."

Trajan was up for hours after Elizabeth left. He'd ruined countless relationships because of work, his need to focus on building his career, his company. It got worse each time, but it seemed so out of his control. Work was everything.

But this time was different. It wasn't just his focus on work that left him alone again. Seeing George again and all the memories that returned with him, and Maya driving him to distraction was what made this different. For the first time in a long time, Trajan felt parts of his life getting out of his control, and it angered him.

George Hobbs was waiting for Maya outside Jackson Funeral Home in Alexandria, Virginia. As she arrived with Alissa at her side, Maya wasted no time after introducing the two.

"Why isn't Linda a suspect anymore?" she asked.

"Why do you ask questions you know I'm not gonna answer?" George placed both hands in his suit pockets,

nodding at two elderly women who passed them entering the home.

"When I called you," Maya said, "you said you'd tell
me what you could."

"Calm down, girl." Alissa put a hand on Maya's arm.
"Keep your voices down. Not all of these people passing
by are her children. Some of them actually cared about
her."

George leaned over. "I can't give you specifics, but
I'm pretty confident, considering your situation, that
you won't go to the press. So, I'll tell you, Linda isn't
a suspect because of the time of death and the exit
stamp on her car from leaving the hotel garage. We
found it smack dab on her dashboard."

"Is that all?" Maya asked, not willing to accept this.

"Also," he added. "She has an alibi. A friend came
over to her house on the South Side for a visit. She
confirmed it all. This was around the time of death,
which by the way came instantly if that interests you at
all."

Maya was at least relieved to hear this. No suffering.
"But Linda admitted to stealing that will."

"She's not off the blocks completely," he said. "We're
keeping an eye on her. She claims she can't find the
will anywhere. That might be the key."

"Why?" Alissa asked.

"We found Elaine's appointment book. She had a
meeting with her estate lawyer today."

"I'm certain that was the news she had for me," Maya
said. "She was cutting the kids and the grandchildren
out."

"Not just that," George said. "The lawyer says she
was going to give everything to some old folks homes,
a couple of elderly charities and you."

"Me?" Maya was shocked. "I never . . . man."

"What about the other kids?" Alissa asked.

"That's why I'm here," George said. "One son is in Jersey, the other is from this area. Thought he might show up. Still can't track him down."

"Where is the other son, Craig?" Maya asked. "I think Elaine told me he lived near Newark."

George nodded. "Yeah. A small town near the airport called Berto. We don't have an alibi for him, but he's not a strong suspect. Elaine cut him off years ago."

Maya was frustrated. She wondered if George was giving up on Craig too early. "As far as cases go, George, this can't be good. You guys always say if you don't get the guy within forty-eight hours of the crime, it's not likely you will."

"You watch too much television, Maya." George stepped aside. "Can I usher you ladies in? They'll be starting soon."

A sense of determination hit Maya stronger than before. Not just for Elaine, but for herself. She had to find the murderer no matter what the police were going to do.

"You two go ahead," Maya said as her cell phone went off. "I have to get this. I'm supposed to be at work."

"We'll wait," Alissa said with a scornful stare. "Then you turn it off, okay?"

Maya nodded, flipping the phone to her ear. "Maya Woodson here."

"Maya, where in God's name are you?"

"Mr. Matthews." She recognized his voice immediately, acknowledging her feelings of disdain and anticipation upon hearing it. "Who do you think you are, addressing me like that?"

"I've been looking all over for you. Calling everywhere. Why aren't you at the office?"

"None of your business." She looked at George and

Alissa, both entranced by the angry expression on her face. "What do you want?"

"I want to know where you're at?" Trajan had let his temper grow trying to track her down. He knew he was being ridiculous, but he had no patience lately. Besides, he'd been working on the hotel's prospectus papers with Jerome all day and had struggled to maintain some professionalism, all the while thinking of him with Maya in his arms. To find out she was free about town, probably thinking nothing of him, fueled his fire.

Maya knew this wasn't the time or place for this nonsense. "I'm at Elaine Cramer's funeral. Satisfied? Now, what do you want?"

Trajan gritted his teeth. "For Pete's sake, Maya. You're in the middle of a—"

"Listen Trajan. You either tell me what you want now or I'm hanging up and turning this phone off."

She found it within herself to smile as George and Alissa laughed. She saw George whisper into Alissa's eager-to-hear ears.

"It's about Boston tomorrow," Trajan said.

"I'll be there for the lunch, Trajan. I can keep track of my schedule."

"I need you to meet with Phillip Stafford at the *Boston Globe* tomorrow morning."

"Who is he?" Maya was excited. She hadn't heard of this guy, but she had made several attempts to generate interest at the *Globe*. Nothing beyond a human interest blurb had panned out.

"He's a new finance reporter," he said. "Just came on. Was recruited from the *Times*. I've worked with him. He's good. You need to be at the *Globe* at ten in the morning."

"Fine," she answered. "I'll be there. Anything else?"

"Well." Trajan wasn't so eager to let go of the phone,

but he had no reason to keep her on. "Then ten, right?"

"I said so."

"Okay. Then . . . fine. I—"

"Good-bye, Trajan." Maya hung up before he could reply.

"So when's the wedding?" George asked.

Alissa sidled up to her. "I hear you and this Tre guy got some sparks flying. Why is this the first I'm hearing of this?"

Maya turned the phone off and tucked it in her purse. "I'd rather be covered with honey and tied to an anthill. Let's go inside."

The funeral was brief with very few people there. Maya noticed the only true emotion was on Debra's face, Elaine's granddaughter. It touched her and made her angry at the same time. Reflections of her father's funeral and her mother's funeral tore at her.

Alissa held her as she cried for a moment, feeling as if she'd lost a third parent. The experienced spurred her determination. Maya knew what she had to do, and she wasn't concerned with what anyone had to say about it, including Trajan.

"Maya?" Trajan's voice was calmer now than when he called earlier. "What is it?"

"We'll have to move my appointment with Phillip Stafford to the afternoon."

"We can't," he said. "That's out of the question."

"Then I can't do it," she said. "I have an appointment tomorrow morning that I can't miss."

Trajan stood up, pacing his New York office. "Are you aware of the importance of the—"

"After the lunch or nothing, Tre."

Taken off guard by her return to his informal name,

Trajan knew this was an unwinnable battle. However, he still had his pride. "You better hope this works, Maya."

"It will," she answered. "I'm sure you'll use your undeniable charm on your good friend."

After she hung up, Maya called Alexandra into her office.

"What's up?" Alexandra was chewing a wad of gum and leaning in the doorway.

"Change of plans for tomorrow," Maya said. "I need the earliest flight into Newark, with a flight that gets me to Boston in time for the one o'clock lunch."

"Earliest?" she asked.

"The very first. As a matter of fact, find out what's left tonight. Then, check on the Internet for a Craig Cramer in a town called Berto in New Jersey. Should be easy enough. It's a small town. Get me a room nearby if you can fly me out tonight."

"What's going on?" Alexandra's eyes widened. "You sound like you're ready for business"

"I am," Maya said. "Let's work as fast as we can."

Despite Maya's words, Alexandra stood still for a few minutes before slowly sauntering back to her desk.

Trajan rehearsed his conversation with Phillip in his mind. He had to concentrate hard. That Maya was going to drive him insane. He hated being forced to go back on an appointment and he planned on letting Maya know this the second he saw her.

Turning to his phone, Trajan saw his line blinking. His phone was ringing, but Nadine wasn't picking up. It was risky with all the unsolicited calls he received, but Trajan picked up the line.

"Trajan Matthews," he said.

"Tre." The voice was high-pitched, excited. "Little

Tre? George told me you were hot stuff. Why are you picking up your own phone?"

Trajan had no clue who this was. "I'm sorry?"

"Now, you know who this is boy," she said. "Your Aunt Audrey. Don't you dare say you don't remember me."

Trajan did some speed-thinking. Aunt Audrey from the old neighborhood. "Of course I remember."

She wasn't his real aunt, but a close friend of his mother his entire life. Immediate feelings of guilt washed over Trajan. He had lost touch with Audrey, just as he had with everyone who cared for him from the old neighborhood.

"Don't you know," she said, "I was just pleased as punch when George told me he ran into you. I'd thought you'd gone off and joined the black circus."

He laughed. "I'm in New York still, but I guess that isn't much different. How are you?"

There was a pause, and Trajan sensed bad news. He hated pauses.

"I've been better." Audrey's voice was quieter, slower. "I just went through my chemo."

Trajan felt a sock in his stomach. "Cancer? My god, Aunt Audrey. Is everything—"

"It's gone for now," she said. "I gave it to the Lord and the community prayed for me. I'm working on getting my strength back. Breast cancer is putting down so many black women. I belong to a support group that I'm sad to say is very large."

Not a card, a phone call, a visit the entire time. Trajan knew there was no excuse for this. He thought of Maya and what she would think of him if she heard this. "I wish I—"

"I know, child." Another pause. "We all deal with things our own way. Although a phone call on a Sunday every now and then wouldn't put you out."

"It certainly won't." Trajan knew she deserved more than that. She'd always been there for him, especially when his own mother was in her last days.

"You take my number down and call me. And Tre, the next time you come to D.C. and don't visit me, I'm going to fly to New York myself and take a switch to your rear end."

"I'd deserve it too," he said.

When he hung up, Trajan felt himself plagued with several emotions. He hated thinking of those days when he and his mother were dirt poor. Father nowhere to be found. Everything was always a struggle, forcing them to choose which need was needed most. Then there was the other part. The way they all banded together when someone was sick, church on Sundays, block parties, playing ball on the corner with George. Still, the need to overcome it all, be a success, the exact opposite of what he was supposed to be, was still with him. It still guided his every move.

Then there was Maya. Why he connected her to all of this, he didn't know. She'd had it pretty well since she was young, with her father being successful even before he started the hotel. Despite that, something about her reminded him of the old neighborhood, the good parts that made him feel like a traitor, amoral for leaving it all behind.

Trajan tried to block it all from his mind. He'd gotten so good at it for almost twenty years. He dialed Phillip Stafford's number.

Five

Berto, New Jersey, was an airport town. Stuck between Newark and Elizabeth, it would be forgotten if it weren't for the airport. It was a racially diverse neighborhood, blue-collar working class through and through. Maya saw the unwelcome stares of residents, up at seven to go to hardworking jobs, as she walked up to the Franklin Apartments complex. They may not all be friendly to each other, but they all knew each other. And she wasn't one of them.

The building was a few years from looking run-down. The entry door, which should have been locked, was wide open. Maya took advantage of it, assuming that Craig wouldn't be eager to buzz her up.

The printout Alexandra had given her said apartment 3A. Maya climbed the three flights instead of taking the elevator, which she found an interesting amenity for only a four-story building. She knocked twice, but nothing. Her worst-case scenario was that he'd gone off to work already, but it was pretty early. The number the directory had given was temporarily disconnected for repairs, a recorded voice told her. She had to be on that ten thirty flight to Boston or she'd miss the lunch.

Before giving it a third try, Maya heard a clicking sound behind her. Someone was unlocking the door. She turned around as 3C slowly opened. A woman in her fifties at least, with chocolate skin, black hair up in curlers, and wearing a pink and green flowered house dress stepped one foot out.

"You looking for Craig?" she asked, giving Maya a suspicious once-over. "This early?"

"I'm a friend of the family." Maya stepped closer. "He hasn't left yet, has he?"

She laughed. "Friend of the family? Please. Craig don't have no friends, and he don't want nothing to do with family."

"Well, his mother passed away. I thought I would come by and give my condolences." Maya spoke with the most honest tone she could. "Do you know him well?"

The woman shook her head. "Didn't nobody know him well. He kept to himself. Not the nicest fellow. I've been here ten years. Marlo Nash by the way. Anyway, the woman before him was nicer. Although she was a bit loose. Had seven different men stay over in less than one year. I kept track. Always wore those midriffs, but didn't have the stomach for it. Know what I mean? Not like you. You're a thin little thing."

"What about Craig?" Maya asked. "You didn't know him well, but did he ever talk about his mother, Elaine?"

"Hated her." Marlo appeared to be the type who made it her job, her life, to know everything about everyone. "He ran with a bad crowd. Used to complain to his boys out on the porch that she was trying to save him all the way from Virginia. You know, bring Jesus back into his life. He wasn't having it. When she cut him off, he was rantin' and ravin' for a while. Then . . . ."

"Then what?"

"Like I said. He used to run with a bad crowd. They . . . to make a long story short, he got shot six months ago. In the back. He's in a wheelchair."

"That's why the elevator," Maya said. "And the ramp outside."

She nodded. "Since then his boys got no use for him. He got no use for anybody. He—"

"Especially got no use for nosy neighbors."

Maya swung around to a pitiful sight in the doorway to 3A. Craig Cramer looked forty even though Maya knew he was thirty at the most. His head was completely shaved, his eyes had darker circles around them than any she'd ever seen. He was hunched over in his wheelchair, his clothes sloppy. He was deathly thin and his skin was as white as a sheet of paper.

Maya turned back to Marlo just in time to see the door slam.

"Who in the hell are you?" he asked, barely lifting his head.

"I . . . I was knocking, but . . ."

"Getting out of bed is more of a challenge for me than most folks. Sometimes it ain't worth it. I thought you were my meals on wheels delivery. They come early sometimes."

"I was coming by to . . ." Maya realized she had no plan. She'd been impetuous. Now, looking at him, she had nothing to say.

"I heard you two batting around. I don't have a mother. Haven't had one for a year now. Don't care if she's dead."

Maya felt a sting of pain hit her. Elaine didn't deserve this. "You wouldn't have any idea who would want to—"

"The cop already came by here. Your D.C. morons had a local idiot drop by. I was here in my waste of a body, waste of an apartment, waste of a life when it all went down. I got nothing to gain from her death. Not even the satisfaction of knowing she's gone. I ain't got nothing to do with it. Like I said, don't care if she's dead."

He winced in some unseen pain. "Don't care if I'm dead."

Maya believed him. Still, she was angry. Had he said satisfaction? "She was your mother, and she was a good woman. She deserved better than what you gave her."

"We all deserve better than what we get," he said. "She was doing fine. Preaching, feeling superior. She had the money, the good life. I got only enough pity for myself right now."

Maya looked at him. "You'll need it. 'Cause you're not going to get it from anywhere else."

She walked away, knowing she had completely wasted her time. Craig couldn't kill anyone. He'd been dead for six months himself.

When Maya arrived in Boston for the luncheon, she was hit with an unexpected reaction to seeing Trajan. Her emotions, her body, focused on him, remembering and wanting. He hadn't seen her enter because he was engrossed in a conversation in the corner of the hotel luncheon room. He stood out for so many reasons beyond how tall and handsome he looked.

She felt a strange sensation on the hairs of her arm. The kiss was back in her psyche, as if it were only a moment ago. Her mind was being slaughtered by her body.

"Fine," she whispered to herself. "You're physically attracted to him. So what? You can't stand him otherwise, so there's no point in even thinking about it. Just let it go."

"Talking to yourself?"

Maya smiled at Jerome as he quickly brushed her arm. "Just prepping for today. How's it going so far?"

"All right. I suppose."

Maya could see a look of distress on Jerome's face. It was subtle, but she knew him too well. He was nervous today, more than in New York, she thought.

"You're thinking about Daddy, aren't you?"

"You can read me like a book, little girl. I'm thinking of him, Elaine, this lunch, later tonight. Everything. These Boston guys are even more abrasive than the New Yorkers. At least that's what Tre says."

"Have you heard any progress on Elaine?"

"No." He pulled at his tie. "I think it's running cold."

Maya couldn't let that happen. "I still have some things in mind."

Jerome's eyes were impatient. "What do you mean? What are you getting involved in?"

"You know how I feel about Elaine," she said. "Felt about her, I mean."

He looked her over suspiciously. "Does this have anything to do with why you weren't in the office this morning when I called? Why Alex was playing coy over the phone about you?"

"You stop worrying," she said. "You concentrate on today, and making Daddy proud."

"Just promise me," he said. "You'll let the police handle this. They know how to do their thing."

"Only if you promise to quit worrying," she said, "and quit with the guilt feelings."

"What guilt?" Jerome's eyes widened. "What would I feel guilty about?"

"You remember what I told you Alissa said."

His lips smacked. "She's got too much time on her hands. I'm fine, just nervous. A good nervous."

"You sure? It doesn't look so good."

"That's only because you know me so well." He winked. "They have no clue, and that's all that matters."

Maya wasn't giving. "If you promise, I promise."

"It's a deal," he answered just before turning to two analysts approaching them.

Trajan had watched the clock closely. He was full of

anticipation, as he always was when these meetings began. His adrenaline was high; he was in his element. In Boston, the world of venture capital and mergers and acquisitions, it wasn't easy to get the attention of analysts. Besides, Pharaoh wasn't in cities like Boston and New York. Not yet, but that would change soon. In all, he expected thirty guests, and it looked as if it would work out.

As usual, he expected the excitement to last until the meeting was over. But as soon as he saw Maya standing near the door, talking with Jerome and the two men from Phoenix Securities, a sense of calm came over him. It was a passionate calm, unexpected and forewarning. Just at the sight of her. He wanted to tell himself he'd wished she'd never come, but he knew that wasn't at all true.

"Damn," he whispered to himself. "I'm in trouble."

Maya avoided Trajan, greeting everyone except him. She passively nodded in his direction when he introduced her as the presentation went on. She found the audience receptive to her discussions of extensive community outreach and public relations alliances that would make Pharaoh an attractive buy with an excellent reputation. She spoke of possible expansion into the faster-growing cities outside Boston, which intrigued them. She answered every question with ease until the last.

"What about the recent murder at your headquarters hotel?"

He was a young man, with red hair and freckles. Sharply dressed, clean-cut and attractive. Trajan blinked, turning to Maya. Careful, he thought. Careful.

Maya cleared her throat. "As you might know, Pharaoh Hotel has been rated in the top five of the safest hotels in every city we're in for the last seven years. You see, our hotel is more like a home than a place to sleep for a night. That atmosphere creates . . ."

"Of course," the young man said impatiently. "But there was a brutal murder of a resident of Pharaoh recently. I happen to have a friend who is a reporter. He informed me that this murder was preceded by—"

"Excuse me, Matt." Trajan stepped to the microphone. He had to stop him before he mentioned the burglaries. "Let me clarify this."

Maya felt herself gently, smoothly edged to the side. She was more shocked than angry. She tried hard to keep her expression still.

"The incident," Trajan continued, "was unrelated to the hotel in any way. It was a personal vendetta situation. A domestic squabble. Absolutely no one else was in danger."

Maya felt her blood boiling.

"Did you catch the guy who did it?" The question came from an unidentifiable attendee in the back.

Trajan refused to appear affected. "I believe it has all been resolved. It should be of no significance to the hotel or its marketability. As Ms. Woodson stated, their safety reputation is more than impressive. She can continue now."

When Trajan stepped aside, nodding to Maya, he froze. The look in her eyes was like a dagger. He was certain that if she could strangle him, she would at this moment. But if she got mad, she got mad. He couldn't let her get to him. Not now.

Maya pasted a smile to her face, stepping back to the podium. She felt a sense of confidence gone after having been brushed aside, then "allowed" to continue.

Although she answered the last few questions fairly easily, Maya wasn't the same after Trajan's interruption. Her eyes bore into him as she sat back down, but he wouldn't look in her direction. She knew it was on purpose. He wasn't getting away with anything. After Jerome made his final comments, the potential investors seemed impressed, expressing so in their parting words before heading back to their offices. Trajan nodded a good-bye to the last attendee, and as he expected, no sooner did he turn around than Maya let him have it.

"How dare you?" Her temperature was already steaming.

He leaned back a second, bemused that he was attracted even to her anger. "Listen, I know what you're upset about, but I did what I felt was necessary."

"That's what it's all about, isn't it?" Maya followed him to his chair, where he reached for his appointment book. The fact that he couldn't even stand still to listen to her only angered her more. "What you feel. You have to control everything. It's all about you."

"What would you have me do, Maya?" He turned back to her, ready to match her for all she was worth.

Maya threw her arms up in an exaggerated motion. "How about nothing? I was at the podium, Trajan. I could've answered the question."

"You hesitated." Trajan noticed she was back to using his full first name, and he found himself feeling ridiculous for being upset over that. For caring at all. "Hesitation is murder in this game. You told me you were prepared to answer any question."

"I wanted to answer with care," she said, offended even more because he was partly right. She shouldn't have paused. "We were talking about murder."

"Yes Maya, murder. The murder of someone close to you, and you weren't prepared to deal with it. I'm not willing to risk losing Boston because you get a feather in your throat over a dear friend."

"You son of a . . ." Maya wanted to slap him, but she refrained.

"Hey, hey." Jerome entered the room. "I'm coming back from the men's room and I can hear you both."

"Sorry, Jerome." Trajan gripped his appointment book, turning to his client. "Just a little disagreement."

"Just be glad there's no one in the hallway." Jerome's face softened as he turned to Maya. "Maya? You look like you're about to lose it."

Maya tore her eyes away from Trajan. She was almost shaking. "I'm fine, Jerome."

Trajan watched as Jerome's eyes looked tenderly at the young woman. Jerome loved her, that was obvious. But in what way? Common sense told him it was like family, but something in the back of his mind said that wasn't all there was to it, and it drove him crazy.

"Why don't you and I go outside for some air?" Jerome reached for her shoulder.

Maya nodded. She looked up at Trajan. He seemed taller than usual, but she wasn't intimidated. Her eyes were like stone.

"I could've handled it," she said calmly before leaving the room.

Trajan stood alone among leftover chicken Kiev and russet potatoes. Jerome was Maya's source of comfort and Trajan envied him for that.

As the housekeeping end of the catering department entered, Trajan took a seat in a chair along the wall, checking his watch repeatedly. He had plenty of people to call. He needed to follow up with his secretary, Nadine, on his messages. She'd been making more mistakes than usual recently. He had to stop in on a client or two.

But he did nothing. Nothing but think of Maya, and it drove him crazy that she made him second-guess his actions, his motives and priorities. He was certain that stepping up to the question of murder as he had was the best thing to do. Maya was good, but she could be inconsistent once her personal feelings got involved. He wouldn't let her, or his temporary attraction to her, ruin anything long-term. He clenched his free fist. He couldn't even pinpoint what he was so angry about, but he knew she was at the core of it.

"Sir?" The young man stepped cautiously to him. "The room. We need to clean for the next group. It's gonna get pretty loud and distracting."

Trajan nodded, taking the hint. It was time for the *Boston Globe* anyway, and he held no discomfort at the thought of interrupting Jerome and Maya's love fest. Trajan anticipated a long afternoon.

Maya gave him the silent treatment in the cab to the *Globe*. She had wished Jerome could come and act as a buffer, but he had appointments of his own. She felt Trajan staring her down, but she refused to look at him. He was forcing a power play on her, and she wasn't going to lose. She threw New York out of her mind, she decided that all the assumptions she had made because of that night were drastically wrong. Trajan was making himself her enemy, and she could accept that if necessary.

The elevator on the first floor of the building opened and everyone inside got off. A long, useless habit he had with women, Trajan reached for Maya's elbow to guide her in. She quickly jerked away.

The door closed and Trajan pushed the button for the floor. "I'm not diseased, Maya. I was only trying to—"

"I can step into an elevator myself." Maya kept her eyes on the floor numbers. "Why do you even have to be here? I can handle an interview myself."

"This is what Jerome hired me to do," he said. "And I'm going to do it, whether you want me to or not.

Besides, Phillip Stafford is an old friend of mine," he said. "I can do you some good in breaking the ice, and I have a right to say hello to my friends."

"Sure you didn't come to answer my questions for me? You never know, I might hesitate."

"I know you think I'm a cold bastard," he said. "But I do have compassion."

"I guess I'll have to take your word for it, because I sure as hell haven't seen it."

"You haven't tried. Besides, I don't show it for everything. I keep it in perspective."

"I guess you reserve it for people like Elizabeth. Well that's fine. I don't need your comp—"

"Not that it's any of your business, because I still don't know how you know about her in the first place, but Liz and I aren't together any longer."

Maya paused, turning to him. She was alarmed that her senses went wild at this news. It mattered to her. It really did. She was speechless. This was no good.

Not knowing where it came from, Trajan sensed a window of opportunity, a short moment when her guard was down, and something urged him closer to her. He knew at that moment, he wanted to touch her, be near her. He wanted to kiss her again despite everything that told him he didn't, shouldn't.

He reached for her, but just as he did, the elevator stopped and everything went black.

"Oh my God." Maya's heart jumped. She was already anxious in elevators of tall buildings. "What happened?"

"I'm sure it's just a glitch," Trajan said with uncertainty. "It'll start back up in a few—"

"Tre." Maya fought off panic. "When I was ten, my mother and I were stuck in an elevator for three hours. I almost lost my mind. I can't take this."

"Calm down, Maya." He reached for her, wanting to take her fear for her.

Maya let out a gasp as the elevator jerked, tossing her forward. She fell into Trajan's arms and he grabbed her.

"Tre?" Maya held on tight, feeling safer in his arms.

"Don't worry," he said. "I've got you, Maya."

Maya looked up, her eyes adjusting to the dark. She found an unfamiliar comfort this close to him. He was looking down at her, and she could see compassion in his expression.

"Maya." He whispered her name, his arousal coming immediately, fueled by a sense of protection. For this moment he could believe she was his woman, and he would keep her from harm. "I won't let anything happen to you."

His mouth was on hers in an instant. Without the hesitation of last time, Maya returned his kiss fervently. She felt her knees go weak, her body ignite like a volcano.

As her arms wrapped desperately around his waist, Trajan kissed her deeper. He pulled her tighter. He wanted her so much as he raised his hand to her head, entwining his fingers in her hair. His other hand caressed her back with an urgency.

Maya felt his tongue enter her mouth and her mind left her. Her stomach began to ache at its core, and her hands squeezed into his skin. She wanted him to the point of insanity. She never remembered feeling such fury in passion. From just a kiss, although her body told her this was so much more than a kiss.

Trajan's desire forced a hungry, wanton groan from him. This woman. There was nothing but this woman, and he had to have her. Completely.

The pressure of his body against hers pushed them both hard against the wall of the elevator. As he kissed her possessively, Trajan's hand slid down her side, grabbed greedily at her buttock before pulling her leg up to his waist by the thigh. He positioned himself between her. He couldn't imagine ever getting enough of this woman.

A second jolt of the elevator separated them both, returning them to the world they'd left. The lights flashed on, causing the two to close their eyes in pain. In a second, the elevator moved up less than a foot and the doors opened fast.

Maya opened her eyes, blinking them rapidly to adjust. She was face to face with four people waiting impatiently to get on the elevator.

"What happened with the elevators?" A large woman with fire-red hair asked. "We've been waiting forever."

Her mind scattered, Maya couldn't answer. She stepped out with weak legs, whispering "excuse me" to no one in particular. Her fear and desire were fading, leaving her to wonder what had just happened. In a second, she'd been overcome with an animal-like desire for a man she was so certain she hated. It was more than she could fathom. She had to get herself together.

"Some mishap," Trajan answered the woman as he stepped out. "I'm sure it's fine. It only lasted a second, but if you want to be sure, wait for the other elevator."

"None of them are coming," the woman mumbled as she stepped inside.

Trajan wasn't listening to her anymore. He fought to get control of his emotions as he followed Maya. He'd been completely taken over by her closeness, her vulnerability, her beautiful eyes that seemed to shine in the dark. What had taken over was instinctual and beyond his control. It had been so unlike the way he carried himself.

"Tre! Tre, this way!"

Trajan turned around, trying hard to clear his head.

Phillip Stafford stood at the other end of the hallway with a confused look on his face.

"Phillip." He smiled with an upward nod. He turned to call Maya, but she had already started toward Phillip.

Trajan introduced them, taking a moment for familiar references. He sensed an extreme irritation radiating from Maya, but only for him. For Phillip, she was charming. All smiles and witty sarcasm.

They followed him to his office, listening as he gabbed away. Maya pulled herself together. She had to think of Pharaoh now. She had to think of her father, her mother and Jerome. Not Trajan. If only he would go away it would be easier.

Only he wouldn't. Phillip insisted he stay in the office during the interview in case he was needed for a question. So he sat in the corner and Maya felt his eyes on her the entire hour. She was certain she'd fooled Phillip, appearing only concerned about the interview. He hadn't seemed to notice that her mind raced, her heart pumped fast, and she felt herself close to breaking a sweat under Trajan's constant stare.

What had made her open up to him like that? So fast. It was as if no matter how horrible he was to her, she never learned her lesson. She'd opened up to him about her childhood fears, and proceeded to practically make love to him in a public elevator.

She caught his eyes a few times when Phillip turned away to check his notes. His expression wasn't what she'd call flat, but it gave nothing away. Was he mocking her? Making fun of her loss of control? Was he basking in the power of making her open up to him? She would give anything to know what he was thinking. Or would she? What was his reason for kissing her? Was he playing a game with her? Was he just trying to show her up? She wanted to strangle him.

Maya knew she was getting into something over her

head. How serious she wasn't sure. There had been no romantic horse ride or wine over dinner to excuse this kiss away. On the contrary, she should have been too scared to even think of a kiss. Especially a kiss like that. She couldn't have imagined what would have stopped them from making love if they had been alone. Thank God they were in public. What was she saying? She hadn't meant it that way. No, she had, but . . . oh that horrid man!

The hour seemed more like two to Trajan. He couldn't take his eyes off Maya. Between his growing attraction to her and his admiration for her professional skills, he'd become entranced by the woman. It was as if she'd put a spell on him. But he knew he had to find the antidote for whatever was in him that pulled him to her, made him want her. Made her opinion matter so much to him. When the interview ended, he was eager to talk to her to clear the air. He had no explanation for what happened, but he'd have to come up with something. Otherwise, every second together would be unspeakably difficult.

"Maya." He approached her as soon as she sat up from her chair, and he felt more vulnerable than he was used to. Much more than he was comfortable with. "I need to talk to you."

Maya looked up at him. She was being betrayed by a body that urged her to agree with him. No, her mind screamed, barely an echo. Don't talk to him. Remember the last time. Get away from him.

"No," she whispered, turning away from him. "Stay away from me, Trajan."

He was hurt by her words, her rejection. "I didn't mean for . . . whatever that was that happened to happen. I want . . ."

"Do you two have any more appointments today?"

Phillip stepped between them, completely oblivious to what was going on.

Maya was grateful for the move, although she thought it a bit rude. Any distance between her and Trajan was good. It helped her clear her head. She waited on pins and needles to get away from him.

"No," she answered, roping her purse harshly over her shoulder. "Trajan and I are finished for today. We're going our separate ways."

Trajan was frustrated. He never took no for an answer and was horrible at rejection, so unused to it. "Maya, we should—"

"Good." Phillip slapped his hands together, rubbing them aggressively. "Tre, my man. We gotta get reacquainted. And I'm talkin' the traditional way."

Trajan knew what he meant. He and Phillip had been drinking buddies in their Wharton days. "It's only a quarter to four."

"Late enough." He slapped Trajan on his back. "Let's hit it."

"I'll catch a cab to the airport," Maya said, although her flight wasn't for almost three hours. She held her hand out to Phillip. "Phillip. Again, it was so nice meeting you, and you have my card for any follow-up."

"Same here." Phillip's smile was wide. It was obvious from the excitement in his eyes he was a party animal through and through. "Good luck with this guy. He'll drive you crazy, but he's worth it. He's good."

"He's definitely something," she said, smiling harshly. She gave Trajan a second look. "I'll see you in Philadelphia."

Trajan nodded, saying nothing. He could tell she wanted nothing to do with him, and as she left the office, he felt his shoulders slump just a bit. He considered himself a wimp for letting her hurt his ego. He knew he was stronger than that. But something about this woman brought on all the exceptions to the rule. He may be in the dark somewhat, but he wasn't insane. That kiss had been two-sided. There was no questioning that. Obviously, Maya chose to react to it with anger and resentment. Trajan thought he'd be better off having resented it as well. But that wasn't about to happen.

"Why the long face?" Phillip asked. "I thought it went well. Looks like you have another winner."

"This is a winner," Trajan added, a smile creasing his lips again. "A sure thing."

"You ready?" Phillip grabbed his keys and wallet from his desk.

Trajan nodded. "Yeah, I'm ready. I could use a drink right now."

Maya ate much more than she should have at the airport restaurant, drowning herself in fried food and magazines that told her how to fix everything that she didn't even know was wrong with her before she read them. When Jerome arrived for their joint flight, she greeted him kindly, but pretended to sleep during the short flight. She knew he would be concerned about her mood and probe further, and she wasn't in the mood to explain something she didn't even understand.

She felt a sense of dread and a nagging desire to cry her eyes out, but she refused to. She was developing feelings for Trajan Matthews. That was clear. But what was she going to do about them? That was the question of a lifetime.

"I think that went well," Trajan said as he and Jerome stepped onto the business streets of downtown Philadelphia. "I mean, Lincoln Pembleton is the hottest analyst in Philadelphia. In the East Coast for that matter. He seemed receptive, enthusiastic. For him to suggest an opening price of seventeen dollars a share is a great sign. We'll have to be strong with the follow-up, but . . ."

He stopped talking, noticing Jerome was barely paying attention to him. When they were alone together, he'd been distant and cold all day. Trajan hadn't bothered to complain, since Jerome turned it on the second they met an investor, broker or analyst. Trajan wondered if Jerome sensed the latent jealousy that Trajan had developed since acknowledging his feelings for Maya. Did Jerome know about what was going on between the two of them? Whatever that was.

Jerome looked down at his watch. "We have to be at the *Inquirer* at three. I'm starving. I didn't get a second to eat at the lunch."

"These hot dog stands will have to do," Trajan said as they approached one. "We don't have time for anything more."

They got the hot dogs and sat on the stone-edged seat of a nearby building. Trajan wondered if he should say something. The tension seemed to have been there from the start. When Jerome showed up without Maya, telling Trajan she'd passed on Philadelphia, Trajan wasn't sure what he should feel. He thought he'd be happy to avoid dealing with his attraction to her and her mixed messages. On the other hand, he wanted so much to see her. Part of him had been excited to see her beautiful eyes and that bud of a nose.

"Jerome." Trajan waited for his business partner's full attention before continuing. "Is there something you want to tell me?"

Jerome frowned, confused. "What?"

"I've noticed your distance today. Is there a problem?"

Jerome nodded. "It's Maya."

Trajan braced himself. What should he say? There

heart & soul's got it all!

Motivation, Inspiration, Exhilaration!

FREE ISSUE RESERVATION CARD

YES! Please send my FREE issue of HEART & SOUL right away and enter my one-year subscription. My special price for 5 more issues (6 in all) is only $10.00. I'll save 44% off the newsstand rate. If I decide that HEART & SOUL is not for me, I'll write "cancel" on the invoice, return it, and owe nothing. The FREE issue will be mine to keep.

Name	(First)		(Last)	
Address				Apt.#
City		State	Zip	MABP

Please allow 6-8 weeks for receipt of first issue. In Canada: CDN $19.97 (includes GST). Payment in U.S. currency must accompany all Canadian orders. Basic subscription rate: 1 year (6 issues) $16.97.

BUSINESS REPLY MAIL

FIRST-CLASS MAIL   PERMIT NO. 272   RED OAK, IA

POSTAGE WILL BE PAID BY ADDRESSEE

heart&soul

P O BOX 7423
RED OAK IA 51591-2423

was an attraction, undeniable, but there was no relationship.

"She's very upset," Jerome continued. "She said she couldn't come because she had too much to do for the NAACP banquet, but I know that's not it."

"Listen, Jerome." Trajan knew he was more successful at heading things off than reacting to them. "About Maya and me. I—"

"It's the murder." Jerome looked at the rest of the hot dog as if he'd just lost his appetite. "She's getting too involved."

Trajan's sense of concern for Maya took over, and he adjusted "Is she putting herself in danger?"

"I found out she was in New Jersey yesterday, trying to track down one of Elaine's kids. I think she's up to something today too, but I don't know what."

Trajan didn't like this at all. He'd thought his first concern was for the IPO and how Maya willingly distracted herself from it, but that wasn't what upset him the most. Maya was putting herself in danger, and this upset him in a way that he couldn't deny he cared for her in more than just a physical way.

"Can't you stop her?" Trajan asked, his face tightening, his voice higher-pitched than usual. "She's going to get hurt or worse if she comes across the wrong person."

"I would never let anything happen to Maya," Jerome said with a calm, very certain tone. He leaned his head back, eyeing Trajan suspiciously. "What's going on with you two that you'd care so much anyway?"

Trajan's instinct was to deny everything to save the partnership. But he wanted to say something, if for no other reason than to get his own clarification on Maya's relationship with Jerome.

"You seem very concerned about a woman you can't seem to do anything but fight with."

"It's complicated," Trajan said. "With our relationship—"

"You mean you and me? What would that have to do with Maya?"

Trajan wasn't about to make assumptions. "All I'll say is that Maya and I don't get along well, but that doesn't mean I don't like her. I wouldn't want her hurt."

Jerome laughed bitterly. "So you'd want me to believe this was out of a gentleman's concern? Except I've seen the looks tossed between the two of you. The way you look at her when she doesn't know."

Trajan felt a sense of relief that it was at least out. "I'm sure you're used to men looking at Maya. She's very beautiful. You can't be jealous of that."

"Jealous?" Jerome let out a loud laugh. "Do you think Maya and I are lovers?"

Trajan's spirit lifted. "You aren't?"

"Damn, Tre! The girl is seventeen years younger than me. Besides, she was a baby when I met her. The thought is pretty perverted if you ask me. No. We aren't lovers, but we're family and I look out for her. I love her like a daughter."

Trajan could laugh now. Inside, he struggled with this feeling of new inspiration at the news. "I guess I saw the closeness, and thought . . . I'm not sure what I thought."

Jerome tossed his napkin into the nearby garbage. His expression changed suddenly. He was somber again, almost depressed.

"No," he said. "Even if I were a suitable lover for Maya, I wouldn't think of it. I would never deserve someone like her."

Trajan thought this quick change mysterious. "Who would you say is? I guess I'm asking if she is involved with anyone."

He nodded. "Not recently. She's looking for a man like her daddy. The late, great Nick Woodson."

Trajan sensed a level of contempt in Jerome's voice and found it odd. Jerome had always spoken of Nick with such regard, as if he worshiped the man. He'd always suspected there was a strong competition between the men when they worked side by side. It would have been expected.

"You'd like to be considered, wouldn't you, Tre?" Jerome stood up, stretching his arm.

Trajan followed suit, never one to give much away in his expressions or demeanor. "You forget. She hates me."

"Ahh, but she's attracted to you. I know Maya."

They started down the street. The interview at the *Philadelphia Inquirer* was only three blocks away.

"Would you say I was anything like her father?" Trajan asked. "You say that's what she's looking for?"

Jerome looked him over. "Not really. You'll have to soften up. Nick had some flaws, but he wasn't as rough around the edges when he dealt with Maya."

Trajan ignored the insult, assuming Jerome didn't realize he'd said it. "Flaws? From hearing you and Maya talk, I'd say Nick Woodson was perfect."

Jerome's face was all serious as he straightened his tie. Stopping at the corner and waiting for the light, he kept his eyes straight ahead.

"There's a lot Maya doesn't want to believe," he said. "As well she shouldn't. It's good for a daughter to worship her father."

"Whatever the case," Trajan said. "I've got to fix this rift between us, and you've got to convince her to stay out of this murder investigation."

The road show made its way back to D.C. for an unexpected second visit based on good word of mouth from last month's meeting. Maya felt the hair on her arms stand on end as she anticipated seeing Trajan again. Since their last kiss, he was all she thought about, although she did everything not to. There was no point to it.

She'd spent the morning with Jerome working on various PR activities coming up. When they weren't discussing work, he spent most of the morning trying to convince her to quit her one-woman investigating crusade. Through it all, Maya only wanted to know about Trajan.

Did he ask about her? Was he upset she hadn't come to Philadelphia? Did he care? Did he mention anything to Jerome about the kisses they had shared?

Part of her had given in. She'd given in to the dreams and odd fantasies during the day. Still, she was determined to fight it. Trajan Matthews was not the man for her. She'd only end up the next Elizabeth, and God only knew how many more there were before her.

Still, seeing him as soon as she walked into the luncheon room at the Renaissance stirred desire within her. She pressed her lips together as her stomach twirled. He was gorgeous and people gravitated toward him. Older men with lots of money of their own soaked up his every word.

Trajan felt a bolt of energy surge through him when he saw her. He hadn't thought to kid himself into believing he'd wanted anything but to see her again, and now that he had, he wanted nothing but to hold her in his arms and seduce her.

They nodded hellos to each other, not comfortable with anything else. Each thought only of the kiss in the elevator in Boston, the kiss in New York after the romantic ride, and the so many close calls in between.

Trajan did his best to concentrate through the luncheon. It was a good one. Some heavy hitters had shown up. He couldn't remember a woman who had ever distracted him from his work like this.

"Northern Virginia," he started as everyone else sat down, "as part of the D.C. metro area, is becoming well-known as the Silicon Valley of the east. Technology and telecommunications companies dominate. New tech startups pop up every week. Very seldom do they hire locals to fill their positions. Your unemployment rate was half the rate of the national average, which itself is at an all-time low. So what they have to do is relocate thousands of people each year. Where do those people stay until they find a permanent apartment, condo or home? Living out of a suitcase is good for a week at a time, tops. Pharaoh has the alternative."

"Tre, you had them hooked from the beginning." Jerome slapped his back after the last attendee left. "You were on some supernatural flow today."

Maya joined the men. She'd kept her distance from Trajan, afraid to be alone with him. Now that she was near him again, the tension coursed through her veins. She felt as if she had to fight a force pulling her to him.

"You were good, Tre," she said, blinking as he looked at her for a moment. "You too, Jerome."

Trajan nodded a thank you, finding a silly sense of pleasure in her using his nickname again.

"I'd love to stay and shower the compliments." Jerome checked his watch. "But I have other business to attend to. Still running a company, you know."

Maya felt panic set in. "I'll come with you."

"Maya." Trajan reached for her arm, enjoying the electricity that hit him when he touched her.

Maya felt the heat of his hand on her bare arm. She felt her face, then her whole body, flush with warmth. She couldn't look at him. Her eyes focused on the space around him. Jerome was already leaving.

"No, Tre." The words were almost a whisper as she pulled away.

"This is business, Maya."

She mustered the courage to face him.

"Jerome and I have a follow-up interview at the *Post* at three. Can you join us? Just in case." He would never admit to himself that he simply wanted to keep her around him.

"No." She smiled, hoping to appear unfazed. She knew she wasn't cutting it. She would never admit to herself how much she wanted to be with him. "I have an event."

"Important?" She made him so conscious of how he came across. He didn't want her to think of him as she had before. Since Boston . . . he could barely think.

"My goddaughter's play." Maya noticed a change in him immediately. Softer. Still strong and a little distant, but not as aggressive. "I really . . ."

"I understand." He nodded. He was becoming familiar with her smell. She wore the same perfume all the time.

He understood? Maya's eyes widened. "No reprimand? No accusations of unprofessionalism or lack of commitment?"

He smiled an embarrassed smile that made Maya's knees go weak.

"No more of that, Maya." His head tilted to the side. "Can we call a truce? No more insults or arguments."

Maya nodded, a voice inside asking, *no more kisses?*

"If you can't come today," he went on, the rest of the room around them evaporating. His throat was dry. Was he doing this? "How about tonight? I have a dinner meeting."

"With who?" Maya couldn't remember a dinner setup for the night, but she couldn't remember much right now.

He shrugged. "Something spur-of-the-moment I set up this morning. Jerome can't make it. It's very informal. Casual dress, all that. Can I count on you?"

Maya opened her mouth to say yes, but as she gazed into his arresting eyes, no words came out. She caught herself, swallowed hard and forced a "yes" out.

Trajan nodded in compliance. It made such sense. Why hadn't he thought of it before?

"Good. It's at seven. Can I pick you up?"

Maya wasn't comfortable with that. It sounded like a date and that was dangerous. But she wouldn't make waves. If she and Trajan could get along, get rid of the tension, she'd ignore her own questions.

"I'm at 2345 Speer Street in Georgetown," she said. "Right off M Street. Do you need directions?"

He shook his head. "I'm a native, remember?"

As if by instinct, Maya's eyes blinked flirtatiously, her head lowering. She nodded a good-bye before leaving. She had to get out of there before she embarrassed herself.

Even though her mind told her this evening was about business only, she let herself anticipate something else entirely.

Amani's play was a pleasant distraction for Maya. She loved the kid, her goddaughter. The school had set their ambitions high with a modified rendition of "The Wiz." All the children sang off-key and messed up all their lines. It was one of the funniest things Maya had seen in a long time. She had never seen so many home video cameras in one room.

At the tiny reception in the gymnasium of the elementary school they snacked on punch and pastries. Maya was immersed in the suburban family culture. Mommies and daddies as proud as ever of their angels.

It was bittersweet. She thought of fond memories as a child, but at the same time felt deprived. With thirty around the corner, Maya wanted forever after with a loving husband and children, and she didn't see it happening any time soon.

Alissa always read her emotions like an open book, bringing the topic up as soon as they were alone on the wooden bleachers.

"Thinking about Mr. Right and the kiddies again." She handed Maya a foam cup of fruit punch.

"I'm patient," she answered. "I know my man will come. It just gets a little harder to wait sometimes than others. These kids are so precious. The looks on all these parents' faces, even when their kid was a tree in the background. They were in tears. I want to feel like that, share love like that with someone."

"True love doesn't fall in your lap, girl. What are you doing to make it happen?"

"I'm not going to go out searching for a husband," Maya said. "The desperate spinster is not the role for me."

"You don't have to hunt one down," she said. "But you do have to make yourself available. Working twelve hours a day and hanging out with Jerome isn't gonna help you."

Maya sighed. "But when I do take a risk, what happens? My last few boyfriends were huge disappointments."

Alissa wiggled her nose a bit. "Now, how about Dennis? He was okay. You were looking hard for reasons to kick him to the curb."

"No." Maya jumped on the defensive. "No, no. I wanted to love him."

"You wanted to change him. Make him into your daddy. Or your vision of your daddy. When he wouldn't become Nick Woodson, Jr., you got rid of him."

"Whatever." Maya wasn't giving up. "You can spin it how you want to."

Alissa pushed her playfully. "Now, don't get so depressed. You must have some prospects."

Maya shook her head no. Her mind, her body, thought of Trajan. No way.

"What about that Trajan Matthews?" Alissa said as if reading her mind. "The black Roman emperor."

Maya laughed to ease her embarrassment. "Funny, Ally."

"Well? When I was talking to George at the funeral last week, I got the impression that you and this guy have some pretty shiny sparks flying between you two."

At least, Maya thought. She felt weird keeping the details from Alissa. It was just . . . well . . . Trajan was different. She couldn't tell.

"Tre is nothing like Daddy," was all she said, her eyes straight ahead.

"Tre?" Alissa smacked her lips. "You're using pet names now. You must be keeping something from me."

"Everyone calls him Tre."

"You didn't answer my question from before."

Maya faked a cough.

"Fine," Alissa said. "Play elusive. I'll call George. Doesn't make a difference to me. He gave me his card. I didn't know cops even had—"

"He's a detective, and he can't tell you anything. He doesn't know."

"Know what?"

"Nothing." Maya shifted in her seat. The bleachers were so hard and uncomfortable. The gymnasium was freezing.

"This is sounding spicy. You better give."

Maya sipped an empty cup. "There's nothing to give. He's a callous, cold, feelingless, money-hungry tyrant. He has no couth, no concern, and his priorities are so out of whack, I can't even begin to explain it to you. He's a complete ass."

Alissa said nothing. She waited for Maya to look at her, then smiled. Her eyes narrowed.

Maya was irritated. "He insults me constantly, has no respect for my father's vision. He specializes in insulting me. He had the nerve to call me unprofessional."

Alissa never changed her expression. Maya's annoyance grew.

"All he cares about is his own success," she continued. "Not people. He's . . . he's . . ."

"He's the guy you'll be coming to this gym with to see your kid mess up the one line she has in her first play."

Maya stared at her. There was that fear and excitement again. It would seem impossible. Wouldn't it?

Six

As soon as Maya appeared in her doorway dressed in a playful polo dress, a shade of hunter green that delighted her skin tone and flirted with her thighs, Trajan knew this was about more than he'd intended. He'd tried to convince himself this was about convenience, about a truce. That was all shattered with one smile.

"I can see I'm not overdressed." Maya sat back in the comfortable leather seats of the rented Buick Park Avenue.

"You're referring to my polo and shorts?" Trajan smiled, keeping his eyes on the road. It wasn't easy with her so close to him. The dress hiked up her thighs as she sat down. He could see from the corner of his eye. "You don't approve?"

"Don't be silly." Maya approved. She approved too much. Looking at his strong, muscular legs and arms, she felt the summer heat getting to her.

There was an awkward silence at the red light. He stole a glance. Her hair fell over her face, hanging without order over her shoulders. Only lipstick, but a soft shade of red that highlighted her face. That nose. It was just as adorable in a profile as up front.

Maya adjusted the vent in front of her, focusing the air on her face, which was getting hotter every second. "So, who are we meeting? What firm are they with?"

"I know these people from way back."

"I assumed as much." Maya noticed they were leaving the business district, not toward the city, but southeast. "For it to be okay that we're dressed like this. Where exactly are we going?"

"You'll like them," he said. "They'll definitely like you."

"You mean they'll like Pharaoh." She wasn't stupid. Maya knew something was up. There were no companies where they were headed, and the few restaurants weren't necessarily fit for business meetings.

Trajan nodded.

The silence returned. Maya's anticipation grew. She tried to ignore the voice that said it wasn't wise to entertain the thought she was entertaining. Especially with him. As they drove down a neighborhood street, Maya heard the music first. She saw a couple with a little girl around five years old walking down the street, the woman holding a plastic round cake holder at the straps.

The two orange street blockades came into view. The block party had already started.

Maya turned to Trajan as they stopped. He smiled mischievously.

"Go ahead," she said, her eyes narrowing. "Explain yourself. You have one minute."

He spoke fast, in one breath.

"This is my old neighborhood. We're having a block party, and my aunt begged me to come, begged me to bring someone. I didn't want to, but I never visit, so I had to. Besides, you agreed."

Maya tried to keep from laughing. She couldn't believe she wasn't angry with him. "I agreed to a business dinner. I don't know your family. I don't—"

Trajan was out of the car already. Maya watched with her mouth wide open as he moved the barriers. He jumped back in the car.

"As I was saying when you left me in the middle of a sentence," Maya continued. "I don't—"

"They're great." He winked at her before hopping out to replace the blockades.

Maya folded her arms across her chest as he parked the car. "I'm not getting out."

"Come on, Maya. They're good people." When she hadn't blown up in anger, Trajan knew he had won this one. The rest was small stuff. She was getting out of this car.

"But they're your people. I don't even know them. Who will they think I am?"

He sighed. "I'll tell them you're a friend. You can survive one night of friendship with me."

She shook her head. "You took me for granted. You deceived me."

He wouldn't let her frustrate him. "Maya, that's a little stretch."

"You tried to make me think everything was fine this morning, so I would be dulled into complacency and—"

"Everything is fine! What was wrong?"

He'd regretted saying that the second he heard it come out of his mouth. Everything hadn't been fine. This relationship, or whatever it could be called, was confusing at least. Nowhere near fine.

"Look, Maya." He lowered his head, took a deep breath and raised it again. "Can we start over? I can't explain the kisses or the arguments any more than you can. But if we start over, maybe we won't have to."

"I don't know." Maya was torn. She loved the idea of a clean slate, but part of her didn't want to forget the kisses. Another part thought maybe they'd gone too far for a clean slate to be an option.

"My Aunt Audrey made grilled pork chops, smoked turkey and her famous cheddar garlic rolls."

"Food doesn't sway me," she lied.

"Baked, soft and mushy sweet potatoes with butter and cinnamon sugar. Greens, corn on the cob, barbecued ribs, fried chicken."

"Stop." Maya's stomach grumbled.

"Homemade pound cake and hot peach cobbler with vanilla ice cream melting all over it."

Maya bit her lower lip. "I hate you, Tre."

Trajan smiled victoriously. "I can accept that. Now, get on out of this car, woman.

Maya was enjoying herself right away. George greeted them on the way, not an inch of surprise on his face at seeing them together. Trajan's Aunt Audrey hugged her tightly, as if she'd known her forever. Everyone made her feel welcomed immediately, most of them vaguely aware of her father and the hotel. She was flattered by their compliments, but grateful that no one treated her differently for it. The food was abundant, home-grown and rich. Maya filled herself up, urged by Aunt Audrey, who complained about her weight as if she was being starved.

Trajan watched Maya all night. He enjoyed watching how she naturally warmed to people, and how they naturally warmed to her. She was a beautiful person inside and out, and it made him feel like a better person just from being with her.

Urged on by some pre-teen girls, Maya went into the street and held the rope for double-dutch. As the sun set, the streetlights illuminated the scene. Laughing, eating, joking, meaningful conversation about much of nothing and innocent play. It was all beautiful, and Maya was caught up in the moment remembering her childhood, and grateful that Trajan brought some of it back to her.

"You got some serious issues, boy." George handed Trajan a beer as they stood against a tree.

Trajan smiled, emotions waving through him as they had all evening. "How did you know?"

"You got that look on your face," he said. "Like you just gave in to something you've been fighting. Like that look in between a perp denying everything and confessing it all. I know it well."

"So I remind you of a perp, a criminal?" Trajan laughed, surprised that he was so readable.

"You know what I mean."

Trajan nodded, looking up the tree. "Remember this tree?"

George nodded. "The only one on the block big enough for me to hide behind."

Trajan looked down the street. "Who's living there now?"

"Last Audrey told me, some middle-aged woman and her mother. Nice folks. She says they keep to themselves."

Trajan had thought to walk that extra block, but didn't. He'd expected to feel apprehensive, maybe a little afraid, but he didn't. He could see his old house from where he stood and he felt fine. He had George, Audrey and especially Maya to thank for that, even though they didn't know it.

"You take the good with the bad, brother." George drank his beer.

Trajan nodded. "It's not that easy. I mean, I have a lot of good memories. Mama was so good to me, would do anything for me. Give me anything."

George looked away. "I know the story. But she had nothing but love to give you."

"You don't know how hard it was for me, man." Trajan felt his fists clench. "Fighting every inch. Seeing her spend her life just trying to keep her head above water."

"I grew up here too, brother. Remember?"

"But you had a dad. A good dad that made some money."

"So what are you saying? By ignoring where you came from, you can gain . . . what?"

Trajan shrugged. "I'm here, aren't I?"

Trajan watched Maya in the street, laughing. She was beautiful, so comfortable around everyone.

"Issue number two."

"Enough." Trajan held up a hand to stop him. "Don't drag her into this."

"She's already in it, man. I could see that from the start. I think you did too."

Trajan nodded, taking a sip. He watched as the music blared and the girls tossed the ropes aside to dance. Maya was as sensual as she was playful.

As if by nature, Trajan started for the street, soaking her up with his eyes. When she swung around, her eyes caught his and she stopped, but only for a moment.

Maya felt her body warm as he headed for her. She kept dancing to the strong bass of the hip-hop song. She was inviting him to join her, wishing for nothing else in this world. Only a few hours ago, she would have never guessed Trajan Matthews could get down to a rap song, but he showed her the contrary as he joined her.

A few hours ago, Maya would have never thought she wanted to kiss him again, but as soon as the song changed to a slow tune and he took her in his arms, she knew she did.

"Your aunt thinks I'm your girlfriend," she said, looking up at him. The night had cooled considerably, but she was just as hot as the midday sun.

"So my plan is complete." Trajan loved holding her. She was soft and feminine to touch. He liked having her close. Her smile was like wine to his system.

"Plan?" Maya's hands were at his shoulders. He smelled like cologne and sun, and her senses liked it.

"My plan to keep the matchmaking at bay." He wanted to kiss her again.

"So you've used me again." She playfully punched his arm.

He pulled her closer, looking down at her. Her lips were so moist, inviting. "Hey, you got sweet potatoes out of it. I think you came out good."

She nodded. Maya could hear her heart beat fast. "If your aunt is a matchmaker, you might want to avoid her, but I think I need her number."

"Now Maya." She smelled too good. "There's no way you're in need of a matchmaker."

"Thanks for the compliment, but it's hard out there."

"Especially for those of us committed to our work."

There was a silence as they both contemplated a relationship with the other. But no, they told themselves. Business before pleasure, Trajan thought. Look for something you can handle, Maya thought.

"When you do find someone," Trajan said, in a whisper because her closeness was getting to him, "I know you'll make him happy. You won't put him second to work."

"What about you?" She appreciated his compliment more than she expected to.

Trajan grinned apologetically. "I'm married to my business."

There was that lovely mix of compassion and confusion again. "Not forever, Tre. You've got to want more."

The music stopped, but they separated only inches. Their eyes were locked. Trajan saw more in her.

"I do want more, Maya. I want everything."

The silence between them was louder than the noise of the next song. It was louder than George's voice as he called to Maya. Neither one heard him until he was right on them.

"I hate to break up this magical moment," he said, "but if I leave it up to you two, you'll be standing here till tomorrow."

Maya blinked, turning away. She removed her hands, smiling nervously. Trajan pulled at his chin, needing something to do with restless hands. He tried to calm his desire for Maya.

"Maya," George said. "Can I talk to you for a second? I'm back on duty, so I have to head out."

Maya nodded, unable to speak. She avoided eye contact with Trajan as she passed him. They sat at the edges of the hood of George's car.

"It's Elaine Cramer."

Those words were enough to distract Maya from watching Trajan dance with two teenage girls.

"Have you found something new?" she asked.

He shook his head, his expression somber. "We've gone cold. It's frustrating as hell."

"What about Steven, her youngest son?"

"We haven't found him. I'd like to hold on to him. I think if he was innocent, he'd show up somewhere. Still, what's the motive? Just like Linda and Craig, Steven was written out of the will over a year ago."

"He's transient," Maya said. "Maybe he didn't know until now. Or maybe he knew and he was out for revenge."

"A year later? Farfetched."

"A year later to make it seem farfetched. You know, getting away with a crime because its simplicity and obviousness would lead to you. But it has to be more complicated, everyone assumes."

"He's a transient, but no real criminal record. He gets in bar fights all the time. He's always out of work. His credit is shot to hell. He owes everyone all the money in the world. Still, no crimes."

"Not even a misdemeanor? Elaine told me the boys were constantly in trouble."

George nodded. Shook his head. "Her version of trouble and the law's version differ."

Maya sighed. She'd have to find Steven. "So, what do you want from me?"

"Everything, anything you can give. You know her best. We need to know everyone she knew. Good or bad. Anything she'd told you over the past month before she died. Any names she mentioned that struck you as unfamiliar. It seems like a lot to ask, but if you sit and concentrate, you'd be surprised at what you could remember."

"I'll do whatever I can," she said, touching his arm comfortingly. "I know you're frustrated, but I appreciate you not giving up. I know it would be so easy to file this under the cold file and move on."

"That's not my style." He smiled at her. "It's not yours either. You don't give up on people you care about. You're my kind of girl."

Maya laughed, crossing her legs in front of her. She tilted her head to the side. "Same to you. And speaking of girls, where's that fiancée of yours?"

"Vancouver." He whistled slowly. "Can't stand it, being away from her. Like torture."

"That's so sweet." She tugged at his arm. "You are a big romantic, George."

He nodded and spoke with pride. "Can't help it. When a woman gets a hold of a man's heart, there's no fighting it. Kind of like Tre."

Maya laughed. "If you're gonna try and tell me Tre is a romantic, I take back everything I just said about you. You're either a liar or insane."

"I'm neither. There's a romantic in Tre. It's just been lying dormant for thirty-five years."

He winked at her, but Maya only rolled her eyes.

"Dormant for thirty-five years?" she asked. "That's pretty dormant. Sounds more like dead and buried to me."

"Romance is never dead and buried. Tre is just waiting for the right woman to awaken it. We've been talking almost every day since hooking up again. I think he's finally found that woman."

Maya ran her fingers through her hair. "Not me. No. We're business partners. The business of stocks and trading."

"Which has somehow led you to the business of . . . let me think . . . love." He leaned back, forming his words into a melody. "The business of love. That's got a nice little ring to it. Did Tre tell you I'm a songwriter? That's my hobby."

Maya stood up, patting him on his enormous thigh. "Don't quit your day job."

His laugh shook his entire body as Maya walked away.

Trajan and Maya stayed at the party for a couple more hours. They spent most of their time at a distance, both thinking it would help quell the attraction they were feeling. Both hoping to keep out of trouble. It only served to increase it, make them more aware of it. Whenever their eyes met, lightning struck. Each time, it was harder to turn away.

After walking Trajan's aunt to her home down the street, they both agreed to call it a night. The ten-minute drive seemed like an hour, both struggling for polite, irrelevant conversation when all each could think of was the taste of the other's lips. By the time Trajan turned down Maya's street, they'd given up and accepted the thick silence.

They both saw the parking space at the same time. Right in the front of Maya's brownstone. Maya felt fate was tempting her.

Their eyes met. Flash. Maya turned away as Trajan slid into the space.

"This is a miracle, you know." Maya swallowed hard. "There's never a space on Friday nights. There's barely space ever, but especially on the weekend."

Trajan parked, leaning toward Maya as he opened his door. "I guess I'm a lucky man."

Maya hurried out of the car as he walked around. She couldn't explain why it was so important to her that he not get the door for her.

"You don't have to walk me to my door," she said as they walked anyway.

"It's late." Trajan was looking for excuses. He didn't want to be away from her, although he knew he should leave. "Besides, no matter what you think, I am a gentleman."

They reached the door, standing on the porch.

"Maya." Trajan paused, knowing he had to leave now or else he'd ask to come in. He was good at seducing women. He could admit that to himself. So close to throwing all his charms at Maya. He wanted her enough. But then he knew he didn't want her that way. He wanted her to want him with her eyes wide open. "Thanks for coming with me."

He seemed so calm. Maya felt like pulling her hair out.

"I really mean it. Tonight would've been unbearable if I hadn't come with someone."

"No problem." She played with her keys. "I had fun."

She inserted the key in her door and turned it. "I'll see you next week."

"Good night."

Maya opened the door as he turned to walk away. She wasn't sure what caused her to call after him. She was almost home safe.

Trajan turned, desire crossing that line where he could turn it off and go about his business. He was going to kiss her. He needed to.

"Why did you bring me tonight?" she asked. "I mean the real reason."

Trajan's first thought was to stick with his original story, but Maya deserved honesty. He wanted to be honest with her, and something told him it would be okay.

"I wanted . . . I needed to show them I still . . ." He didn't even know how to say it. "I left them behind. I hurt them. You remind of the good parts, the reason why I loved them. I can't really explain it."

"You don't have to." Urged by emotion, Maya reached her hand up to his cheek. His skin was soft and smooth. "I understand."

She did, Trajan felt that right away. Probably more than he understood. Her heart was like that, he realized.

Trajan didn't hesitate. He wrapped his arms around her waist, pulling her to him. His lips melted into hers. He wanted her with a desire he had no control over because he'd never felt it before.

Maya's mind left her the second their lips touched. Her arms moved swiftly, instinctively, up his arms, around his neck. Her stomach ached, her knees quivered. She pressed her lips harder against his, heat like lava flowing through her.

"Woo hoo!"

"Get it on!"

"Show some skin!"

Trajan and Maya sent the three young men standing on the sidewalk an ugly glare, sending them on their way.

"Let's not give them a show," Trajan said.

Maya opened the door, and Trajan walked in the foyer. Maya closed the door behind her, locked it and peeked out the window to see if anyone else was out there.

She heard herself inhale sharply as a stroke of lightning hit her. Trajan was behind her, one hand wrapping around her stomach, the other gently, but not too gently at her chin. His mouth, his tongue, was hot on her neck as he tasted her soft skin. Kissing her desperately, roughly. Maya was consumed with passion. Her arms reached behind her, grabbing at him.

Trajan moaned. The feeling of her body next to his made him feel like a man in a way nothing else could. He swung her around forcefully, pulling her to him. The taste of her lips, as hungry as his, sent him soaring.

There was enough electricity between them to light up a city. Maya felt waves of insanity flow through her as his hands slowly creased her dress up . . . up.

Trajan's lips greedily laid claim to her neck, her chin, before returning to her mouth. He knew this would happen, and he let go of his restraint. He moved with Maya to the living room, letting her pull his shirt off of him. The desire in her eyes excited him beyond words.

Maya's lips trailed his chest slowly down before she welcomed him to the sofa. The world was erased as he joined her. She bit her lip in anticipation of the delight.

"Maya," he said as his hands hastily ran her tiny dress up her body and over her head. He tossed it aside and returned to her mouth. As his tongue parted her lips again, his body parted her legs.

Maya felt as if he heard everything her body begged for. He was sliding out of his pants as his tongue blazed a trail of flame over her neck and chest. She wrapped her legs around him, her hands at his shoulders. When he unclipped the front clip of her bra, his hands pushed it to the side as they cupped her breast. Gently at first, then with more urgency. Maya let out a moan.

Trajan's mouth kissed her breast tenderly, his tongue caressing its nipple. His hands grabbed her at the waist, lifting her body to him as his tongue teased both breasts, sending Maya to insanity.

"Trajan," she whispered passionately.

Trajan's hand slid down an inch to the tip of her panties. As his tongue made its way down the middle of her stomach, he pulled at the edges of the fabric. Slowly, torturously, he began to slide them down, revealing her completely.

The ringing of the phone right next to their heads was barely heard. The world around them was being erased. Neither of them was thinking of anything but making love right there, right then.

Her panties were off, and Trajan's mouth returned to Maya's breasts as he kissed them with a sweet roughness. Her nails were digging into his back. She barely heard Alissa's voice, but as soon as Trajan's name was mentioned, her eyes widened. So did Trajan's.

"What I guess I'm saying is . . . I may have suggested you and this Trajan guy should hook up. It's wishful thinking on my part. I was thinking of what you said earlier today. You hate the guy. You think he's a cold-hearted jerk, a complete ass was your word, right? Who am I to say otherwise? I just hate seeing you alone. So sometimes I push when I shouldn't. Forget what I said. I'll talk to you tomorrow, hon."

Trajan was already sitting up, hurt and desire welling up within him, leaving a bad feeling. The two didn't mix well. He didn't know what to say.

Maya tried to think as she sat up, but her body's passion and her mind's shock made it hard. Trajan's expression said everything. She was horrified.

"Tre . . . Tre, I . . ." She reached for her dress on the floor, feeling suddenly ashamed of her nudity. She held it against her chest. "It's not what you . . . It's—"

Trajan stood up, putting his clothes on faster than he ever had. "Stop, Maya. You don't need to go further. As a matter of fact, please don't."

She slipped the dress back on, standing up. "You have to understand. This was all before."

He held up his hand to stop her. He was putting on a good display, but he wasn't sure he could keep it up if she continued.

He just had to get out of there with what little pride he had left.

"Maya." His tone was harsh as he avoided her eyes. "I really don't need . . . want to hear anymore. Before or after, it doesn't matter. It's how you feel."

"Not now." Her stomach hurt, she was so upset over this. "After tonight . . . I didn't know you—"

"Weren't a cold-hearted jerk, a complete ass?" He headed for the door, wanting to be as far away from the same woman only seconds before he couldn't be close enough to.

"I was trying to cover my feelings when she . . ." Maya followed him, her heart on her sleeve. "Don't go. I can explain this."

"Look Maya." Trajan stopped at the door. It was painful, even looking at her. She looked so sexy in a disheveled way. "No matter what, this is for the best. We're business partners in the middle of a major project. This . . . this just isn't professional."

Maya knew he was right. Still, the words cut at her. "I-I know. You're right."

"It's my fault," he said. He was so angry at her, hurt by her words. Despite that, he hated seeing her hurt, and wanted to hold her. What was happening to him? "I shouldn't have brought you to a family event. It was inappropriate."

It stung Maya to hear that, thinking of how right the

whole thing had been for her. "Tre, I understand. You don't have to blame yourself."

"My point is, regardless of blame, we need to maintain professionalism here."

Maya just wanted him to leave now. This rejection was more than she could take.

"Good night, Tre."

He nodded his good night and left.

Trajan sped to the hotel. He tried to block the voice on the answering machine, but he couldn't. He'd known that Maya hadn't thought highly of him, but to think she thought so little was a shot to the heart. He'd been so stupid to let himself start falling for her.

Now it was too late. He'd already developed these feelings for her and gotten slapped in the face the moment he wanted to act on them. Not the exact moment. He'd been wanting to make love to her for a long time. Since the first moment he kissed her, he would have to admit he knew she was different if he was going to be honest with himself. But this . . . this was a surprise. Tonight, he realized he wanted her more than he'd wanted any woman.

A jerk, a cold-hearted ass. Trajan was confused. She thought that at the same time she'd been ready and willing to make love to him.

Still he couldn't curse her and erase her from his mind. No matter what she thought, he couldn't help but wonder if he had a chance. It wasn't for now. There was no way he would merge the personal and professional again. That wasn't his style. In that sense, this could all be a blessing in disguise.

But what about after the IPO came to an end?

No. He shook his head, staring at himself in the bathroom mirror. *One night of passion doesn't mean a thing,*

Tre. She'll wake up the next morning and still be the exact opposite of you. She'd never be satisfied with who you are. Don't set yourself up. Just let it go.

Easier said than done.

Maya refused to cry. She told herself over and over again that this wasn't so unusual. She'd been attracted to men that were no good for her. As attracted as she was to Trajan? She'd been rejected before. Had the rejection stung as much as Trajan's? She got over it all and moved on.

Alissa's message was a blessing, she said to herself, staring in her bathroom mirror. She didn't have the energy to wash her face.

Entering her bedroom, it seemed larger and emptier than usual.

She imagined herself and Trajan on the large bed, making love, tossing the red satin sheets and pillows aside. Maya closed her eyes, imagining how satisfying it would have been. How close they'd come. It had been a long time for her.

How would she face him at work? They had several cities to go with the IPO. Maya tossed and turned all night. She wasn't so stupid she could convince herself that professionalism was what Trajan's rejection was about.

He hated her after hearing Alissa's message. The words were cruel and true. She knew she thought things of Trajan that completely contradicted her behavior tonight.

How would she deal with this? She had to focus her mind on the IPO and her emotions on Elaine. She'd allowed her preoccupation with Trajan to distract her recently, and that was how she'd gotten herself into such trouble.

So, it was decided. Maya knew it wasn't as if she'd had a choice. She just had to accept that whatever this physical magnet was that drew her to Trajan Matthews, it was over. She'd be lucky if he even spoke to her again. And that was for the best.

The next two weeks were hard on Maya and Trajan. Maya sucked up her pride and prepared herself to see Trajan again in Chicago. The luncheon was at the beautiful Four Seasons Hotel, but even a leisurely trip up and down Michigan Avenue didn't calm her.

He was so polite, it irked her to no end.

"Hello, Maya," he'd said. "How are you today?"

As if they'd just met.

She wanted to scream that she was an emotional mess since last week, but the look on his face held her back.

"Fine, thank you," she'd answered.

Maya was certain she was going crazy. She knew she should have been grateful that Trajan was so civil. Instead it made her angrier. It was as if he didn't even remember they'd been naked an inch away from making love only four days ago. Despite it all, she focused on her job. Accompanying Jerome on interviews with the *Chicago Sun-Times* and the *Chicago Tribune,* she was on her game. She was also aware that Jerome's mood was improving, and that pleased her.

"Have I been that obvious?" he asked as the two rode the cab back to O'Hare Airport.

"Gloom and doom," Maya said. "I'm glad you're finally getting out of it."

He squeezed her hand in his and winked at her. "Thanks for worrying about me. It's nice to have someone do it."

"I love you, Jerome." Maya always wondered why he never married. He'd come close a couple of times, but never all the way. No kids either. Sometimes she wondered if he felt he didn't deserve it. He'd always told her that Maya and her mother were his family.

Jerome sighed, glancing out the window. "I'm getting into the swing of it now. It's really a great thing, and it's going better than I thought. It just got off to a bad start."

"Elaine?"

"All of that. Plus the normal jitters."

Maya squeezed back. "I haven't made it easier. I haven't been there for you."

"You're not my mother. You have a job to do and a life of your own. Besides, you've had other things on your personal agenda."

It was Maya's turn to turn away. She shrugged, knowing Jerome understood her body language.

"Tre isn't the one?" he asked.

She shook her head, fighting the sigh.

"I think you both fooled everyone at lunch today."

"What?"

"If I didn't know you so well, I would've been fooled too."

Maya turned back. "I won't embarrass you or this company. I wouldn't do that to Daddy's memory."

"I would never think that," he said. "And I know Tre wouldn't do anything to hurt his reputation."

There was an understanding silence between them.

"When you want to talk about it," he said, "you know where I am."

"Yes," she said, finding relief in the familiarity of his comfort. "Always there for me.

Trajan was doing his best to appear unaffected and keep his distance from Maya without making it obvious. Being near her was hard. He was consumed with ways to prove himself a better person than she'd thought,

but he tried to focus on what he knew best. Especially
in Detroit, where past experiences threatened his calm.

Detroit's LFM, short for Laggerty, Francis and Math-
ers, was the largest securities firm in Michigan, and the
third largest in the Midwest. It was created in the early
1900's by Sean Laggerty, Robert Francis and Alex Math-
ers, three of the richest men in the Midwest. It was a
powerful firm, holding the money of some of the Midwest's wealthiest families, including Bloomfield Hills,
Michigan, one of the wealthiest cities in the United
States. They were also just coming off a racial discrimination case that included some ugly allegations.

Remembering the obstacles he faced, being black
and especially successful in the business of money, Tre
tried hard not to let personal feelings interfere. When
LFM approached him to work closely on a formal rec-
ommendation of Pharaoh, he knew it was a good thing.
Whether they were just trying to look good or were
genuinely out to right some wrongs, it wasn't something
he could pass on. In the end, LFM's much-publicized
interest garnered a front-page article in the *Detroit Free
Press*, and piqued the interest of high-quality analysts
and brokers from the area. Detroit had the highest at-
tendance of the road show so far.

Trajan wasn't only grateful for the success, but getting
caught up in its fervor allowed him to think of something besides Maya for once. Although not for long.

Maya was hit hard in Detroit. She watched as Trajan
wrestled with his feelings about LFM, knowing it
brought up bad memories for him. Every fiber of her
being wanted to reach out to him and comfort him. He
was doing everything he could to maintain his professionalism, and was doing a pretty good job of it. She
was getting to know him well, unable to do anything
but stare at him when she was around him, and she
could see what others weren't seeing. He was still avoid-

ing her, and it tore her apart even though she knew it
was for the best.

Maya was feeling it in Miami. It could have been the
hot, humid summer, but she knew it was more than
that. The luncheon at the Ritz Plaza Hotel went well,
as did the morning interview at the *Miami Herald*. It
was Maya's ability to control her attraction to Trajan
that was failing her.

They spent the afternoon with the head analyst of an
Internet trading giant. As they toured the city at his
escort, Maya found herself focusing on the way Trajan
always touched his left thigh when he sat patiently. How
he gently touched his stomach as he laughed. How he
so smoothly erased any concerns of the analysts regarding the company.

She also noticed the tinge of jealousy she felt when
Trajan and the analyst, a friend of his from his Wall
Street days, discussed an ex-girlfriend of Trajan's.

"I'll admit," Trajan said as they all sat around the
deck of his friend's twenty-four-foot boat. "I was head
over heels in love with her."

"College boy fool in love he was." Johnathan Black
handed Maya a glass of wine before sitting next to Trajan. "He was mad for this girl."

Jerome laughed. "I can't picture Tre acting a fool
over a woman."

Maya could only think what a lucky woman. She
looked at Trajan, hoping to see something in his eyes,
but his eyes were set over the water. He was remembering a love he'd had, and she couldn't help but feel a
need for his attention.

Johnathan slapped him on his arm to get Trajan's
attention back. "What was she, a beauty pageant
queen?"

Trajan felt embarrassed because of Maya, so he

smiled, not looking at her. "She was a Ms. Brooklyn Heights. Let's change the subject."

"She broke your heart?" Maya asked, needing to know.

Their eyes connected with a flash.

"Yes, she did," he answered. "She left me for a football player. He was the star quarterback, and she was looking for a meal ticket when he went pro."

"She sure did," Johnathan said. "Allen Madden. He broke both legs in a car accident his senior year. No one drafted him. Last I heard, he's selling bathroom tile in Jersey. And our boy here is setting the world on fire."

Everyone laughed, and Maya pretended to be amused. She found a few seconds of delight as Trajan's eyes stayed with hers, but only for that moment. It wasn't enough to satisfy her. She wasn't sure how much longer she could pretend.

Trajan pictured a perfect day and night in Miami. He loved the city, having visited several times. He pictured Maya on his arm as they danced at the crazy night clubs, lay out on the beach in the afternoon, and ate the rich Latin food he had come to love so much. They would top the night off by making mind-blowing love with the balcony door open, so the hot breeze could fan their passion. He pictured it, but could only wish for it to happen.

By the time they reached Atlanta, Trajan felt his resolve fading. He was stealing moments, when Maya was preoccupied with someone or something else, to simply stare at her and soak in her beauty. He delighted in watching her do something as simple as eat her lunch at the glorious Ritz Carlton in Buckhead. She separated her food in a compulsive way and always wiped her mouth with a napkin before taking a sip of water. She covered her mouth with a feminine charm whenever she laughed with the reporter from the *Atlanta Journal-Constitution*. Her questions were nonstop and her eyes were wide with pride as they toured Spelman College, a thriving, leading African-American university. He would never get bored with her. She was too full of life.

He found himself dreaming of her at night, alone in the bed of his condo, which seemed so big and lonely now. He found himself feeling an almost boyish excitement when he knew he would see her again. Whenever he was home, his friends would try and set him up with women they knew were perfect for him.

"You'll forget all about Elizabeth."

"She's beautiful. Six feet tall. Used to be a model."

"Runs her own interior design firm. Worked for the best. Self-made wealth."

"Harvard grad, Tre. An Ivy League girl from a prominent family."

He wanted nothing to do with any of them. He wanted Maya, but he couldn't have her. He wasn't sure what to do, and that was an unfamiliar position for Trajan.

Seven

Maya and Jerome were working in her office when Alexandra's voice came over the intercom.

"Maya's there, right?"

"Were in a meeting, Alex." Jerome always spoke louder than necessary into the speaker phone. "Take a message."

"Okay, but it's that cop."

Maya sat up. "George Hobbs?"

"George?" Jerome asked. "What are you, friends with this guy now?"

She waved him silent. "Put him on, Alex. There could be new news about Elaine."

Jerome sat up, pushing the volume button up. "Fine, Alex."

"Hello?" George's deep voice came over. "Maya?"

"Hey George," Maya said. "You're on speaker phone. Jerome is here. How are you?"

"I'm all right, and yourself?"

"Busy." Maya smiled as Jerome rolled his eyes in annoyance.

"I heard you left a couple of messages for me. I'm assuming it's about Mrs. Cramer."

"I was looking for any new leads." she asked. "Jerome and I are very concerned. It's been weeks."

"I wish I could tell you what you want to hear, Maya. Problem is, the case has gone cold. I've been focusing on a new case with some stronger leads today. A wealthy Georgetown banker with a 22-caliber bullet in his head."

"Elaine's case isn't closed, is it?" Maya asked.

"No. It won't be closed until we find the killer."

"But how will you find the killer if you aren't looking?" Jerome asked. "I'm interpreting your words as saying that you aren't looking anymore."

"I wouldn't say that exactly, sir. Listen, Maya."

"Yes, George."

"I have to go, but remember what we talked about. If you ever think of anything—"

"I know," she said. "I'll give you a call."

After they said their good-byes and Jerome clicked off the speaker phone, there was a short silence.

"What if they never find him?" Maya asked, her stomach hurting as she thought of this man or woman walking around free, certain to hurt someone else.

"Someone who would kill so easily," Jerome said, his tone uncertain. "You've got to believe he's a killer for a living. He'll get caught or get his eventually."

Maya nodded. "But I want him to pay for Elaine. She deserves justice."

"Everyone who is murdered deserves justice." Jerome ran a frustrated hand over his hair. "The police have to solve the cases they can. If they occupy all their efforts on cold cases, they won't solve any."

Maya tapped her nails on the table. Thinking, thinking.

"I've lost you, haven't I?" Jerome asked.

"No, no." Maya leaned forward, trying to focus on the work. "I'm here. I'm here."

"Well, I'm not." Jerome sighed, looking away. "I can't wait for this to all be over."

"It'll never really be over, Jerome. After this, we'll be obligated to two publics. Not just our guests, but our shareholders. Their demands are going to conflict sometimes."

Jerome rolled his eyes.

"It's not too late to pull out," Maya said, noticing the look of being overwhelmed on his face. It was rare. He was usually in control. "I'll support you in any decision you make, Jerome."

He smiled as her hand covered his, looking into her eyes. "Sweet Maya. You would, I know. I couldn't pull out. Nick would never have pulled out."

"Daddy would've done what was best for the company. And you know better than anyone what that is."

"I've been so convinced of that for so long. I think it's coming back to haunt me."

"Haunt you?" Maya asked. "I don't understand."

He shrugged. "Neither do I, really. I have no place to complain. It's all going better than I imagined. With you and Tre working hard as oxes."

"I'll always be here, Jerome." She squeezed. "Why don't we take a break and finish this over lunch."

"Georgia Brown's?" He licked his lips. "I could go for some fried catfish."

"So could I. I'll meet you in the lobby in ten minutes."

Maya waited until Jerome had left before logging onto the Internet at her laptop. In an instant, a related thought occurred to her. Georgia Brown's restaurant, soul food, family, friends, nosy neighbors. Marlo Nash. Maya looked her up on an e-switchboard and found her number. She picked up right away.

"I remember you," she answered after a moment's hesitation. "The friend of the family. Coming to tell that no-good his mama passed."

"I was wondering," Maya said. "About the other son, Steven. Do you know anything about him? Have you ever seen him?"

"I can't . . . recall. What kind of information are you looking for?"

"Just where he hangs out. Where he might be found."

Marlo made a thoughtful moaning sound. "He's a transient. I know that."

"Has he ever visited Craig?"

After a short pause. "No, he ain't never come here. But I did hear Craig talking about him to old Bernie Jesley. He's one of them functional alcoholics. He could be full of Crown Royal and talk, walk and drive as quick and straight as a priest. One time—"

"Marlo, what was Craig saying about Steven?"

Another pause, short this time. "They were on the front steps, so I heard it out my window. It caught my attention 'cause Craig don't never talk to nobody, and he was chatting with Bernie like schoolsgirls.

"I figure they were discussing siblings, 'cause Craig went from Linda to Steven. He hated how Steven acted like the world was against him. Like he was a very good man, but the world thinks of him as white trash. So Craig had said something like it wasn't what the world thought of him that was causing him to sleep with another man's woman."

"Who is this woman?" Maya asked, grabbing pen and pencil.

"I remember the name, 'cause it was different. Some girl named Tatiana something or other. She was supposedly a girlfriend of one of Steven's boys he runs with. Had kids with him and everything. I guess that didn't matter to Steven."

"What about a last name?"

"Nuh-uh," Marlo said. "Just Tatiana. She's in the D.C. area. Maybe Steven stays by her now."

"Anything else?" Maya knew she couldn't get anywhere without a last name.

"Not that I can think of. I'll keep my eyes and ears open for you. Sounds important."

"It is, Marlo. Thank you."

Maya gave her phone number to the woman and listened to a few more minutes of mindless gossip before hanging up. She had hoped for more on the basis of luck. She had to figure out what she could do with Tatiana. She was certain Craig wouldn't help her. Besides, she couldn't even call him.

It hadn't passed by Maya either that Jerome's presence was the only thing that kept her from asking about Trajan while on the phone with George. She'd thought of him constantly since seeing him last in Miami. She wanted him with a desire that frightened her because it was so clear. She'd always been one that needed a strong emotional attachment to any man before becoming intimate. With Trajan, who she barely knew, she could see herself tossing that aside for a night with him. That scared her to death.

She anticipated seeing him again at the Los Angeles luncheon tomorrow. Although his utmost civility threatened to drive her crazy, Maya knew it was better than nothing.

She tediously tidied up her desk, not allowing herself to see beyond her current attraction. She wasn't at all prepared to deal with the outcome of this, whatever it was. Maybe some fried catfish would clear her mind.

Maya was just in time for the Los Angeles luncheon, her flight running late. She expected an ugly look from Trajan, but got none. Again the civility, she thought, unable to believe she actually yearned for his obstinance and impossibility.

The luncheon went smoothly, by all standards. The Los Angeles group was more focused on expansions and acquisitions than financials. Trajan wanted to tell all, whereas Jerome and Maya wished to keep the details out. They handled it well, but the disagreement was a cause for conversation after the luncheon attendees were gone.

"Most of those deals aren't more than verbal agreements yet, Tre." Jerome spoke with a calm tone, although irritation slipped out occasionally.

Trajan pretended to focus on his appointment book as Maya approached. As good as she was at this, he didn't want her here anymore. She was too much of a distraction for him. It was bad enough he was thinking of her every second of every day. She seemed more beautiful, more perfect, each time he saw her.

"I only referred to them as agreements," Trajan answered. "Not which kind. These guys are in Los Angeles. They're used to verbal agreements. It's that type of city."

"Can we agree on something?" Maya asked. "From this moment on, we only discuss the deals we have on paper."

"This is an IPO, Maya," Trajan said. "They're expecting us to impress them. We need to talk in risks. We can't compete with those high-tech startups in Silicon Valley who have IPOs every day by playing it safe."

"Maya is right," Jerome said. "If we say an acquisition is a go and it falls through, it will slap us in the face, and we'll get our butts kicked. Stick with what's on paper. Try to stretch the truth somewhere else."

Trajan sighed with a nod as Jerome turned and headed for the phone, touching his beeper.

"Jerome was supposed to be the risk taker," Trajan said.

Maya clung to her organizer pushed tightly against her stomach. "He was. Daddy was the conservative one.

I guess he's changing. There's nothing wrong with that, Tre."

Trajan didn't want to argue with her. There was a strong part of him now that never wanted to argue with Maya, only wanted to say yes to her. Make her happy. He didn't know what to do about that part.

"What's important," he said, "is that we impressed a bunch of guys in a city where they have a thirty-second attention span."

There was a silence as they both smiled cordially at each other, each preferring a kiss. Maya felt tortured with kindness. She envisioned him taking her in his arms, and she wouldn't fight him. She wouldn't fight him at all. Trajan felt like he deserved an award for self-control. He wanted to grab her, kiss her, force her to take back any opinion she'd had of him in the past and say that she loved him. He was losing his mind.

"I'm sorry I was late, Tre." Maya needed the conversation. The silence was too much. It made her mind wander to unacceptable thoughts. "My plane got in only minutes ago. I came right over."

"That's fine. So did I. I haven't even checked in yet."

Maya found herself insane for being disappointed. She'd wanted him to be angry. Did she actually like the old Trajan? She couldn't possibly.

Trajan was pleased when Jerome returned. He had to concentrate on work, what he did best. He could control this.

Jerome relieved his hand firmly on Maya's shoulder. "Your day full?"

"I have a million calls to make," Maya said. "Are we still having dinner?"

"Sorry, kid. I forgot to tell you. I'm staying in Anaheim tonight. An old friend from Howard has a little setup."

"That's fine." Maya couldn't hide her disappointment. "I'll order room service."

"No way." Jerome reached his other hand out to Trajan's shoulder, connecting the three of them. "Tre knows the city. He'll take you out."

Trajan's stomach tightened. Maya's entire body tensed.

"We need to get going, Jerome." Trajan stepped away, nodding toward the door.

"Don't you need to check in?" Jerome asked.

"No time." Trajan was already headed for the door. "I'll leave my bags downstairs and check in later."

Jerome nodded with a quick step. "Look, Maya. We have a business meeting, an interview with the *Los Angeles Times,* then another meeting. I'm off to Anaheim, so Tre should be checking in around six or so. You two work it out then."

"Jerome, I don't think—"

"Maya." He leaned in, an eyebrow raised. "You need to work it out then, if you know what I mean. This tension is like molasses. There's no way these luncheon guys didn't sense it."

Maya nodded, even though they were both gone. She remembered the last time she and Trajan were alone. There was no way she was having dinner with him. She didn't trust herself.

When Maya checked into the Los Angeles Hilton where the luncheon had been held, she was stressed out. Aside from contemplating how she could avoid an evening with Trajan, there was at least one convention going on, and the wait to check was painfully long. When she finally reached the desk, there were no reservations in her name, and no extra rooms available.

With considerable complaining, the clerk finally found her room. Not under her name, as it had been at the other hotels, but under TM Investor Relations.

She knew leaving reservations in Trajan's secretary's hands would eventually lead to a problem.

After tossing her bags on the bed and washing her face, Maya went to work. Her first call was to George Hobbs for an update on the investigation.

"I don't have any news for you, Maya," he said. "I wish I did. It ain't right that anyone gets away with anything, but especially killing an old woman."

"I hear you," Maya said. "It's so frustrating. It's as if she was just wiped away, and everything goes on as usual. No more clues about Linda's supposedly missing the will she stole? I still think there's something there."

"We don't have cause for a search warrant. Her garage ticket time and her alibi says she's not a suspect."

"Is her alibi reliable? Her friends might be pretty shady. She sure is."

"The woman isn't a pillar of society," George answered, shifting papers heard in the background. "Titi . . . that's her name. Titi's got no record at all. Thirty-two, a clerk at a grocery store."

Maya got the connection immediately. "What is Titi short for?"

There was a short silence, with only ruffling papers being heard. "Tatiana Morris. Why? She sound familiar?"

Maya thought a second. Her first thought was to tell all, but a sudden burst of self-determination against her better judgment hit her.

"I think so, George," was all she said. "Let me check something out."

"I'm getting this idea you're playing detective here, Maya. You shouldn't be. Tell me what you know."

"I don't really know anything yet, George. I need to check on one thing. I promise I won't do anything stupid."

"Why don't I believe that?"

"You've been a cop too long," she answered. "I'll call you later today, tomorrow at the latest."

When she hung up, Maya went straight to her laptop. After the plug-in and log-on, she found only one Tatiana Morris in northern Virginia. Baileys Crossroads.

What to do? Maya asked herself, pacing the room. She knew she should call George, but she couldn't fight the urge to visit Tatiana herself. Maybe she could get some answers on Steven. Or maybe she could break the phony alibi Tatiana had concocted for Linda. Were Linda and Steven in on this together? That made sense.

She had no right to keep this to herself. She knew that much. She also knew she would be in San Francisco, Denver and Dallas before getting home. Clues could be lost between now and then. So she called a skeptical George Hobbs and told him all she knew. She felt better after forcing him to promise to check it out right away. After finishing some other work, Maya decided to head out. If she could genuinely be gone, then there would be no obligation to an evening with Trajan Matthews.

She enjoyed a soul food dinner at Roscoe's Chicken and Waffles, and went shopping on Rodeo Drive. She couldn't eat enough or buy enough to make her think of anything but Trajan.

It was after nine when Maya returned to her room. She was exhausted. Throwing her bags to the floor, she kicked off her shoes, noticing she'd left the television on.

No. She became suddenly alert. She'd never even turned the television on.

Seeing Trajan laid out, shirt half open, pillows behind his head, on the king-sized bed floored Maya. She froze in place as he turned to her with a look so casual, as if he'd been expecting her all along.

"What are you doing here?" She stood in front of

the television, since it seemed to be what was holding his interest. "This is my room."

He sat up with a smile. "Correction, Maya. This is my room. Let me—"

"This room was checked out to me." Maya hated how calm he appeared.

Her bud nose squeezed when she was angry, making him want to smile. "Calm down, Maya. I'll explain. I'll take complete responsibility. Nadine was supposed to make hotel arrangements for all of us, as she has at every hotel. She sent the hotel a list of our names with three rooms attached. Whoever came first, second or third would get the rooms in that order. When I told her to cancel Jerome's arrangements because he'd be in Anaheim, she accidentally thought it meant both of you. Therefore there was only one room attached to all of our names."

Maya's hands were on her hips. She saw his bags near the bed, clothes hanging out. "All I want to know is when you're going to your room."

"This is my room," Trajan said. "It was listed for me. The front desk gave it to you by accident. She searched back to deleted files and found your name."

"You're saying I'm on the street?" Maya felt her temper heading up. "Why couldn't you just get another room?"

"I tried." He noticed the skepticism on her face. "I did, Maya. There aren't any rooms anywhere. Not here or for miles. There are two major conventions right in the heart of the city. It was impossible."

Maya's hands remained on her hips. "How many did you try? There had to be a room somewhere."

"We tried twelve hotels. Nothing. The closest was an Accent Inn. Shady chain at best, and it was over an hour's drive away."

Maya's brow raised. "Well?"

He looked at her, incredulous. "Maya, this is my room."

"A room we're paying for as the client. So technically it is my room."

"No chance, babe. You haven't paid for it yet. This comes out of my pocket and I bill you."

"After a significant markup."

He winked. "Capitalism is a beauty, isn't she?"

"I am not, I repeat, not leaving this room," Maya said. "And you are not staying here."

Trajan said nothing, leaning back again.

"Tre!" Maya felt her hands form in fists. "I'm tired. I'm living on Eastern Time. It's midnight for me."

"Where do you think I'm from? Hawaii? Besides, we both have to be in San Francisco for lunch tomorrow. Thinking back, maybe it would be better to book a hotel in San Fran, but we had expected a dinner meeting that fell through. Either way, neither of us has the time to shop around for another hotel. We'll have to deal with it."

Maya knew what he was suggesting. She felt her stomach tense. He had already turned his attention back to the television, tilting his head to the side. Maya paced the room. She was the client! She was his boss!

She hated him. She couldn't possibly stay in the same room with him. If this ever got to anyone, the rumors wouldn't end. Forget the rumors. She couldn't handle the thought of a night in the same room with him after what had happened between them at her apartment.

Trajan laughed at the commercial with a dog tossing a frisbee, his master running to get it. Maya's eyes bulged. It took everything in her not to curse him out loud. No, he wasn't going to do that to her. If he could play aloof and careless, so could she.

Maya blocked his field of vision again, caught his eyes and said, "You're on the sofa, so get up."

Trajan blinked before accepting the victory and moving to the sofa.

Maya took her entire suitcase into the bathroom. She couldn't chance forgetting anything and needing to step outside again. She locked the door loudly. She had no reason to suspect he would try to enter. Despite that, as she showered, Maya felt her stomach tense with an exciting fear. She tried humming songs to herself for diversion, but there was nothing to it. She was naked, and he was just outside her room. No song could cover that up.

Trajan took the opportunity to undress and get into bed. He only had trunks, which he put on before taking one of the bed pillows and grabbing the extra linen out of the closet. He felt his anticipation grow despite the resolve he had come to as soon as he realized they would most likely end up in a room together.

Initially he'd been hit with all sorts of reasons why he'd rather sleep in the car. Temptation was what it came down to. The more time he'd spent around Maya, the more he cared for her. The more he wanted her. The thought of spending a night . . .

No, he knew that was an impossibility. He didn't doubt he could handle it. He was Trajan Matthews. A stubborn little woman wouldn't destroy his resolve. Couldn't possibly.

Keep it light, he told himself, anticipating her return from the bathroom. Don't even entertain such thoughts. No matter what you think you feel, she's a client tonight. Nothing more. It would be the same as if Jerome was here.

Such hard-fought resolve was shot out of the cannon as soon as Trajan heard the shower running. Images began floating in his mind, twinkling desire running through him. Thoughts of the last time he'd touched her, so certain they would make love, flooded his mind.

Maya was grateful she had packed her big cotton bathrobe instead of the short satin one she usually wore at home. She was able to completely cover the one-piece, spaghetti-strapped, gray cotton nightie that went mid-hip. It seemed so harmless night after night alone. Suddenly, she noticed it slid around her curves suggestively. However, it was all she had packed that wasn't for work.

She decided she'd sleep with the robe on.

Maya played off the anxiety she felt after returning to the room. Seeing Trajan on the sofa, which faced her bed, without a shirt on threw her.

"Where are your clothes?" she asked.

Trajan smiled. He was good at presenting an exterior that didn't remotely resemble his interior. Right now, all he wanted to do was touch her skin. She was glowing, runaway strands of wet hair in various spots against her face.

"I hadn't planned on a fashion show," he answered. "My only tops are dress shirts."

Maya pursed her lips together and raced for the bed. She pulled the covers up to her neck. "There's a bathrobe in the closet."

He pretended to ignore her, flipping the channels. He had to put forth a strong effort to concentrate on the television. Maya reached to turn off the light next to her, the only light in the room besides the television. The darker the better, she thought.

Trajan found a news channel.

"Sex in the workplace," the anchorwoman said. "It's becoming more commonplace as people revolve their lives around their jobs."

Trajan swallowed and clicked the remote.

A nighttime soap opera came on, with a dangerously tan couple rolling around on a kitchen floor. They were practically naked, making X-rated sounds.

Maya tightened her grip on the covers as Trajan clicked.

"Are you lonely?" The voluptuous woman, clad in a revealing nightie, asked with pouting red lips. "Call me. I'm waiting for—"

Click.

The familiar talk show host faced the camera as the words "RECORDED EARLIER TODAY" flashed along the bottom of the screen. "On today's show, people who are having sexual relationships with someone they find morally repulsive. Why can't they stay away from them? What's the pull that—"

Click.

"Nothing is more romantic than a weekend getaway." A tall, beautiful woman walked with confidence through a hotel lobby. "You and the one you love in a romantic, luxury hotel suite together. The possibilities are endless. Call for our weekend packages and—"

Click.

"Why don't you give me the remote," Maya said, unable to take it anymore.

"You think you could find better channels?" he asked, feeling the heat of embarrassment.

"Better than you."

Trajan's eyes narrowed. "You think I'm doing this on purpose?"

Maya didn't answer.

"In some kind of master plan to seduce you, huh?" He stood up, walking to her. He dropped the remote on the bed. "Don't flatter yourself."

Maya's mouth flew open. "How dare you? I never suggested anything."

"You'd better not," he said. "I'd have to throw it right back in your face."

Maya sat up, the covers falling. She was too angry to

notice her robe had come loose, exposing her thin nightie.

"What could you possibly throw back at me? That I had something to do with us being stuck together?"

"No," he answered, distracted by the skin revealed on her chest. It was glowing in the light of the television. So soft and tempting. "But if we're making wild accusations, it's more likely it would be you."

Maya's eyes widened. "What delusions would bring you to that?"

"If I recall right, it was I who ended our last . . . encounter."

Maya kicked the rest of her sheets off in a rage and stood up on her knees. He towered over her still, but she didn't care. "You make it seem like I was trying to seduce you. I recall us both stopping at the same time."

"Thanks to your friend's lovely voice mail." Trajan hated that those words still affected him, but they did. "Despite your cold words, you expected me to—"

"I didn't expect you to do anything. I was just trying to explain that message."

"Give it up, Maya. There's no explaining that. It spoke for itself."

Maya let out an aggravated groan. "It doesn't matter. None of it matters. You can stay here with your shirt off and watch your X-rated television. Hell, sleep in this bed. It won't have any effect on me."

Her words hit Trajan hard. "So now you're saying what happened between us in your apartment meant nothing?"

Maya held her chin up. She was lying through her teeth. "Not then, not now."

"How about the elevator?" Trajan wasn't going for it. He knew how their encounters had made him feel. She had to have felt something.

"Hardly remember it."

"And outside your hotel elevators in New York?"

"Must've been someone else," she said. "I don't re-call that encounter at all."

"So." He stepped to the very end of the bed, closer to her, looking into her eyes. "My kisses have never had any effect on you?"

As his eyes seemed to bore into her, Maya suddenly realized her robe was on the bed. It had fallen off her in the process of her kicking the covers around and standing up sharply. With the light from the television, the shine on his chest, his arms glistened. His muscles were tight. She could smell his seductive cologne.

"I asked you a question, Maya. Speechless isn't your style."

Her pride found a voice even though her body was melting. "No. Neither you nor your kisses mean any-thing to me, Tre. And I would appreciate you not sug-gesting—"

When he grabbed her arms, Maya knew what was coming. Deep inside, she had to understand that she wanted it. And the moment his lips touched hers and her body ignited in flames, she knew that she did. She'd wanted this all along.

Trajan couldn't help himself. The passion he'd felt since meeting her, the desire that had developed since first kissing her, and especially the tension that had grown between them over the past weeks spurred him on.

He pulled her to him, trying his best to be gentle with her soft skin. His lips pressed into hers, firing him up. His intention had been to prove her wrong, embar-rass her into admitting she'd felt something. But that was all wiped away as the sweet softness of her full lips touched his. He only wanted to love her, to make love to her.

Maya's body melted into his. She knew in a second

the evolution of this event was coming, and she completely opened herself up to it. Her arms wrapped around his neck, her lips opening wide for him.

Her emotions whirled and skidded all over the place, but Maya was crystal clear. As his tongue explored her mouth, she returned with her own. As his hands caressed her hips, her body swayed to music only they could hear.

As she moved in his hands, Trajan felt himself lose control. As his manhood hardened, he tried to tell himself to be patient, but it was hard. Her tongue teased his mouth, those lips swaying back and forth.

Passion pounded her veins as his hands squeezed her. His lips devoured her from within as she felt his hard thighs rub against hers.

She was taken over by desire as he stepped away. Trajan's eyes were possessive as he slowly lifted a hand to her left shoulder, and wrapped her strap around it. He did the same with the other hand and at the same time slid the nightgown down her body.

Trajan joined her on the bed, watching with a greedy desire as she lay back.

"You're the most beautiful woman I've ever seen," he said, his voice husky with desire. "Ever."

Maya's eyes closed as his hands slowly pulled her panties off. There would be no interruptions now.

As she felt his mouth caress the inside of her thigh, Maya's back arched. Her head went back. It was such sweet torture.

"Trajan," she moaned, relishing in the seduction.

"Please wait, baby." His words came as a whisper, as with all the strength he had, he separated himself from her. "One last thing."

The few seconds he took to gather protection from his suitcase and return to her seemed an eternity to Maya. But all the agony of waiting was erased as he placed the package on the nightstand and returned his attention to her.

She would be ready soon, he thought. He wouldn't have to wait long. Now, his need was at full force as he enjoyed delighting her, teasing her. His eyes never left hers as he sat up and removed his thin cotton night pants.

The sight of his arousal sent a shiver through Maya. She ached for him more every second. Her hands pulled at him desperately as his mouth, his tongue, his teeth played with her breast and her now hardened nipples. She was swallowed by the tantalizing, sensuous mastery he held over her.

Trajan felt a certain wicked sensation as he applied the protection. He enjoyed teasing her as slowly, slowly they approached their final destination.

Maya's body wriggled underneath his as he positioned himself on top of her. She loved his weight on her, felt fiery sensations as his hardness brushed against her thighs.

Their eyes connected as he entered her. Slowly. Maya let out a moan. Trajan followed with one of his own as their connection liberated them from this world. As he moved, she moved with him. Their bodies were white-hot, dancing, building.

Trajan's lips claimed hers when he wasn't speaking words of passion. Maya called out his name as his thrusts came faster, harder. Sweet agony and hysteria consumed her.

Maya's body arched, her nails dug into his back as a crescendo of fire and magic spread through her. She let out a scream as Trajan buried his face in her neck and let out a shuddering groan.

He laid his sweating body next to hers, covering her left thigh with his own. Exhausted, Maya turned her head to him. Their eyes met, and they both smiled.

Trajan leaned over and kissed her passionately. He wrapped his arm around her, and they were both asleep in minutes.

Maya let the hot water of the shower stream down on her. The smile on her face told everything. Her entire body was smiling.

After last night, the most intense lovemaking Maya had ever experienced was repeated as she and Trajan awoke the next morning. They barely spoke, as if their bodies had done all the talking necessary. Maya languished in the bed as Trajan quickly showered, needing to be in San Francisco earlier than she. She listened to him shower, filled with sweet excitement.

Maya wanted to shower alone, to reflect on how in the world she got to such a wonderfully confused state. Her only intention had been to focus on the public offering. Then came Trajan, and despite all that had happened since, he'd taken her life in a new direction.

She wanted to focus on the good. If she wasn't already in love with Trajan, she was certainly close to it. The public offering seemed to be going well, although it was far from over, and Jerome seemed to be more positive. Still, Maya wondered if she was in over her head, stretching herself too thin over all that was going on.

In the end, there was still no conclusion to Elaine's murder, and Maya knew she couldn't be completely happy with everything else until that was resolved. Until then, it would be a thorn in her side, as well as Trajan's, which she soon realized as she stepped out of the bathroom.

"What is this?" Trajan held up the pad she had placed on the table yesterday.

Maya was surprised. "That's . . . hey, why are you reading my . . ."

"These are notes," he said, trying to control his temper. He loved this woman, but his patience was wearing thin. "Notes on this woman's murder."

"Elaine Cramer," Maya said, snatching the pad from him. "She has a name, and these notes weren't meant for public consumption."

"You're still investigating on your own, aren't you?" He followed her to the bed, where her clothes had been laid out.

Maya tipped her head back. "I'm just helping. Someone has to. The police department has practically given up."

"They're doing what they can, Maya. Leave it alone."

"I can't, Tre." Maya sat on the bed, looking up at him apologetically. "I feel like I have to do this."

"Well stop feeling that way. Do whatever you have to to get rid of this feeling. Stay out of this."

Maya couldn't fight the protective anger that rose within her. "Are you trying to give me an order?"

"Take it however you want it," he said. "Whatever will make you listen to me."

"Ordering will not." Maya sighed. "I hope you don't think that because we've slept together you have some type of ownership over me now."

"Don't be ridiculous." Trajan tried to explore his own feelings, to make sure she wasn't right. "However, I do feel it gives me a say in your well-being. I saw what you wrote. You plan on visiting that . . . who was it? Steven? His girlfriend, Linda's alibi. How do you know so many names?"

"I was very close to Elaine, remember?"

"It doesn't matter," he said. "You're not doing this."

"I am doing this, Tre. And it does matter. That's why I'm doing it."

She shot up from the bed and began getting dressed.

Trajan didn't move. He wasn't giving up, and that was a big problem for her.

"It's dangerous, Maya!" He refused to give up. There was too much to deal with now. He couldn't be worried about her safety. "Jerome was supposed to talk to you about this. We discussed this."

She swung around, facing him. "You and Jerome discussed this? It's so like men. To decide on your own what's best for the little woman without even consulting her first."

"That's not what this was about."

"Yes it was. You wouldn't be this concerned if I were a man."

"If you were a man, you wouldn't let your personal feelings interfere with your job." Trajan regretted the words as soon as he said them. "That's not what I meant. I—"

"That is what you meant." Maya felt the pain of his words mix with her anger. "I really expected something different after last night, but I should've known better. My safety isn't a concern at all. You're talking about the public offering again. We're back to that being number one. Before us, before justice for Elaine."

Trajan slammed his fist on the end table. "Listen to me. I'm concerned about your safety. I'm also concerned about this public offering. That's my job!"

"But you're not concerned about an innocent woman, brutally murdered?"

"That's what the police are for!"

"They aren't doing anything!" Maya's stomach hurt, she was so angry. "I know what you care about, Tre. The bottom line and appearances. Don't worry, I won't let it get out or leak to the press. And I'm doing my job."

Trajan realized how the change had only been in his

mind. All that mattered was Maya's opinion of him, and it was exactly the same as before.

"Fine, Maya." He tightened his tie, glancing at his watch. "You want me to be the bad guy, even after last night."

Maya sighed. She could see she hurt him. "Tre, I don't . . . I mean . . . I can't let this go."

"What does that have to do with how you feel about me? Yes, I'm concerned about the publicity and I'm concerned about you taking time away from work. But you interpreted that to say I was no different than what you thought about me before. What stopped us from making love the first time."

Maya felt like she could cry at any minute. "How are you different? Tell me. I want to believe. Because if you were different, you would understand why I have to do this."

"Why did you make love to me, if you thought I was the same man?" Trajan felt his throat dry up. He was angry and hurt.

"I . . . I . . ." Maya wanted to tell him she was falling in love with him, but the look on his face stopped her. "I don't know. I know I wanted you. I don't understand most of this."

"Neither do I, Maya. But I haven't used that confusion against you. I was genuinely concerned about your safety. You just don't want to believe that."

Maya shook her head, running her hands through her hair. It was up to her to say something, but she had nothing to say. She was ashamed to admit to herself she was giving up.

Trajan grabbed his overnight bag. "Thanks for last night, Maya. If you want to continue it like I do, you let me know. Right now, I've got to get to work."

Maya winced when the door slammed. She refused to cry, feeling no right to such tears.

What is wrong with you? she asked herself. *Are you into self-sabotage?*

She wasn't sure how or if Trajan had changed. She was just sure she was falling for him either way. Only that wouldn't satisfy Trajan. He had too much respect for himself to put up with her indecision and mixed messages.

Was it her? She wondered, was it all her? Alissa would have a field day with this situation. Maya wasn't one to psychoanalyze too much. When it came down to it, Elaine's murder was standing between them. It tainted her mind and her heart to a point where not even the good that occupied the same space could be enjoyed. She had to get it out of the way before she could fix things with Trajan.

She only hoped it wouldn't be too late.

Eight

Jerome pulled Maya aside as the San Francisco luncheon came to an end.

"What is wrong with you?" he asked, his tone borderline harsh. "You look miserable."

"I'm sorry, Jerome." Maya had hoped to disguise her feelings, push them down, but the second she'd walked into the luncheon room of the Hyatt and saw Trajan, they came full force to the top. She wasn't herself, and it was visible.

"I know this is about Tre," Jerome whispered. "He looks worse than you. You barely spoke to each other. The only times he looked at you, he had this expression on his face like someone had knocked him in the gut. I'm very disappointed."

"I can't even begin to explain." Maya had noticed Trajan's reaction. She'd hurt him terribly and she felt miserable for it. "I tried to hide it. I think the luncheon went well despite it, don't you?"

"Thanks to Tre warming them up last week. I think they were so excited to hear about us, they let it pass. I hope at least."

"I hope so too." Maya could see Jerome's point. She was losing control. She was allowing her personal feelings about Trajan and Elaine interfere with her work.

"I think you need a break," Jerome said.

Maya's eyes widened in surprise. He was very angry

with her, and she wasn't used to that. "What do you mean?"

"You need to skip Dallas, Denver and Seattle. Go back home, Maya."

"Jerome, those are the rest of our cities. What about my interviews with the *Dallas Morning News, Seattle Times* and *Denver Post*?"

"If you can't do them via phone," he answered sharply, "then I'll do them for you. I know you don't like this, Maya, but I think you know it's best. If we don't appear to be a united front, nothing we say, no matter how good, is going to get through."

She nodded in agreement. She hated it, but it was true. "I'm letting you down. I'm letting Daddy down."

"Don't you even think that. You just need some time off. Not just for you. I love you too much to ignore your pain. I won't be able to do my job being worried about you like this. And the last thing we need is three people who can't function."

Maya loved him for never forgetting to remind her that she mattered, no matter under what circumstances.

Jerome squeezed her shoulder. "Now, I've got to mingle with these guys. You go get your head straight and your business in order. We'll reconnect when I get back."

Trajan watched as Jerome squeezed Maya's shoulder. He was a source of comfort to her because she loved and respected him. He ached for that from Maya. He'd have to have it in order to be with her. He couldn't live with her knowing she wanted him, but having no respect for what he did or who he was. He realized unfortunately, that the two were one and the same. And that was his own problem.

Their eyes met and he was stricken with compassion for her. She had so much going on and she felt so deeply. The look on her face before she turned and walked out spoke to him so clearly. She was leaving. He wouldn't see her for a while and it tore at him. He didn't think once about how it would affect the public offering. Only how it affected his heart. And it was wrenching.

Maya had thought of nothing but Trajan over the past week. Since returning to D.C., she'd wanted to throw herself into work, but he remained number one on her mind. Everything was suffering. Her work, her appearance, her patience. She knew she had to focus on solving Elaine's murder so she could move on. Now, as she stood outside the door to Tatiana Morris's apartment in Baileys Crossroads, she thought of Trajan's words against her pursuing this.

She'd wanted to stay away, but couldn't. Not after she'd spoken with George Hobbs. He'd intended to pay "Titi" a visit, but before he could, a couple of gang murders and an accountant's wife found dead in her car dressed like a clown had kept him occupied. He'd swung by the apartment twice, but no one was home. Tatiana had quit her job a week ago, so he was unable to find her there either. He'd pushed it off after that. He was in between partners at the time, so it was all on him.

Maya understood the pressures D.C. detectives were under. Still, she couldn't help but be disappointed in him. And she couldn't help but pay Tatiana a visit herself. She never considered the fact that she wouldn't be there, or that she would refuse to talk to her if she was there, or that she would lie and deny everything. Her extreme confidence served her well since Tatiana was home, and although she wouldn't let Maya in, she agreed to talk to her.

"How do I know you aren't a cop?" she asked. She

was a pretty, warm, peach-colored girl, with large eyes and very large breasts. She dressed provocatively. She was still young, but her skin said she was on the way to the kind of life that would soon make her look older than she was.

"If I was a cop," Maya answered, "I'd have to show you my badge if you asked. Otherwise, I couldn't use anything you say for anything. Not for bringing you in for questioning, a warrant or an arrest."

"Arrest?" She looked alarmed. "I haven't done anything."

"You haven't?" Maya's brows raised, but she kept the tone compassionate. "You, Linda, Steven. It's pretty unusual that you would be her alibi, although both of you would forget to mention to the cops that you and Steven were lovers."

Tatiana rolled her eyes. "Linda didn't tell because she doesn't know. I didn't tell because I didn't want her to know. Now, I don't care. When I agreed to do this, murder wasn't part of the—"

"Shut up, Titi."

Maya jumped back as a tall man with sandy blond hair in a ponytail, a mustache and beard came forward and pushed Tatiana out of his way, opening the door wide. Her adrenaline started rushing. She quickly looked around. There was no one. It was the middle of the workday.

"Who in the hell are you?" he asked.

"Steven," she said, assuming. "My name is Maya. I was a friend of your mother's."

"I heard about you." He nodded to himself more than anyone. "What do you want? I don't have to answer anything."

"I know, Steven." Maya swallowed. "But Tatiana just opened the bag. Why—"

"Neither of us killed anyone," he said angrily. "There

was no love lost between me and my mother, but I'm not a murderer. I know the cops been looking for me."

"I know the head detective on this case, Steven. Tell me your story and I can act as a liaison for you. A go-between. There was love lost between me and your mother, so I need to find out who did this."

"Gotta be my sister, Linda. She stole the will."

"She claims it's missing." Maya rolled her eyes, appearing cynical to get in his good graces.

"Show her, Steven." Tatiana's voice came from behind.

He closed the door halfway. Maya could hear them arguing in whispers. Finally, Steven opened the door all the way and nodded for Maya to come in. She hesitated out of lingering fear, but for only a moment.

The house was made up of nothing that matched or originally came with anything else, but was neat and somewhat cozy.

Tatiana returned to the room with some papers in her hand. She hesitated, looking at Steven, who leaned against the chair across from the sofa.

"Titi made friends with Linda at my request," he said. "I didn't want her to know. I had heard through the grapevine that Linda was planning on getting Mama's will to take a look at it. See if she could get it altered. I wanted to get my hands on it. I knew Linda wouldn't think about me. So I was going to see about altering it myself."

"How would you do that?" Maya asked.

"Easy. Forgery. A little of this or that. I can't get in trouble for it 'cause I ain't done nothing yet."

"But you did get your hands on the will." She nodded toward Tatiana.

"We got lucky," she said. "I was just over to drop off some CDs Linda let me dub. As I always did, the second Linda went to the bathroom, I searched the house. It was on her bed. I grabbed it, hid it, and left as soon as I could."

"Didn't she suspect you?"

"Linda's always misplacing stuff, so I'm figuring she thought she'd misplaced it for a while. After that, she called me a couple of times asking me weird questions. Never hitting it on the head, but just like, 'Did I leave something over there? Did she give me something last time I was over.' After the cops started bugging her, she hasn't peeped."

"Give it to her, Titi," Steven said.

Tatiana handed her the papers. "Give those to the cops. We don't care about the will or the money anymore. We had no idea Linda was gonna murder her for it. Tell the cops that."

Maya glanced at the will. As she opened it up, a letter on canary-colored stationery fell onto her lap.

"What's this?"

"That was attached to it," Tatiana said. "It's about murder. I think Linda was really up to something. It's definitely not Steven's mom's murder. I think she's killed before."

Maya felt a shiver run down her spine. What had she uncovered? She put the papers into her bag. "Why didn't you take these to the cops?"

Steven shook his head vigorously. "Don't want nothing to do with the cops. I'm white trash to them. I don't stand a chance whether I'm talking the truth or not."

"The cops are still going to want to talk to you," Maya said, standing up. "I can't stop that."

"But you said you'd do what you can, right?" Tatiana's hands were wringing tight.

"I will. I promise."

Maya was unfolding the letter before she got down the front steps. Her eyes raced over it. She looked at the stationery. G. Stevenson, MD, 255 Lance Lane,

Reston, VA. She'd never heard Elaine mention that name. She read on, taking in groups of words, too impatient to read the whole letter yet.

Addressed to "LIAR"
. . . we made a deal . . .
. . . blackmail is a dirty word . . .
. . . faking a drunk driving accident . . .
. . . clever payoff, but loose ends . . .
. . . you're still a murderer . . .
. . . want my money or . . .
. . . Woodson . . .

Maya's chest caved in. She felt herself begin to hyperventilate. Just then the letter was ripped from her hands.

"What do you think you're doing?" George Hobbs's usual smile was nowhere to be found.

"Give me that!" Maya reached for the letter, but George held it up. There was no way she could reach it. "George, you have to let me read it. My name—"

"Tre told me you were going to try this."

"Tre?" Maya felt a tug at her heart at the mention of his name.

She loved him. She was struck with a blow of realization. Now, at the worst of times to awaken to this, she knew beyond a doubt she was in love with Trajan Matthews.

"What did he say?" she asked, still trying to reach the letter.

"He's worried about you. He said you'd keep trying to investigate this murder yourself even though you told Jerome you wouldn't. You know I can't let you do that."

Maya tossed any sense of joy at Trajan's concern from her mind. That simply didn't matter right now. "Look,

George. I know what you think, but you have to let me read that letter."

"This," he said, folding the letter and putting it in his pocket, "is evidence. And so is this, I assume."

He snatched the will, which was sticking out of Maya's purse.

"Take the will," Maya said, "but just let me read the letter real quick. It has my name on it. I think it might be—"

"What? Your name?"

Maya was feeling overwhelmed by the thought. "It makes no sense, but I think that letter is about my father's death."

George's brows narrowed. "Tre said your father died in a car accident over a decade ago."

"He did." Maya wondered exactly how much Trajan spoke about her. "I can't explain it but I . . . just let me—"

"No, Maya." He held a hand up to stop her. "This is a serious investigation. You might not think I take it seriously, but I stopped by here to follow up on your lead for the third time this week because I want to solve this. Good thing I did. You would've taken this evidence and ruined—"

"I was going to give it to you," Maya said. "I promised them—"

"Who are you to make promises?" George's anger was growing. "You're not a cop."

"They know that." Maya followed him as he started toward the house. "They didn't do anything. They explained it all to me."

"Fine." He stopped her. "We'll call you to testify in court if we need you. For now, you stay out of it. Go home, go to work. Give Tre a call. He'd like to hear from you. Just stay out of this investigation."

"George!" Maya saw the surprise on his face at the

desperate tone of her voice. "I only read bits of that letter, but what I did read makes me think Elaine had a letter blackmailing someone about my father's death."

"Which was an accident?" he asked with disbelief.

"So I thought." Maya's mind was racing, her stomach turning. "So everyone thought. I distinctly read 'faking a drunk driving accident.' "

"So Elaine knew something about your father's murder? Don't tell me. You think one of her kids is involved."

"I don't know, but the letter was with the will that Tatiana stole from Linda's house and it has my name on it. It says Woodson. I read it clearly."

"Tatiana told you she stole this stuff?" George bit his lip in frustration. "Look, Maya. I'm not asking you. I'm ordering you to stay out of this. Let me do my job."

"The letter." Maya felt herself near tears.

George placed a hand on her shoulder. "Calm down, sweetheart. I'll read the letter. If it even remotely suggests what you're saying, I'll copy it and give it to you and tell my captain. I have to admit it as evidence first. That is as good as it's going to get for now."

It wasn't good enough for Maya. "When will that be?"

"Tomorrow."

Maya threw her arms in the air. "No. That's too long. I'll go crazy."

"As good as it gets, Maya." George was unwavering. "Now, you have to go."

They both turned as the front door opened and Steven stood in the doorway. He eyed George suspiciously.

"I made promises," Maya said to George. "They didn't kill Elaine."

"Your promises mean nothing, Maya." George spoke with disappointment in his eyes. "They don't have anything to do with me, except make my job harder. Now leave."

Maya hesitated. "When tomorrow?"

George sighed. "By noon."

Maya suddenly remembered what tomorrow was. "The stock is trading tomorrow. We're having a celebration lunch in the Douglass Conference Room at the hotel. Will you come? Can you bring the letter then?"

George nodded. "I'll try my best, Maya."

Maya reluctantly turned and headed toward her car as George entered the house. She sat for a while, trying to make sense of what little she knew. Her mind was all over the place. She couldn't do this alone.

Her first thought was to go to Jerome at the hotel, but he couldn't handle this. She had nothing but speculation, and to drop it all on Jerome the night before the stock traded would just be cruel. Jerome loved her father just as much as Maya did. He wouldn't be able to function if he knew Nick had been murdered.

No, Alissa was the only person she could go to.

"It doesn't make sense, Maya." Alissa placed the last dish in the dishwasher.

Maya leaned across the kitchen table, staring at the back of her hand. "You read ten words tops, all spread apart. From that you want to assume murder and blackmail, involving Nick no less?"

"I don't want to assume anything. I can't help it. Besides, if I read everything else wrong, I know my name. I saw Woodson."

"You sure? You haven't been thinking very clearly lately."

"My head is spinning," she said. "I can't even . . ."

"You don't know anything yet, Maya."

"I know. That's all that's keeping me from losing it

right now. I guess I'm holding on to the hope that I'm wrong. But I don't think so."

The loud hum of the dishwasher stretched the silence.

"What do we have, hon?" Alissa asked. "Let's go backward."

Maya smiled, appreciating the "we." "This letter that I think has something to do with Daddy's death was stolen from Linda's house. Tatiana said it was right with the will, which was all she intended to take."

"So the letter could either be Linda's alone, or what Linda stole from Elaine's apartment along with the will."

"I think it was Linda who stole the will and the letter from Elaine. She meant to steal them both."

"What was Elaine doing with it?"

Maya felt a headache setting in. "I'm stumped. Something big is missing here."

"So maybe it was just Linda's all along, and Tatiana just happened to pick it up."

Maya considered this. "Then, the 'liar' in the letter was Linda. She was the one being blackmailed."

"Why would Linda be blackmailed, Maya? Do you even remotely think she could've had something to do with Nick's death? That was ten years ago."

"The world is a small place, Ally." Maya wasn't counting anything out. "Maybe Elaine found out and was going to tell me or someone else."

"Okay." Alissa leaned back in her chair. "That's enough. This is too much speculation. You could be setting yourself up for a major misunderstanding."

"I can't forget about it."

"You can until tomorrow, when George gets you some answers."

Maya stood up, pacing the room. "What if—"

"What if what? Nothing will change between now and

then. Go home and prepare for your big day tomorrow. Call me as soon as you get the letter. We'll figure out what we have to do then."

Maya leaned back against the sink of the prairie-style kitchen. She figured, as long as she was here . . .

"Oh yeah." She didn't look up. "I'm in love with Tre Matthews."

Alissa sat in silence, with eyes wide. Maya finally looked at her, a sarcastic laugh finding its way out.

"That's how I looked when I found out," she said. "It just hit me."

"These things never just hit you," Alissa said. "Not if you're honest with yourself."

"It's been building, but I never . . . I never thought love. I thought it was physical. You know . . ."

"Sex." Alissa winked. "Why don't you sleep with him and see what happens? Maybe it is just sex."

Maya blinked, biting her lower lip. Alissa's mouth dropped.

"When?" she asked. "And how dare you not tell me."

"Los Angeles." Images of their lovemaking flashed in her mind. She remembered it so clearly, and wanted it again. "And I couldn't tell you. We had a horrible fight the next morning and I've been devastated ever since. Just thinking about it hurts."

"It's been a while for you," Alissa said. "How was it?"

"Ally, that's clearly not the issue now."

"Isn't it? Think about it. You have this man you thought you hated, now you realize you love. You have this IPO driving you across the country. You're still dealing with Elaine's death. Do you want some advice from someone who loves you?"

"Please." Maya spoke from her desperate heart.

"Let go of Tre, Elaine and this letter for one day. Tomorrow, think about nothing but the IPO, your job.

You're gonna drive yourself insane if you don't. Everything will work its way out eventually."

Maya nodded at the simplistic solution, but inside she wasn't at all confident. She wasn't sure of anything, and she felt like it would all get worse before it got better.

When Trajan finally saw Maya walking up the street toward her apartment, he felt a sigh of relief leave him. It was late, and he was getting worried. The first and only thing on his mind when his flight touched down in Dulles was Maya.

He loved her. Despite himself, and her for that matter, he had found a way to fall in love with her. Making love to her had been the icing on the cake. He'd intended to explain to her what he himself didn't understand, but she was nowhere to be found.

He waited, thinking of nothing else he could do. Now, as he leaned down in the driver's side of his rental car, he caught a distant glimpse of her face as she passed by and headed up the steps to her brownstone.

She was upset, overwrought; that could be seen even in the dark. She walked with a stride of exhaustion. Tomorrow was a big day, and Trajan could see it was getting to the poor girl. The last thing she needed was some man she didn't seem to care much for telling her that he loved her.

He felt compassion for her beyond anything he'd felt for anyone as long as he could remember. She reminded him of what was good in his life before he'd lost his way. Maya would bring him back. That was, if she was willing.

* * *

Maya took a deep breath as she entered Jerome's office. Her smile was convincing, and as everyone turned to her, it became contagious.

"Good morning, everyone." Maya's eyes veered to Trajan, and she regretted it immediately.

He was staring right at her, looking his usual devastating best. Her heart flipped over and the hair on her arms stood up. The room was erased and time slowed. She could sense more than anything that he wasn't happy, and her first reaction was to reach out to him. She was halted by the acknowledgment that she was the cause of his pain, and it made her stomach turn.

"The market opens in a few minutes, Maya," Jerome said from behind the desk. "We'll be opening at sixteen and a half."

"We're taking bets," David Hanley said. He appeared smaller than usual standing next to Trajan. "Do you want in? Where do you think we'll close?"

Maya swallowed hard, forcing herself to turn away from Trajan and his avoidance. "That's pushing our luck, Dave."

Jerome wrapped his hand over hers, and Maya felt comforted. She was unnerved by the fact that for the first time since her mother died, she preferred the comfort of someone other than Jerome. Even with Elaine, Alissa, or any of the lovers she'd had, when times were hard, only Jerome could soothe her. Now, she wanted Trajan. But that wasn't going to happen.

She looked at Jerome, wishing she could tell him about the letter. No, not today. Let him be happy today. "Are you condoning this? Betting on our market value."

"It's out of my hands. It's turned into a regular Atlantic City here." His smile seemed strong and confident as he leaned in to whisper. "What have you done to Tre?"

Maya's eyes widened. "What?"

"He's a mess, and he's only getting worse. Are you okay?"

"I'm fine," she lied, squeezing his hand. "It'll be a great day."

Trajan felt his pager vibrate, distracting him from Maya. He had to think about the stock today. He couldn't let his feelings for her interfere with his managing this day. As much as he wanted nothing but to be with her, he had to stay away from her.

"I have to make a call," he said, excusing himself from the room.

He didn't even look at me. Maya felt nauseated. No, she'd made a promise to Alissa, to herself. She couldn't think about Trajan today. At least, not so much.

The stock opened at sixteen and a half a share in heavy trading. In less than an hour, it was at twenty-two dollars. Despite the early celebration that filled the conference room, Maya couldn't enjoy any of it. If she wasn't agonizing over Trajan, who appeared to want nothing to do with her, she was agonizing about getting her hands on that letter. She was obsessed with the idea of catching Elaine's killer.

"Psst."

Maya's trance as she gazed outside the large conference room window was broken when Jerome approached with a worried expression.

"Where are you right now?" he asked, offering her a glass of wine.

"It's not even noon, Jerome." She accepted the glass, but placed it in the windowsill. "A little early for alcohol."

"You should know. You've been checking your watch every ten minutes."

Maya didn't respond, pressing her lips together.

"Besides," he added. "It's sparkling juice."

Maya retrieved the glass and took a sip. "What's the latest?"

"Twenty-three and a quarter." Jerome spoke calmly. "You're going to be a very wealthy lady by the end of the day."

"There you go with those hasty predictions again." Maya. briefly touched his cheek. "It's nice to see you happy."

"I wouldn't say I've been unhappy. Just stressed. I guess I finally let your optimism get to me. This is the right thing. Nick would've been proud."

Quiet tears came immediately. Maya hated herself for her lack of control. She felt as if she had lost control of every aspect of her emotions and her life.

"What is it, Maya?" Jerome wrapped his arm around her. "I hope those are happy tears."

"No, they aren't." Maya wiped her cheeks with the back of her hand. "I can't keep this from you any longer. It's about Daddy."

Jerome led her out of the conference room and into the attached bedroom, where he closed the door behind him. Maya told him everything. Jerome's mouth dropped, and his eyes narrowed. She wasn't sure she had ever seen him so angry.

"Where is this damn letter?" He stood up, running his hand over his head. "How dare this detective not show you!"

"He'll be here later today. What should we do?"

Jerome shook his head. He rubbed his fists as he always did when he wanted to try and calm himself. "I have to think. When is he coming again?"

"Probably noon." Maya looked at her watch again. "Eleven thirty."

"I know someone," Jerome said. "He can get us the information the cops won't. You hold down the fort here. I'll be back in an hour."

Maya called after him as he stormed out the bedroom door, but she got no response. She regretted telling him in one sense, but felt better knowing that someone who felt about her father the way she did knew about it. Jerome would get them answers. She could always count on him.

Trajan was ready to bust the bedroom door down. His blood pressure was rising and he was ready for a real drink. No more of this weak juice. When he saw Maya begin to cry, and Jerome lead her into the bedroom, he could think of nothing but finding out what was upsetting her. And fixing it, whatever it was. They'd been in there for what seemed like forever. It was driving him insane.

"Tre!" George slapped his hand on Trajan's shoulder as he turned around. "You were supposed to call me when you got in last night."

"Sorry, man." Trajan forced a smile for his buddy. "I got tied up."

"With what?" George asked. "Or whom, should I say? Did you see Maya?"

"Not exactly."

"Delaying the inevitable, man. You two are going to be together."

Trajan laughed. "From your mouth to God's ears. I just don't know."

"Don't start again about the two different worlds you both came from. You're from the same place where it really counts. You have that in common that stays with you. And face it, you're both in the same world now. You're both rich."

"But she's still in that place we came from in her heart, no matter how much money she has. I haven't been in that place in a long time, George. I'm not real enough to her."

"She slept with you, didn't she?" George whispered.

"Now, I don't know her too well. Most of what I know is from what you told me about her. But what I do know would tell me that she isn't the type to sleep with someone just for sex. She obviously cares."

"But how much?" Trajan hated doubting himself. He wasn't used to it, but he wasn't used to a lot of the feelings Maya stirred within him. He wanted Maya in his life more than anything. "Not enough to love. She wouldn't love me, and that's what I need from her. Nothing less."

George nodded compassionately. "They're a complicated species. I'll give you that. But sometimes I think we make them out to be more complex than they are."

"Maybe I'm making it worse like this," Trajan said. "But it's only because I'm not willing to go two or three rounds with Maya. I want all twelve."

"Pardon the pun, brother, but put your gloves on and ring the bell yourself. Don't wait for the ref."

"Very weak pun." Trajan laughed. "But I appreciate the effort. By the way, what are you doing here?"

"I'm here to see the sister in question." George explained yesterday and the letter. "Where is she anyway?"

"You have to keep her out of this, George." Trajan led him to the bedroom, happy for an excuse to get in there. "I'm assuming you plan to."

"I'll do what I can," George said. "But she's a spit-fire."

The second Maya saw Trajan in the doorway, she stood up. She knew she needed to have his arms wrapped around her, whether he wanted to or not. Nothing else would soothe her. The only thing that stopped her from running to him was George's massive figure appearing right behind.

"George!" Maya felt anticipation racing through her veins. "Do you have the letter?"

George frowned. "No, Maya. I can't give you the letter."

Maya had to catch her breath, she was so shocked. "But you have to. I have to know what—"

"Sit down, Maya." Trajan took her by the arm and sat her on the bed. "Let him explain."

Maya felt a sudden sense of comfort with his hands on her. Still, the thought of not getting that letter was too much.

"Maya." George stuffed his hands in his pockets. "I almost got taken off this case when my captain found out about you and your promises to Tatiana and Steven. Not only is Tatiana in trouble for lying to the cops, but she stole evidence."

"I'm sorry." Maya regretted not being able to do more. "I know that was wrong. I wish I could take it back."

"Forget that." George went on. "At issue is the letter. You were right. It does have something to do with your father."

Maya felt dizzy. She knew what she'd read. "Oh, my God. I knew it. Who killed my father?"

"It's under investigation, but I can't tell you more than that right now."

Trajan felt Maya squeeze his hand. He squeezed back. "If this is true, Maya, it's more reason for you not to get involved. This is dangerous."

"I have to know," Maya said. "Jerome and I have a right to know. It's Linda. I know she has something to do with it."

"Linda claims to have gotten it by accident," George said. "Her latest story is she brought along a bunch of papers of her own to conceal the will when she grabbed it. She left those papers on the desk near the bedroom. She stuffed the will under those papers and ran out. She's thinking the letter had already been on the desk.

When she got it home, she opened it up and read it. She wasn't sure what it meant, but said she was planning on using it against Elaine in the future. To get some money for herself and her daughter."

"If that's true then it's easy," Maya said, not believing such an easy story. "Whoever the envelope was addressed to is the murderer."

"Linda can't remember what it said." George rolled his eyes. "I know, I know. Very convenient. She remembers she saw the hotel's name and address and could swear it was addressed to her mother. She thinks she tossed the envelope as soon as she opened it."

"And never bothered to look again after she read it?" Trajan asked. "This woman is either an extreme idiot or she's lying."

"There's no way Elaine killed anyone," Maya said. "She was in Germany the entire year of my father's death anyway. We'd talked about that a long time ago."

"Are you sure?" George asked. "She could've paid—"

"Come on, George," Maya said.

"I've told you too much already. I've got to get back to work."

"You can't leave me hanging like this!" Maya yelled. "When will I get more news? I can't tell Jerome this. He'll go crazy."

"Look, Maya." George's face was stone serious. "Too many unauthorized people know about this already. Out of respect for me telling you more than you should know, don't tell him anything. Don't either of you tell anyone anything. I have a feeling we'll make an arrest, or at least have a suspect name by the end of the day."

"You'll let me know?" Maya was already thinking of ways around this. "As soon as you can?"

"Yes I will." George nodded. "Bye, Maya. Tre, look after her."

"I will." Trajan wrapped his other arm around her shoulders as George left the two of them alone.

Maya rested her head on Trajan's shoulder, not even stopping to think whether or not he wanted her to. It felt so right. The only thing that could be right, now that her world was going crazy.

Trajan held her tight. He'd never let her go. All bad was forgotten. Love made it that way. "It's going to be okay. Don't force yourself to take it all in right now."

"My father was murdered." Maya wiped the tears from her cheeks as they kept coming. "He was really murdered. I was hoping, giving anything that I'd read wrong. That the stress of it all was making me see things, think crazy, but it's true. Why?"

"I'm not a cop, Maya, but I don't think you should accept anything until it's proven true. Your father's death was investigated and it was concluded it was an accident."

"They make mistakes all the time, Tre." Maya thought of her mother, dying with the belief that she'd lost the love of her life because of the luck of the draw. "I have to find out what that letter said. Linda, Steven and Tatiana read that letter. I'll ask them."

"No you won't." Trajan said. "It's too dangerous."

"Then why haven't they hurt me before now?"

"You didn't know about the letter until now."

"Tatiana and Steven gave me the letter," Maya said. "They would never have given—"

"No, Maya. You have to stay out of it. You can wait another day."

"I've waited ten years, Tre." Maya stood up. "Ten years of believing, forgiving, but not forgetting how much was taken away because of a careless, stupid mistake. I can't wait another second. Not for myself, for Jerome or Mama."

A knock on the door from the conference room was followed by David Hanley poking his head in. His smile quickly turned to a nervous frown.

"I'm sorry to interrupt," he said. "It's important."

Maya wiped her face. "What is it, Dave?"

"The stock is at twenty-seven. The guys at International Leveraged Markets are getting nervous. They say it's going too good, if there is such a thing. He wants to talk to Jerome."

"He stepped out," Maya said. "He'll be back soon."

"I'll take the call." Trajan stood up. "Tell him five minutes."

After the door was closed, Trajan took hold of Maya by her shoulders and turned her to him. She looked into his eyes and found a sympathy and warmth she could have never thought him capable of only a month ago.

"You understand," he said in a whisper, "that I'm here for you. That nothing else means anything to me."

"I know." Maya was filled with a warmth stronger than her pain.

Trajan gently stroked her neck with his fingers. "Sit down here. I'll be back in a few minutes. We'll make it through this."

With a quick kiss on her forehead, Trajan left the room. Before he could close the door, Maya was headed out the other door. She was in the hallway and at her desk in less than a minute.

Clicking on the Internet switchboard, she typed in all she knew, wondering why she hadn't thought of that before. All she remembered from reading the letter.

FIRST NAME: G
LAST NAME: Stevenson
ADDRESS: Lance
ADDRESS2: Reston, Virginia

There was only one. Geoffrey and Samantha Stevenson, 255 Lance Lane. The names meant nothing to her now, but Maya was on the road to answers in a matter of minutes.

Nine

Samantha Stevenson was an elderly white woman, with salt and pepper hair tied in curlers. She was petite underneath her paisley housecoat. She'd been crying, Maya noticed as soon as the woman opened the door.

"Can I help you?" she asked with a weak voice.

"I'm sorry to bother you." Maya felt butterflies in her stomach, heard the tremor in her voice. "My name is Maya Woodson. I'm here to ask you about a letter I think was written by a Mr. Geoff Stevenson about my father."

"Geoff is my husband." Samantha's eyes closed slowly, briefly. "Was my husband. I believe your partner is already here."

As she opened the door wider, George appeared from behind. He held a look on his face that would have scared Maya to death if she could feel much of anything right now.

"Mrs. Stevenson," he said, turning to the woman. "You can return to the sofa. I need to talk to Ms. Woodson for a moment."

Maya took advantage of the opening to step into the house. If George wanted her out, he'd have to physically force her out, which she was aware would take nothing out of him. Still, she hoped he wouldn't do it in front of someone.

"What are you doing here?" he whispered, his eyes slits of anger.

"Do you have to ask?"

"I told you to—"

"I know what you told me," she said. "But finding out after ten years that my father was murdered has left me unable to reason. I want the truth now."

"Damn woman." He clenched his hands in fists. "Tre is gonna have his hands full trying to handle you. I can order you to leave this home, you know. I am an officer of the law."

"You'll have to arrest me," Maya said with as much defiance as she could muster.

George gritted his teeth. "Don't think I won't. Now, I don't have time for your nonsense. You're going to sit down and keep your mouth shut."

"Dr. Stevenson," George said as they convened on the sofa of the antique-littered townhouse living room, "was killed in a robbery attempt only two weeks ago."

Maya felt certain there was more to his death than a simple robbery. She could tell from the look on George's face that he did too.

"No suspects were found," Samantha said. "Not yet."

"Before this, Dr. Stevenson was a prison psychiatrist at Fairfax County Prison, right in the district. He retired five years ago." George nodded toward a dusty cardboard box. "These are some of his personal notes from work."

"Mrs. Stevenson." Maya ignored a disapproving moan that emitted from George. "We were talking about any problems your husband was having with acquaintances before his death."

She shook her head, obviously not at her wits. Maya assumed she was on Valium to handle her grief. "No. No enemies."

"You sure he never mentioned Nick Woodson?" George asked.

"We've established that there were money problems," he told Maya. George looked at Samantha, who was staring into space. "I can't believe I'm saying this, but I think it's good you're here, Maya. Mrs. Stevenson, I know you already said this, but I need you to repeat it. Do I have your permission to look through his papers?"

"Yes, of course," she answered, attempting a gracious smile. "I don't know what you'll find to help solve a robbery that happened in the district, but go ahead. I have to check my stew."

After she left, Maya leaned in with a whisper. "She must be medicated heavily."

"I just hope she remembers she gave us permission." George opened the box. "You take a stack. I'll take the other."

"For someone who didn't want me here, you sure could use me."

"Don't worry." He winked at her. "I'll get you for being a thorn in my side yet. Look for anything, mostly names that might be relevant."

It took twenty minutes and Samantha excusing herself to rest before George hit a jackpot. Maya had just returned from the bedroom.

"I think we should call a doctor," she said, concerned. "She's very weak. I don't think she's eating."

"She was just making stew," George said. "Besides, how healthy do you expect a woman of at least seventy-five to be?"

"I think she's overmedicating."

George gripped the black-and-white-speckled journal. "You better sit down. I found something."

Maya saw the look on his face as she did what she was told. He was more than serious. She braced herself.

"It looks like this guy kept a little book for each patient. He had to have left patient files at the prison, so he kept these notes for himself. This one is for a Reid Lucas, an inmate. It starts March, six years ago."

"Go on," Maya said after a long pause. "What is it?"

George was reading quickly, sifting pages. "Damn. I don't know. I don't think you can handle this."

"It couldn't be worse than—"

"It's worse, Maya." His eyes held an apology.

Maya felt her stomach clench. "There's no turning back for me, George."

George sighed. "All right. I'm gonna paraphrase here. It looks like Reid Lucas bared his soul to the doctor. He committed many more burglaries than the two he was convicted of. More on that. . . . more, more. He starts to tease the doctor about a murder he might have had a hand in."

Maya caught her breath. Who was this Reid Lucas? This man that stole her father from her.

"He teases and teases," George continued. "Then finally, he admits that he fixed the brakes, which was apparently his specialty. He worked at an auto shop for ten years. He fixed the brakes in a car that killed a big-shot local businessman for money."

Maya swallowed. "He wanted money?"

George blinked at her, looking down at the paper. "Maya. I gotta stop there. Tre told me how much you—"

"I what?" Maya leaned forward, wringing her hands together.

"How much," George said calmly, "you love Jerome Newman."

Nothing registered for Maya. She stared blankly at George for several seconds before connecting his words. She laughed.

"You're insane," she said. "Are you—"

"Maya. It says it right here. Lucas didn't fix those brakes because he wanted money from your father. He did it because Jerome paid him money to."

Maya sat speechless, refusing to accept this. "He's a liar. He's a criminal and a liar. Jerome loved my father as much as I did. He still does. He was devastated when he died. He was everything to me and my mother."

"What would Lucas have to gain by telling this?"

"Early release," she said, trying to think quickly. She felt sick to her stomach. "Attention."

"Then why would he tell his psychiatrist, the one person who couldn't tell anyone else?"

Maya searched for words. She shook her head vigorously. "To amuse himself. To tease this doctor. For fun. No, George, this is crazy."

"Maya." George stood up just as she did. He grabbed her arm. "Calm down. You could be right. I'll make a visit to the prison. I'll talk to him. If he's not there, I'll track him down."

"Let's go." Maya grabbed her purse and headed for the door.

"Maya. There's no way you're going to the prison. Why don't you call the hospital, and get someone to check on Mrs. Stevenson. I'll call Fairfax to set up an appointment for *myself* to drop in on Mr. Lucas."

Maya felt anger take her over. "I know he's lying. My father's death was in all the papers. Everyone knew about him and Jerome being partners. He used that. There's no way."

"We'll see."

The tension mounted for Maya as she checked on Samantha, got the name of her doctor and called. Fortunately for Mrs. Stevenson, it was an old, family doctor that cared for his patients the traditional way. A dying breed. Someone would be by in less than an hour. Maya returned to the living room, determined to convince George to bring her along.

George was already out front, standing near his unmarked car in the driveway. She joined him.

"I want to face this liar, George. I want him to have to look in my face and repeat this horrible lie."

George shook his head. "You won't get the chance. Neither will I. Reid Lucas was murdered in a prison fight over a year ago."

"No." Maya's hands formed into fists as she leaned against the car. "What's next? How do we go on?"

"No more we, Maya. You're out of this. You're too close to the suspect."

"You suspected Jerome before this, didn't you?"

"I read the letter, Maya. You have to think about this."

Maya threw her hands in the air. "There's nothing to think about, George."

"Elaine Cramer is dead," George said. "She had this letter. She lived in the same hotel as Jerome Newman."

"So, now he's a double murderer." Maya let out a cynical laugh, just as memories flashed in her mind. Elaine asking to see Jerome the morning of her death. Jerome upset over Randy mixing up the mail again.

"No," Maya said. "No way."

"You forget Dr. Stevenson. A triple murderer. Possibly. Dr. Stevenson was having financial problems, so he dug into his own past and discovered an opportunity to blackmail Jerome. Divulging the information would cost him his medical license, but he didn't care since he never intended to use again."

Maya flashed back on Jerome's mood. No, she told herself. He was like a father to her, all the family she had left.

"I don't want to hear this," she said. "You've burned

all your leads and you're making up suspects. You have nothing concrete."

"No, we don't. But we do have enough for questioning. I'm going to bring him in."

"You're crazy." Maya fought any speck of doubt that tried to make itself known in her mind.

"Don't you go near him, Maya. It could be dangerous."

"Now I'm in danger from the man that has been my father for ten years? You have no idea how ridiculous that sounds. Jerome would never hurt me. He'd never hurt anyone."

"Look. If you're right, you'll be proven right by the end of the day. If you taint this, it'll only make things harder on Jerome, and could ultimately get you in trouble."

"Bye, George." Maya rolled her eyes and walked toward her car.

She didn't look back until George drove off. The sound of his tires on the smooth road passed by her just before the sound of someone else's tires on gravel rock behind her caused her to turn around. Looking past the driveway into the alley, she saw the very end of a large ruby red luxury sedan speeding down the alley.

Maya blinked, her pulse quickening. She couldn't ignore that she saw it. She couldn't ignore it looked just like a Lincoln Continental. She couldn't ignore that it looked exactly like the Lincoln Continental that Jerome drove. A chill ran down her spine. Her whole life would seem a lie if she even began to accept what George was saying. It wasn't possible. No, there were thousands of Lincoln Continentals on the streets. It was a popular car.

Don't let his craziness get to you, she told herself.

Craziness. It was insane. Maya started her car, angry at herself for even considering it to the point of denial.

She would stay quiet about it, but not for George's sake, not to help his investigation. She wouldn't tell Jerome because even the suggestion that he would kill anyone, especially Nick, would tear him to pieces. She loved him too much for that.

Trajan watched as Jerome paced the living room floor of his penthouse.

"Jerome," he said. "Why don't you sit down? You're all wound up."

Jerome stopped only briefly to look out his window. He looked in Trajan's direction, but not at him, before pacing again.

They'd been searching for Maya since noon when Trajan returned from the phone call and Maya was gone. He immediately called George. He hadn't been able to reach him all day. When Jerome returned later in the afternoon, he became immediately anxious. Trajan found him no help at all.

Now it was almost five. The stock market closed, everyone left to prepare for the celebration dinner, and the two of them waited anxiously.

"Tre." Jerome walked toward him, his arms folded across his chest. "You don't have to be here. Maya is my responsibility."

"I understand what you're saying." Tre stood up. "But things between Maya and I have changed."

"Really? So I can count on you?"

"To?" Trajan was trying to see Jerome's point. He realized Jerome was more than anxious. Something was really wrong here.

"To take care of her," he said.

"Of course." Trajan analyzed the situation, going over Jerome's behavior the past few hours. "Either way, I think I'll stay."

Jerome didn't appear happy with the decision, but before he could respond, a knock came on the front door, and he turned and raced for it. When Maya came face to face with Jerome, she wrapped her arms around him, hugging him tighter than she had since she was a child.

"Jerome." She felt tears coming. "Oh, Jerome."

"Where have you been?" Trajan was at her side in seconds. "Are you okay?" Maya nodded as she leaned away from Jerome. She was anything but okay. She saw the look in Trajan's eyes and was touched by its sincerity.

"I've been driving around for a while." She lifted her head to Jerome. "I'm sorry I deserted you on our big day."

Jerome blinked, letting her go. He headed for the bar. "No problem. It's been a bittersweet day for both of us. Drink?"

"No." Maya noticed Jerome's jittery movements. He'd found something out.

Trajan felt like a ghost in the room. He wanted so badly to be close enough to Maya that she would include him in whatever she was feeling right now.

"Come sit down." He led her to the sofa. "I've been . . . we've been looking for you all day. Maya, I . . ."

He was truly concerned, and Maya loved him for it. She placed her hand over his, and felt him calm immediately. "I'm fine. Physically at least. I wasn't in any danger. I was with George."

"Doing what?" Jerome joined them, sipping a brandy nervously. "What did you find out?"

"Daddy was definitely murdered." Even though the words came from her own mouth, Maya felt like they were being spoken from far away. "I guess I was trying to believe it was a lie, a horrible misunderstanding. It hit me today that someone murdered my father."

"Tre." Jerome stood up, heading for the door. "I need to speak to Maya privately. Family business."

Trajan was reluctant. He didn't want to disrespect Jerome in his own home, but he didn't want to leave Maya right now. "Maya, I—"

"Jerome." Maya turned to him. "I need to speak to Tre for a moment."

Jerome was obviously displeased, but he took a deep breath. "Fine. I'll go make some tea. I know it calms you."

"Maya, I was going insane," Trajan said.

"I'm sorry." She sighed. "I had to go. I wasn't going to be satisfied with Tatiana or Steven. They didn't know what that letter meant. I didn't trust Linda because I didn't think she was safe. I had to go the source. It's complicated, and George—"

"What?"

"He's crazy," Maya said with a convincing nod. "He's going to mess up this entire investigation because he wants to follow false leads."

Trajan sensed an uncertainty behind her forced conviction. "I think he's a good cop, Maya. But regardless of that, let's focus on you. Forget the dinner tonight. Let me take you home. I'll stay with you."

"I need to be with Jerome tonight, Tre." Maya saw the look of pain in his eyes. "It's not that I don't want to be with you. But Jerome and I need each other."

"I understand," was what Trajan said. *I want you to need me* was what he wanted to say. He had to do what she wanted. He loved her to that point, whether it was what he wanted or not. "Can I call you later tonight?"

"Tomorrow." Maya knew she was hurting him, but she could only deal with so much right now.

Trajan wanted to kiss her, but didn't. Reluctantly, slowly, he let her hands go and stood up.

"Tre." Maya called after him as he reached the door.

She hated herself for asking it. "When did Jerome return today? You know, from his lunch errand?"

"Why?"

"I'm just worried about him. He's devastated by all this too."

Trajan thought about it. "He was gone pretty long. He got back about three."

That wasn't what Maya wanted to hear, but she smiled at Trajan as if it was. When she was alone, Maya fought back tears. For the past few hours she'd accepted the truth of her father's death if not the explanation. She was doubting herself, her own love for the only family she had left. It shouldn't be so hard for her to fight it, and that was what upset her the most.

Maya was certain all she needed was to be with Jerome. They would share their memories and their feelings, as they had so much in the past. That would erase the doubts. They'd lost that closeness over the past months, so caught up in work and the IPO. A return to that would cure everything.

"Where's the tea?" she asked as Jerome returned.

"I put it on the stove." He sat down beside her. "You always get mad at me when I nuke it in the microwave. Be patient."

"We're alone now, Jerome. You found something out. I can tell just from looking at you. This guy you went to see at lunch. What's going on?"

Jerome's eyes narrowed, his face concentrating. "I don't want to talk about that guy right now. He's not going to come through for me like I need him to. That's not what I want to talk about anyway."

Maya felt better as Jerome's eyes softened. His hand reached up and gently touched her shoulder. "You're like my daughter. You know that."

Maya nodded with a warm smile. "I've always felt that. We'll get through this, just like we have in the past.

With Daddy, Mama and now Elaine. We won't let them get to us."

"Them?" he asked. "What has George told you? Come on, baby. You can tell me."

Maya had wanted to keep this from him, but she couldn't let the first time he heard of it be when he was brought in for questioning.

"I'm sorry, Jerome. I didn't want to tell you this, but the investigators are screwing everything up. They think the investigation leads here. We won't help them. They want this to be easy. They don't want to have to work because it's complicated. They—"

Maya was shocked by Jerome's sudden smile.

"Precious Maya." He let out a short, emotionless laugh. "Precious Maya, always loyal. Such a good girl. It's why I love you so much."

Maya shook her head, not understanding his expression. "It's not funny, Jerome. They intend to bring you in for questioning. Tonight maybe. I was with George today."

"I know," he said. "I saw you."

Maya felt the world stop. Something snapped in her head. There was a pause that, although short, seemed to last forever. She blinked once, again, staring at him.

"That was your car." Maya felt her body shaking. "God, no. No."

Jerome frowned. "I thought I'd taken care of everything, but I haven't."

Maya was horrified. The room was spinning. She felt herself almost step out of her own body.

"It was ten years," he said. "I spent so long scared to death, but nothing happened. I was making up for it, finally living again. I had a feeling with this IPO. It was too good to be true. Too good."

"No," Maya said. "No."

Jerome's expression turned sympathetic. "You have to know, I loved your father."

Maya's mouth opened, but nothing came out. Her life, their life, flashed before her eyes. She blinked, hoping to come back to reality, but it wouldn't happen.

Jerome sighed regretfully. "I loved him. I worshiped him. And I love you. That's why I'm here. That's why I stayed. I knew the police were onto me, but I stayed because I had to tell you that before I said good-bye. You have to believe I love—"

Jerome almost fell of the sofa from the force of Maya's slap across his face. He bounced back, his eyes filling with stinging tears that wouldn't fall.

"Maya, you can't hate me," he said. "I've made up for this. I've spent ten years making up for this."

"Jerome." Maya could barely see through her own tears. "Please tell me you . . . You couldn't have. Daddy. He loved you, guided you, gave you everything. You're family."

Jerome pressed his lips together. "You're in denial, Maya. And you can thank me for that. For the past ten years, I've fed your fantasies about a man that weren't true. No, Maya. There's so much you don't know. Even more than you've chosen to forget. Despite that, I couldn't just run away. I stayed, risking it all because I couldn't leave without saying good-bye to you. I can't explain this, and you have no need for my sob stories, so—"

"You killed Elaine, and that doctor." Maya felt her head spinning. "You killed my daddy."

"You could never . . . never understand."

Maya tried to stand up, but her knees gave way and dropped her back to the sofa. "Why?"

Jerome's eyes filled with vibrant, hateful rage, his entire face tightening. "Why? Oh God, Maya. You could never begin to understand. You wouldn't be able to accept it either. Not if I spent hours telling you. But I don't have hours even if I wanted to. But Pharaoh closed at thirty-two dollars a share today. That would've never happened if I hadn't done what I did."

Maya felt a sting of pain as she realized her fists were clenched so tight that her nails were piercing the skin of her palm. The pain awakened her. She turned to the phone next to the sofa and reached.

Jerome grabbed her with one hand, pulling her to him. With the other, he stuck a cloth napkin in her mouth. Maya panicked. The napkin hurt, but it was Jerome's eyes that really scared her. They were almost demonic. Maya had never seen him look anything similar to this. She didn't know this man.

Maya fought, but she was small and weak from exhaustion, and within minutes, Jerome had dragged her to his bedroom where he tied her to his bedpost. She tried to spit the napkin out, but each time she tried, it became harder to breathe.

Worse than anything, Jerome said nothing throughout the process. Not a word, a groan, a mumble. When finally he removed the napkin to replace it with tape, Maya took a deep breath and yelled out.

"I'll get you for this! I'll get you for killing my—"

He taped her mouth. "I know my time is short. I'm only doing this because I need time to get away. It may not last, but I'm not ready to give up yet. I just wanted to see my little girl one last time."

She struggled as he stood at the bed, watching her. With those eyes. His face took on a look of regret, sorrow, but the eyes remained the same. Like nothing Maya could ever remember seeing, and she realized how deceived she'd been. Maya was filled with rage, and as he slowly, casually turned and walked out of the room, she knew she would see him again. She would see to it.

* * *

Trajan clicked the remote incessantly, not taking half a second to see what was on any of the channels. He couldn't figure out the true source of his discomfort. It went beyond the latest news, or Maya dismissing him. Something, he couldn't put his finger on what, told him something bad was about to happen. He wouldn't let anything happen to Maya. He should feel she was safe with Jerome, but he didn't. His behavior all day made Trajan believe he wouldn't be there for Maya when she needed him most.

He needed to go back up there. Trajan was convinced, and as he leaped off his bed, his cell phone ringing was all that kept him from leaving. He checked the number.

"Finally." He turned it on. "George. Where in God's name have you been? I've been calling you all day."

"Some serious work going on here, man. I got your messages. You still looking for Maya?"

"No. I found her, but she's pretty torn up. What can you tell me?"

"I can tell you to keep an eye on her. Keep her company, and keep her away from Jerome Newman."

"Why him? He's all she's—"

"I can't give you details, Tre, but it's serious."

"You'd better tell me how serious, George, 'cause she's with him right now, and he's coming unglued. I have a bad feeling about it."

George cursed in frustration. "Tre, you gotta get her. Come up with some excuse. Aw man, just go get her. I'm still waiting for my captain to green light me bringing him in for questioning. It's crazy, anyone else off the street we can question at will. If a guy has some money, we need permission."

Trajan was already out of the hotel room. "I'm on my way right now. Tell me what's going on."

George told him about the discovery of Dr. Stevenson and his papers. He told him about Maya's doubtful and angry reaction to Jerome as a suspect. He explained that further investigation that day had created greater suspicion, although nothing concrete. Trajan couldn't believe it. All he could think of was how Maya would never accept this and how much pain she'd be in when she might finally have to.

"Look, man," George said. "I'm sorry, but the way this is going, with Jerome's popularity, when it hits the fan, your public offering is going to take a hit."

Trajan thought about it. He realized, with all certainty, that that fact meant nothing to him. All that mattered in his world was Maya. Protecting her and being there for her.

"Forget that," he said. "Just get here."

He turned the phone off, knocking hard enough on the door to Jerome's apartment to almost knock it down. He called out to Jerome, to Maya. He banged on the door. Trajan tried to open the door, moving the knob every which way. Pushing, kicking.

He knew something was wrong, but he didn't panic. He went to the hotel phone near the elevator doors and called security. He told them he was sure he'd heard a scream for help from the penthouse. Lance Snyder was there in only a couple of minutes.

Trajan called out to Maya as soon as he got inside. He ran around, feeling desperation rise in him. When he finally saw her, she was struggling to free herself from the ropes that tied her arms and legs to the bed. The sight filled him with a violent rage.

"I'll kill him!" Trajan rushed to her, untying the ropes. "I'm going to kill him!"

Lance stormed in. "Oh my God! I'll call the police."

"Detective Hobbs is already on his way," Trajan said.

Maya ripped the tape from her mouth, taking a deep breath in. Her mouth, her ankles, her wrists, everything hurt.

"It's Jerome," she yelled as Trajan untied her ankles. "Jerome killed Daddy."

"Mr. Newman?" Lance's mouth dropped in disbelief.

"Where is he?" Trajan asked.

"He's gone," she said. "He left about ten minutes ago."

Trajan reached for her, but Maya slid away from him, trying unsuccessfully to stand up. Trajan turned to Lance.

"Lance, you go meet Detective Hobbs. Tell him what Jerome did to Maya and that he's already gone. He can't be that far, not ten minutes in D.C. traffic."

Lance nodded and was gone.

"Jerome." Maya had to try a second time to stand up. "We have to get him."

"They will, Maya." Trajan could see her hands shaking. "You need to rest. Come to my room and get some rest."

Maya turned to face him, her body racing with rage. "No way. I'm not going to rest until Jerome has been caught. He's going to have to look me in the face and tell me why. Why did he kill the man who offered him everything and asked for nothing in return? Why he killed an innocent old woman who was already suffering the pain of three ungrateful children, but still showed nothing but love to everyone she knew. He's going to tell me why, and I won't sleep a wink until then."

The evening went into the morning with no sign of Jerome. Trajan watched with concern as Maya became

more distant, her anger turning inside. He wanted to
console her, but she pushed away from him every time.

Maya's frustration was building to a crescendo. The
news that Jerome's car was found abandoned at Washington Reagan airport didn't help. Neither did the news
that his noon trip to see a "friend" was actually a trip
to the bank to withdraw cash. George let them know
the police weren't convinced that Jerome was gone.
And in that case, Trajan demanded protection for Maya.

Maya was defiant. She refused to be shuttled off and
kept under lock and key. It took hours of convincing
by Trajan, George and even Alissa, who arrived eventually, before she agreed. When it came down to it, if
Jerome had murdered three people, which was very
possible, it was too dangerous.

After further argument, she agreed to stay at
George's fiancée's house in the northwest Virginia
woods. An hour from D.C., it was secluded and on a
hill, so anyone approaching could be seen from the
front well before arriving.

With her youngest coming down with chicken pox,
Alissa couldn't stay with her, and the police captain
couldn't lend officers to her full-time. Trajan volun-
teered to stay with her as long as necessary, with George
checking in on them regularly, promising to keep Maya
up to date.

Maya had no reaction to the news that Trajan would
be staying with her. Nothing was on her mind except
Jerome and how he'd exploded her life. She had no
idea she was hurting him, and he never considered bur-
dening her by letting her know.

They'd come so close, he thought. Now, Trajan wondered if their window had been closed. Had the insanity
Jerome caused killed their chance for love as well?

Ten

The drive to the cabin house was long and cold. Maya rode with Trajan as they followed George in his cop car. She didn't speak, merely nodding or shaking her head with the occasional shrug in response. At the cabin house, designed in traditional log style, Maya sat on the back porch alone as Trajan and George put away the groceries and George told him about the house.

The tension grew thicker as night fell and Trajan and Maya were alone in the house. There was a magnetic gravity between them that begged them to come together. Maya felt it, although she was a black hole inside.

Trajan was torn between keeping his distance and persuading her to open up to him. Everything in him urged him to hold her, never let her go. But when he saw her sitting on the back porch, staring into the dark night, he knew she wanted to be alone. He approached with some hot tea, but she merely shook her head and turned away. He offered to cook dinner, hoping it would give them a chance to talk, at least be near each other. But Maya refused dinner, understandably with no appetite, before heading off to bed.

Trajan's frustration grew. He had no appetite either, and after some time, he went to bed himself.

Maya tossed and turned in her bed, only fifty feet or so from Trajan's bedroom. She felt cold and lonely. She hated herself for being so cruel to Trajan, but the rage consumed her. It decided what she could and couldn't do right now. She knew she'd feel better in his arms or making love to him. But that would require something of her she wasn't prepared to give. It wouldn't be fair to take from him, after all he was giving already.

Neither Maya nor Trajan slept well that night. The sounds of the insects in the trees engulfing the house drowned out the silence that was as thick as molasses.

The next morning, Trajan was unable to go another day as before. Trajan found Maya, again on the back porch quietly drinking tea. He sat across from her on the wooden furniture, staring out at the woods with her for several minutes before speaking.

"You have to talk about it, Maya. You let this rage and pain build up, and—"

"Tre, I can't." Maya couldn't look at him. She sipped her tea, staring straight ahead. "You couldn't begin to understand."

"That's what I'm trying to do," he said. "Damn, Maya. I'm here for you, can't you see that?"

"No I can't, Tre." She finally looked at him, her heart tearing up at the pained look in his eyes. "I can't see anything right now. I don't mean to hurt you, but I can't answer your questions. I can't calm your concerns."

"I'm not asking anything for me. This is for you. To help you."

"Help me?" She laughed. "What could possibly help me? My life is a lie. I've loved this man for what seems like forever. Thought of him as a father, a best friend. Shared everything with him, everything. I was so certain I knew him. He was my comfort, my mentor. All the memories were a lie. He killed my father and held me in his arms when I found out. My mother cried in his . . . Oh God, I can't even talk about it."

"Yes, you can," Trajan said, glad at least she was getting it out. "It's just you and me here. Yell it out if you have to."

"It won't change anything, Tre. I don't even know who I am anymore. Everything I've built up for myself inside has been based on the people I love. He lived in our home, ate dinner at our table until I was fifteen. He vacationed with us in West Virginia. That was our family vacation, this beautiful cabin. The 'family' vacation was special and he was welcomed with no questions. These memories . . . Tre, he laughed with us at our dinner table the night before he killed my daddy. He was over for dinner, never needed an invitation. He toasted wine and laughed at Daddy's jokes. Had to hold his damn stomach he was laughing so hard. He knew then he was going to kill my father!"

There was a long silence as Trajan waited to see if she would say more.

"Maya," he said calmly. "You're still who you've always been, but you're too scared to depend on yourself to know that. You have to be stronger than that. Because someone in your life lied to you doesn't mean everything in your life related to that person was a lie."

"Is it that simple in the world of black and white?" Maya's voice had a sarcastic tone to it. "Well I'm sorry, but I don't live in that world. Nothing makes sense in my world right now and the last thing I need is you telling me it's my fault."

"I'm not blaming you." Trajan felt his temper rise at her tone and accusation. "I'm just saying you need—"

"What I need," she said, standing up swiftly. "Is for the police to find Jerome and for him to tell me why he did this. How he could've possibly done this. Nothing will help me, console me or heal me until then. At least nothing until I see him pay for it."

Trajan stood up, trying to fight the anger her rejection of his concern made him feel. "So you need nothing from me? I'm useless here? Jerome is the only person who can help you?"

Maya threw her hands in the air. "You don't understand, Tre. I have nothing to give you right now."

"I'm not asking for anything from you." He heard himself yelling, although it wasn't what he intended.

Maya folded her arms across her chest, her eyes staring down at the ground. There was no getting through to him, and she didn't have the energy to continue.

"Forget it, Maya," Trajan said. "Forget it all. I thought we were building something. As untraditional a building as it was, when we made love I thought that was it. We're doing this, we're sharing this. But I can see that wasn't true."

"So what, that means because we made love, I have to make you feel like a king all the time so you don't doubt me?"

"It means you can count on me. That you can use me when you need anything." Trajan waved his hand away. "None of that matters, because it wasn't that at all. 'Cause the first test, you don't even try. I guess it was just a one-night stand, huh?"

"You were the one who walked out of that hotel room the next morning. Not me."

"Because you couldn't think about anything but what you needed satisfied. That's how this is again. All that matters is Jerome, not me, not us."

Maya fought back tears. She turned away from him, listening to his harsh steps as he walked back into the house.

Why was he being so difficult? Couldn't he understand what she was going through? She thought of the night they'd spent together and felt a warmth run through her. But so much had changed since then. She didn't want to lose him, Maya knew that. She just wasn't

THE BUSINESS OF LOVE   233

sure what to do. Everything, everything within her was focused on Jerome and why. Why, why, why.

Maya was at the door waiting when George arrived. She was rubbing her hands together, her heart beating wildly.

"Tell me good news," she said as he approached. "Tell me you've got him."

George sighed. "No Maya, we don't have him." He nodded a hello to Trajan as he entered the living room. "We're working on some leads. It looks like my first instinct was right. Jerome didn't fly anywhere. The car was a decoy. We got the security cameras showing him leaving the airport by foot at eight p.m. His car entered the lot at seven thirty. He was going the wrong way."

"Is that it?" Trajan asked, feeling disappointed for Maya. "Does the airport have cameras outside that would show where he headed, or the car number or plate of a cab he might've gotten in?"

"There are some cameras, but not everywhere. And no, he wasn't seen outside the airport."

"At least he's here," Maya said. "That helps. What other leads do you have? What about the news?"

"His picture was posted everywhere today, and two out of the top three stations ran a quick story with a picture. That's it, honest. We'll see what comes of it."

"You staying for dinner?" Trajan asked. George shook his head. "Well, at least have a drink with me. I could use the company. When you're done here, grab one and join me on the porch."

"What happened?" George asked Maya as soon as Trajan was out of sight.

"What do you mean?" Maya sat down on the sofa. George joined her. She knew what he meant, but hoped he'd lose interest if she played dumb.

"I could use the company? You two won't even look at each other."

"I don't want to get into it, George." Maya reached for the remote and turned the television on. She stretched at her oversized T-shirt. "I don't know what to do."

"How about letting him in?"

"That's very psychiatrist of you." Maya smiled.

"Didn't I tell you my fiancée is a head shrink?" He winked. "Seriously though, if my instincts are right, you're shutting him out, and he doesn't deserve that."

"I just can't deal with a relationship right now." Maya shook her head regretfully. "Why can't he be patient?"

"If you want this to work," he said, "you can't think of dealing with it as an option. You have to deal with it. Despite what you're going through, Tre deserves your effort."

Maya nodded in agreement.

"Look at how he's changed," George said. "Since the short time he and I have gotten reacquainted, I've seen it. He left his business in the hands of someone else to be here with you. Could the man you met a month ago have done that? He hasn't complained about it once. Not to me. I was there on the phone when he handed over operations to his top two guys. Didn't even blink, pout or frown. He just stood there listening to me say that Jerome was on the news, his picture everywhere."

"The old Tre would've blown up over that," Maya admitted. "He would've thought only about the effect on the stock. He didn't say a word."

"And if you'd been looking at him, you'd have seen he didn't even twitch."

"But he's angry with me now. I think I've hurt him too much."

"It can be fixed. If you're coming from the right place with the truth."

Maya was confused. "The truth? I haven't lied to him about anything."

"That's not what I meant, Maya. Not telling the truth. Facing the truth. Maybe you can't open up to Tre because what you think is the issue, isn't."

Maya's eyes narrowed. "You're getting a little deep for me, George."

George stood up. "Sometimes you gotta go deep for the truth, sister. My sweety taught me that. She said let go of everything you think is the issue, and the real issue will float to the top. Just be prepared, because it can be a doozy."

"A doozy?"

"That part's from me." He winked at her before heading off to the kitchen to grab a drink.

Maya headed for her bedroom, determined to do just as George said. She just hoped it wasn't too late.

Trajan sat alone in the living room, poking at his overcooked frozen dinner, while ignoring the game on television. He didn't have much of an appetite. He missed his bed in New York, his office work. He missed that feeling of control. Most of all, he missed that feeling of exciting hope he'd had when he'd thought there was a chance for him and Maya. He wanted to curse the day he met Jerome Newman, but he couldn't. Because of Maya. Anything was worth having met her. Having her in his life.

When Maya entered, Trajan recognized his anger and regret. But with it all, he loved her. Therefore, he was happy. Happy just to see her as she sat down next to him.

Maya reached for the remote and turned the television off. She didn't know how to start, so she just did.

"This is about me and my father, Tre. I don't know why Jerome killed him, but I have an idea. And that idea forces me to admit things about Daddy I've ignored for too long. I want Jerome to tell me that he was insane and Daddy was perfect. That there was nothing there, not that it would make any difference. There would never be any excuse, but I still wanted his version of an excuse. I might not get anything.

"I need to face the reality that Daddy had a lot of flaws. I think both Mama and I pretended they weren't there. After he died, we deified him. The scripture says that the wages man pays for sin is death. So I guess when Daddy died, we erased the drinking, the controlling, the extreme practicalities, the neglect and the occasional cruelty."

"I'm sorry, Maya." He took her hand in his. Words couldn't express how happy he was she was opening up to him.

"I have to let go." She was renewed by the strength of his touch. "I have to let go of so much of what I wanted to believe in order to move past this nightmare. You've shown me that more than anything."

"Me?" Trajan laughed. "What have I done for you but nag you into talking to me?"

"You've let go of a lot," she said. "Oh Tre, I'm sorry I gave you such a hard time. You aren't at all what I thought when I met you, and I haven't been fair throughout."

"You have." Trajan smiled confidently, although inside he was jumping for joy. "I was the man you thought when you met me. But George, Aunt Audrey and especially you, and being back here in D.C., all of it's opened up my eyes. So, we both keep the good and put the bad in its place. It wouldn't do either of us any good to ignore it."

"It's all part of the same." Maya slid closer to him. "I just don't want you to think you have to change me. To be with me."

"I changed because of you," he said. "Not for you. Because I love you."

Maya felt her body sigh. In a time of complete pain and uncertainty, her heart suddenly filled with joy. "Do you, Tre? I haven't frustrated you so much you've given up?"

"You've frustrated me enough to give up all right. But I never would and I never will. Look Maya, I'm a workaholic and I love money and success. That won't change. It just won't be everything anymore. It won't be the first thing, but it will still be there. I need to know you can accept that."

"Oh yes, Tre." She wrapped her arms around him. "I accept it. I have to. I love you too."

They stared into each other's eyes for some time, speaking nothing, but saying everything. They both knew this was it for them.

As Trajan picked Maya up and led her to the bedroom, their lips never separated. Maya let her worries go and let her body take over. She ached to taste him again. Knowing now that he loved her made it ever better than before, which she hadn't thought possible.

They made love into the night, wiping away the pain for at least some hours. They fell asleep in a glowing, exhausted embrace. For that night, all was good, and Maya knew that no matter what was going on, whenever she would be in Trajan's arms, all was good.

Maya slipped her satin tank over her head, watching in the mirror as it slid over her. Her skin seemed to glow. Her entire body smiled. Hope existed within her this morning. Of all possible times in her life, hope was what she felt more than anything. Baring her soul, facing the truth, hadn't been as hard as she'd thought it would. Last night with Trajan was better than she would have imagined.

She felt stronger. She still desperately wanted an explanation, but she was better prepared for what it would be. She could survive if she never got it, although she wasn't prepared to give up on that yet.

Maya continued staring at herself in the mirror. She touched her neck with fingers spread wide. She loved her neck, found it so feminine. She closed her eyes, relishing the memory of the heat of Trajan's mouth right where her hands were.

Suddenly, her eyes flew open as she heard a now familiar voice. Maya turned off the bedroom radio and listened. George was here!

"You used to give details when we were teenagers," George said. "No chance of that now?"

"Not this time," Trajan said. He drank his straight black cup of coffee as he leaned against the kitchen counter. "Not this girl. All I'll tell you is that we're fine now."

"I forgot you were a tease," George said, leaning back in his chair. "I give up. As long as you've fixed it."

Trajan laughed. "I think I could safely say we've fixed it. I gotta tell you, it feels like everything is different now. I woke up this morning with that woman in my arms, and there was a . . . a . . ."

"Completeness," George said.

"That sounds too rosy and sappy for me." Trajan's face held a thoughtful expression. "But that's what I mean, only with the masculine word for it."

"You gotta let all that masculine versus feminine stuff go for love."

Trajan waved him off. "Don't need any of your woman's advice this morning. I—"

"Look. You want a woman to love you, tell her what you mean. No matter how it makes you look. I don't care if you tell her she makes you feel pretty. Say it."

Maya interrupted the laughter, heading straight for George.

"George. What's the news?"

George's face went straight to serious. "Some progress. We got a spotting at the West Virginia border. A store owner is pretty certain it was Jerome. He went west."

Maya caught her breath, feeling a panic. She forced herself to calm down. "West, you say?"

George nodded. "We got quite a few guys out there looking. The store owner says he saw a gun bulge under the shirt. That's what got his attention. He said Jerome was looking pretty on edge."

Maya had moved to Trajan now. His arms wrapped around her as she leaned back into him.

"What'll happen when they find him?" she asked.

"What has to be done, Maya." George shrugged. "We want to get him alive, but if he's trigger happy and on edge, well, we're not gonna let him take an officer down."

Trajan felt Maya stiffen in his arms. "Maya wants some answers from Jerome."

"They have to get him alive, George." Maya made a decision in her mind that she knew could cost her her life, but she didn't know what the police had in mind.

"That's our objective, Maya. The police want answers too."

"Anything else?" she asked.

"He's driving a pretty beat-up red Honda. No one got the plates. I'm on my way that way anyway. They have me on beeper the second they make progress."

Maya sighed decisively. "Well, I'll start breakfast. How about omelets?"

"Yum." Trajan licked his lips. "George?"

"I gotta get going."

"It'll be five minutes," Maya said, tossing her hand

at him. "Look, why don't you two head out for the back porch. I'll bring it to you."

"Looks like you hit the jackpot, Tre." George winked at his friend as he stood up. "Just like me."

"Tell me something I don't know." Tre kissed Maya on her cheek and followed George out.

Maya hoped she wouldn't regret what she was about to do. Her mind was made up, however.

"Why doesn't she want to join us?" George dug into his omelet, speaking with a mouthful.

Trajan had to speak up. Maya had turned the music in the living room on and it was louder than usual, even with the sliding doors closed. "Don't know. Maybe she wants us guys to be alone."

"Well, it gives us a chance to talk about your next big problem, Tre."

Trajan shook his head. "My problem is fixed, man. I'm in love and everything is gonna—"

"New York or D.C.?" George asked.

Trajan paused, turning his attention to the trees, the low-lying leaves still wet with morning dew. "Both for now. Look George, I don't want to focus on that."

"You have to. You love New York, right?"

"I have a business there. My business is stocks. There's no place but New York for that."

"There are investor relations companies everywhere, man. This is the twenty-first century. Location isn't an issue for any business anymore."

Trajan shrugged. "I love Maya. We'll make it work."

"Maya's not leaving D.C. Her family's business is here. And don't say its different now that it's public."

Trajan gave him a stern stare. "We'll make it work. Nothing, not location or anything else, will mess this up. Maya brought me back. Back to who I am. Who I should've never let go of."

"That guy is from D.C. if I recall right."

Trajan laughed. "You're correct there. You want an answer? I'll tell you this. Right now, this situation with Jerome is first on deck. I'm gonna get Maya through this. Then, we'll talk about location. Right now, my location will be wherever Maya is."

"You sound like you're gonna be all right," George said. "Now shut up and eat." The men talked sports and work over a quick breakfast. They'd spoken almost every day since reuniting. Trajan was pleased to know he'd found his best friend again.

They made no notice of Maya's absence after returning their plates to the kitchen. It wasn't until George wanted to say good-bye did either man call out to her.

No response. Trajan turned off the stereo and called out to her again.

He went in search of her after no answer. The moment he realized she wasn't in the house, George called out to him before letting out a curse that echoed through the house.

"What?" Trajan ran to the living room.

"Your car is gone!" George was headed for the door. "I pulled up right next to it and it's gone."

Trajan was right behind him. "Where in the—"

"Why would she leave?" George threw his hands in the air. "How long do you think she's been gone?"

"Wait a second, George." Trajan thought back to two nights ago. "Where did you say Jerome was seen?"

"The West Virginia border. He stopped at a—"

"I know where she's going," Tre said. "She's going to Jerome. We have to find out who is closest to Maya after Jerome. What was the woman's name. Lisa or something. Ally?"

"Let's call her office and get her secretary to go through her Rolodex for her." George trailed Trajan into the house. "Now, where is she going? And how does she know where Jerome is?"

"I'll tell you on the way," Trajan said. "We're going to West Virginia."

Maya entered the "family" vacation home with caution. Her stomach was tied in knots, but she wasn't scared.

The red Honda had been nestled in the trees behind the small house almost half a mile off the road. It was one of twelve houses surrounding a man-made lake hidden between mounds of gigantic trees.

The first door had been unlocked. Doors were rarely locked in this small enclave. Maya treaded quietly around the neatly covered furniture of the living room, past the dining room and the hallway to the room Jerome always slept in when they stayed.

The door was open. Jerome stared at Maya as she entered. He was sitting in a comfortable ottoman, his hand on a gun sitting on the circular table next to him. Maya recognized it as the gun he'd held to her head in his penthouse.

"Been waiting for you, Maya." His tone was flat, his eyes barely open. "Was wondering when you'd catch on. That guy in the store. It was him, right?"

Maya looked with pain at the man she'd loved more than anyone for so long. He was gone. Someone else was here now. This was the man who had stared at her with those evil eyes before. She'd have to accept this too. She'd never get anywhere if she held on to her vision of Jerome. This, what sat before her, pitiful and hopeless, was Jerome Newman.

"Sit down." He nodded to the wicker chair across from him. Maya hesitated. He repeated his command a little louder, and she obliged.

There was a long silence as Jerome seemed to quietly laugh at a private thought.

"We had some times here, didn't we?"

Maya said nothing, her eyes focused on him. She wanted to hate him, but didn't, couldn't. Her emotions were all spent. What little she had left, she couldn't waste on him.

"The boating," he continued. "The barbecues. Playing video games. Even the hot tub, when I was willing to clean it and fill it up."

His smile faded. His expression turned cruel, hateful. "Look at where this room is. Right next to the kitchen. This is where a servant would stay. You, Nick and Rose got to slumber upstairs in the big rooms and have your own bathrooms. Not me. I had to walk to the other side of the house to use the guest bathroom. Doesn't even have a shower."

Maya held her protest and anger in. She wasn't going to appease his dramatic appeal.

"We came here how many times while Nick was alive? A hundred? Once, I could've gotten the big room. One of them. There's always a reason. A reason to give me leftovers. But that's not what I minded so much. I had my own stuff."

Maya pressed her lips together to keep from shouting at him.

"But my sob stories aren't what you're here for." Jerome looked away somberly. "Why, why, why. I loved him, Maya. I worshiped Nick. He was a hard one, but I knew he would be one of the greats. Even though he was an ass. Yeah, he was an ass. He was worse than the man that you've chosen to forget. At work, he was merciless. Loved him still. We had this thing going, girl. It was on. Ten years, and we were ready to bust out. Then Nick went and got his head into that bottle. He was a coward and an alcoholic."

Maya's face tightened, and she gritted her teeth. Still, she said nothing.

"That year before he died. No, for a couple of years before that, I was doing the real stuff. I was moving us forward. He was scared to death. He was going to destroy everything. When he wasn't screwing something up, he was pushing back on projects we needed to take the business to the next level."

Maya wanted desperately to hold her tears, but they fell silently down her cheeks.

Jerome's eyes softened when he saw her tears streaming down her face. "I can't tell you what made me cross that . . . that line. When I decided I had to kill him. I just knew there was nothing else. Nick was lost; there was no fixing him. I couldn't walk away. It had been ten years of my life too. And I couldn't watch it go down the drain. No way. Maya, I swear I tried to make it up to you and Rose."

Maya heard an amazed whimper escape her lips at his words.

"I did." He raised his voice, squeezed the gun, then let his grip loosen. "I have always loved you. I didn't drink. I didn't neglect you. Never said a cruel word to you. I didn't try and determine what it was you were going to do or be. I didn't squander your future financial security. I was a better father to you than he would've been after he gave himself over to that liquor."

Maya shook her head in disbelief. He actually meant what he was saying. He believed it all.

"The rest is pretty obvious." Jerome sighed so nonchalantly, it was as if he was having a friendly conversation. "The guy I paid to do it ended up telling it to the doctor who started blackmailing me. I thought it was over. I didn't know what to do. While I was planning to handle him, one of the letters he so ingenuously sent me with his name and address on it found its way to Elaine's mailbox. That damn mail clerk."

"I didn't know that she had no idea what was in that letter." His tone was argumentative. "She'd called me, left a message that a letter from a Dr. Stevenson was here. When I got there, she acted like she couldn't find it. Said she'd get back to me about it. I thought she was playing a game with me. Yeah, I know that doesn't fit with Elaine at all, but at the time I wasn't thinking straight. All I knew was that I wasn't about to be blackmailed by anyone, let alone two old folks. I did what I had to do. To her, and the doctor. After twenty years of my life, and I have my life in the real sense of the word."

Silence. Their eyes held each other for some time.

"Your turn, Maya," he said with eagerness. "I'm eager to hear what you have to say. Say it."

Maya slowly stood up and stared him down for a full minute before turning to walk away.

"Stop right there," he yelled. "You sit down. You tell me what you have to say. I have held everything together for ten years for you. You talk to me."

Maya started walking, not looking back. The door was only a few steps away.

"Maya! I need to hear you say something. What you think. Tell me you hate me, wish I was dead, want to kill me. Tell me . . . tell me something, anything!"

There was a long silence as Maya left the room and headed down the hall.

"I waited for you! I waited for you, Maya! You come back and talk to me!"

She had reached the living room when the gunshot went off. It was a heavy, dull sound. Maya gripped the edge of the sofa, steadying her weak knees. She refused to look back. She heard police sirens in the distance, relieved that she didn't have to call the police. Trajan must have figured it out.

Maya opened the front door and stood, waiting. She

took a deep breath and exhaled, and in a quiet whisper to herself, she said, "I forgive you, Jerome. I've got to let this all go, so I forgive you."

Epilogue

Trajan leaned back on the sofa in Maya's office, holding his arm out to her as she joined him. Maya nestled in his arms and against his chest. They sighed together.

"The *Wall Street Journal* and the *Washington Post* are both running the story on Pharaoh's turnaround tomorrow." Trajan smiled. "We really couldn't ask for a better scenario."

"You spun your magic, Tre." She reached back and rubbed his smooth cheek.

"No way, baby. You've done the real work. After the disaster, the stock could've taken a dive, but you kept that from happening. You pounded the pavement, went to the investors and kept their confidence."

"Enough with the kudos," Maya said. "You were right beside me, putting in the same time. You risked a lot to support me."

Trajan shrugged. "I've put a lot into hiring good people that my clients have faith in. They won't panic if I take some time off. Nothing was going to keep me from being with you."

Maya shifted in his arms, so now she was facing him. Love, complete and unquestioned, was in her eyes.

"Tre, you could never know how much your support has meant to me. I love you so much."

Trajan kissed her deeply, sincerely. He'd gotten used

to the idea of loving her more than the day before, even though he thought it would be impossible.

The last few months had been trying. Dealing with the aftermath of Jerome's murders, as well as his suicide, had been bad enough. On top of it, the public and the investors saw Jerome as the blood and guts of Pharaoh. With him gone, the company was in trouble. Maya and Trajan worked side by side to save the company. Now, opinion was turning for the better, and the stock was staying steady at twenty-three dollars a share, trading at record volume.

That had been the hardest part. The love that grew between Maya and Trajan was easy, and it saved her. The pain of Jerome's deception and what he'd stolen from her would never go away. Maya knew that. But Trajan's love, and the support of friends like Alissa, allowed her to put that pain in its place and move on.

"You don't have to thank me, baby," he said. "I love you, and I'm here for you. We've been practically hip to hip for the last few months. This hasn't been a favor. Not to me."

Maya wrapped her arms around his neck. "So this works for you? Us traveling back and forth to New York?"

"I can travel just as good as you." Maya couldn't contain her excitement.

She knew she couldn't leave Pharaoh. With Jerome leaving his control and stock in the company to her, and everyone looking to her for strength, walking away or even taking a hiatus was out of the question.

She would have to leave public relations and take on a position in senior management, which was fine since she already knew more about Pharaoh than anyone. At the same time, she couldn't ask Trajan to leave his life in New York behind.

"Tre. I don't want you to regret me or us in the future because you made such a big change."

"You mean if my company suffers?" he asked with a smirk. "It's not gonna happen. I've been talking to my major clients, letting it sink in. They're on board. I won't fail."

"You won't. Neither will I." Maya smiled from ear to ear. "We'll make it all work."

"Besides," Tre said. "I got nothing to worry about if it does get a little hard. I'm gonna be married to a very rich woman."

Maya gasped as Trajan laughed at her reaction. "Don't laugh at me. Don't tease me either."

"I'm not teasing," Tre said, controlling his laughter. "I wanted to ask you a month ago, but I knew you needed more time."

"No I didn't." Maya's heart was doing hurdles in her chest. "Of all the uncertainties I've had over the past few months, being with you was never one of them."

"Let's make it official, baby."

Trajan reached in his suit jacket lying on the side of the sofa. Maya felt the butterflies in her stomach twirl as he pulled out the box and presented it to her.

Maya bit her lower lip in anticipation as she opened the box. It was the most beautiful diamond design she'd ever seen.

"Maya Woodson. Will you do me the honor of becoming Mrs. Maya Matthews." Tre noticed the raised eyebrow. "Oh yeah, forgive me. How about, will you do me the honor of becoming Mrs. Maya Woodson-Matthews?"

"I will." Maya slipped the ring on as Trajan's lips

melted into hers. The kiss was long and made her toes tingle.

"Sealed with a kiss," he said as they finally separated.

Maya hugged him tightly. Everything was going to be all right. As a matter of fact, it was going to be perfect.

ABOUT THE AUTHOR

Angela Winters was born and raised in Evanston, Illinois, a suburb of Chicago. She is the youngest of six children. After graduating from Evanston Township High School, she majored in journalism at the University of Illinois at Urbana-Campaign and worked as a beat reporter for the *Daily Ilini*. She graduated in 1993, and worked in financial public relations, marketing, and executive search. She is currently a recruiter for a northern Virginia financial services company. She lives in Alexandria, VA.

Angela is currently a member of Romance Writers of America, Mystery Writers of America, Sisters in Crime, and Washington Romance writers.

E-mail her at angela_winters@yahoo.com

Or visit her Web site:
http://www.tlt.com/authors/awinters.htm

Coming in September from
Arabesque Books . . .

TRUE LOVE by Brenda Jackson
1-58314-144-8 $5.99US/$7.99CAN
When Shayla Kirkland lands her dream job with one of Chicago's top firms, Chenault Electronics, she's in the perfect position to destroy the company for ruining her mother's career. But she never expects that CEO Nicholas Chenault will spark a passion that will challenge her resolve—and make her surrender to the most irresistible desire . . .

ENDLESS LOVE by Carmen Green
1-58314-135-9 $5.99US/$7.99CAN
Terra O'Shaughssey always did everything as carefully as she could—including managing an apartment building. But when handsome lawyer Michael Crawford becomes her newest tenant, Terra finds his party ways endangering her peace of mind . . . and her carefully shielded heart.

STOLEN MOMENTS by Dianne Mayhew
1-58314-119-7 $5.99US/$7.99CAN
Although widowed Sionna Michaels dreads confronting the man she holds responsible for her husband's death, the instant she sees David Young, her heart is set afire and she's certain of his innocence. There's only one obstacle in the couple's way—the truth about what really happened.

LOVE UNDERCOVER by S. Tamara Sneed
1-58314-142-1 $5.99US/$7.99CAN
When executive Jessica Larson meets FBI anti-terrorist agent Carey Riley in a remote mountain inn, she gives in to her most sensuous desires for the first time in her life. But when a dangerous enemy begins to watch their every move, the two must face down their doubts and fears about getting close . . . if they are to gain a love beyond all they've ever imagined.

Please Use the Coupon on the Next Page to Order

Fall In Love With
Arabesque Books